IN PRAISE OF
LUKE'S PASSAGE

"*Luke's Passage* by Max Davis is an impressive first novel by a talented young writer. The three elements which must work for any successful novel—characterization, plot, and setting—are handled with impressive skill. The development of young Luke Hatcher into a mature man is handled well, and the details of his life are well-researched. The spiritual challenges that Luke faces are daunting, and his victory over them is inspiring. A must-read novel by a new talent!"

GILBERT MORRIS,
Best-selling Author of *Four of a Kind, Charade,*
and *The Pilgrim Song*

"Max Davis brings his characters to life in *Luke's Passage*. This fictional story feels like real life and will truly move each reader. *Luke's Passage* reads like watching a good movie...you can't wait to go back and watch it again."

FRANK C. SCHROEDER
Veteran Film/TV Executive Producer
The Pistol–The Birth of a Legend, Jesus The Christ,
Quo Vadis, Julius Erving's Sports Focus

"*Luke's Passage* is one of those novels that draws you in from the first page. You keep reading just a bit more because you just gotta know what's going to happen next. Then before you know it the characters are like part of your family and your heart and soul gets all wrapped up in their lives. Their pain becomes your pain, their joy, your joy. My wife, Nydia, and I loved this book and recommend it to everyone looking for a book to stir their soul."

LARRY J. KOENIG, PH.D.
Author of *Smart Discipline* and
Happily Married for Life

"Nothing is more powerful than a story and no one tells more powerful stories than Max Davis. *Luke's Passage* pulsates with real life—both its pathos and its joy. Readers of any age will relate to this life changing story."

RICHARD EXLEY
Author of *The Alabaster Cross*

LUKE'S PASSAGE

A Novel

Inspired by a True Story

#55,34

Max Davis

Emerald
Pointe
BOOKS

09 08 07 06   10 9 8 7 6 5 4 3 2 1

Luke's Passage
A Novel
0-97851-371-1
Copyright © 2006 by Max Davis

Published by Emerald Pointe Books
P.O. 35327
Tulsa, Oklahoma 74153-0327

To Alanna

After all these years, I still have to pinch myself.

I can't believe you chose me!

Thanks for being my life partner and best friend.

━▸ ◂━

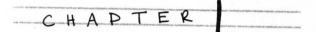

CHAPTER 1

BAREFOOT AND DEFIANT, Luke Hatcher
stepped up to home plate. "You see that big cloud out there?" he
shouted to the group, pointing the bat in the air toward a single
cloud that floated alone like a white ball of cotton in the deep
blue sky. "That's where it's going!"

"You just get ready to bat!" Haley Sparks shot back,
tugging at her shin-length, flowery skirt. She looked like a
restrained prisoner in a straitjacket. At her feet lay a pair of
stockings crumpled in a pile beside a pair of high heels. She
hated wearing stockings and heels and the sooner she got them
off, the better.

A small group of after-church folk, mostly teenagers,
had gathered around the Galilee Baptist Church's baseball
diamond that day to witness history in the making. Some of the

girls, still in their Sunday dresses, had confiscated a number of cardboard hand-fans from the sanctuary pews that bore scenes of the Last Supper on one side and Meek's Funeral Home on the other. Perched atop the rickety, splintery, bleachers, the girls furiously attempted to fend off the humid, South Louisiana heat. The guys unbuttoned their collars and loosened their ties. Luke had untucked his button-down dress shirt and kicked off his penny loafers.

"Oh, I'm ready Little Sis, I'm ready," he barked, blowing his unruly dark hair out of his eyes, grinning large and wide, with two dimples forming in his cheeks. He called Haley "Little Sis" even though they were not related. The two had grown up together only seven houses apart on White Street. Luke had always been fond of Haley, looking after her like a big brother. She was fifteen, a year and a half younger than he, about to turn sixteen, and she had secretly held a crush on him since the fourth grade. But Luke had rarely noticed her in the way she wanted to be noticed—until lately. Over the past year, Haley had miraculously transformed from a straggly, skinny sprout of a thing, into a beautiful blossom. Luke found himself, without warning, thinking of her often, too often. No, she sure wasn't the Haley she used to be. She was most definitely becoming a young woman. And she was more than just pretty. Haley was smart and funny and didn't allow him to be cocky around her. There was a fine line that you just didn't cross with Haley, and if you did, she let you know quickly. She had a fiery way of looking right through a person and getting to the point. She called things just as she saw them, and she had no qualms about telling someone the truth, the whole truth, and nothing but the truth, right to his face. You always knew where you stood with Haley.

But Haley the beautiful young woman was still Haley the tomboy, and she still loved her softball. In fact, she had developed into one heck of a softball pitcher for the Magnolia Springs High School girls' team. It was said she could fire that grapefruit-sized ball so fast it looked like a pea. In fact, she was so good the Hurricanes were hoping Haley could lead them to their first State title that year.

Haley mockingly returned Luke's smile, then inhaled deeply. Her figure was lean and firm, and her hair, long and straight, the color of corn silk. It fell just a few inches shy of her waist, complementing her honey-colored skin. With intense determination, she forced herself to concentrate and not get distracted by Luke's charming good looks. Beads of sweat rested on the tip of her nose. With her forearm, she wiped them off and slowly exhaled.

He was Luke Hatcher, only the best baseball player ever to come out of Magnolia Springs, and he was on his way to LSU, in Baton Rouge, to play for the Tigers. Every girl in town had dreamed of catching him. Yet, it was more than just his devastating good looks and athletic ability that attracted the girls. Luke was a kind-hearted gentleman, humble and always taking up a cause for the little guys. For a moment, Haley reflected back to the summer between her sixth and seventh grade years when she had climbed up a tree to get a Frisbee and fell out, twisting her ankle. Luke carried her home on his back for two blocks. And once in the fifth grade, at recess, when Eli Booty pulled her pigtails and called her Frankenstein's daughter because she was a full six inches taller than any boy in her class, Luke shoved Eli against the tetherball pole and made him promise he would never lay a finger on his "Little Sis" again.

She shook her head and refocused on the task at hand. Stepping back on her right foot, she cocked her arm, paused again for a moment, and then rifled the ball underhanded across the plate. Luke swung, catching nothing but air as the ball whizzed past him and jangled against the backstop. There was no need for a catcher in this contest.

Roger Bridges had set the whole thing up. After Mrs. Watson's Sunday school class finished a couple of minutes early, everybody was mingling in the hallway, waiting for the adults in the main sanctuary to dismiss. Someone was congratulating Haley on winning her latest game when Roger said in a voice so loud that it reverberated down the hall, "I bet Haley could strike you out, Luke."

Roger was really skinny, with a long neck and a protruding Adam's apple and pimples all over his face. He talked in a high-pitched, scratchy voice that annoyed just about everyone. Plus, he wheezed a lot because of his asthma. And those irritating quirks were made more pronounced by the fact that he never shut up. Now he had stirred the group up by saying that everyone knew the best athlete in Magnolia Springs was Haley Sparks and that she threw a ball so hard that not even the mighty Luke Hatcher could hit it. Everyone in Magnolia Springs knew for certain that Roger had a crush on Haley, but she wouldn't give him the time of day. Luke ignored Roger as long as he could.

"Whatsamatter, Luke? Afraid to be shown up in front of everyone by a *girl*? It's just three pitches. Certainly you can hit one."

What Luke wanted to hit was Roger. Hard. But not here. Not in church, of all places. Instead, he reluctantly agreed. Haley, on her part, relished the opportunity. So the bet was on. After church, it would be Haley versus Luke—three swings to get one hit.

"Hey, All Star, surely you can handle a little ol' girl like me?" Haley laughed, elbowing Luke in the side. She just wanted to have some fun.

Luke gave her a smirk. "Let's just get it over with."

When the service was done, the Sunday school gang charged out to the baseball diamond behind the church. A few adults tagged along, curious about all the commotion. Luke always carried a bat and ball in his truck and even though Haley was used to pitching with a softball, she was surprised to find the smaller hardball somewhat easier to handle.

"That's one!" Roger shouted as he ran to retrieve the ball and toss it back to Haley.

Hand claps and cheers peppered through the bleachers.

"Way to go, Luke," Roger continued. "How you gonna play for the Tigers if you can't even hit off Haley?"

Luke pounded the plate with his bat, then backed out of the batter's box and took a couple of practice swings. "Just remember, I only need one hit to do my damage," he barked back.

Haley carefully repeated her routine and Luke swung again, this time catching the ball a fraction too late, sending it high over his head and back behind the backstop.

"Foul ball! Strike two!" Roger spouted, looking into the crowd for the ball, where two young boys were tussling over who got it first and who would get to throw it back. The tug-of-war ended and the ball was sent back to Haley, bypassing Roger altogether.

"One more and you're done, Luke! I told you Haley could strike you out in three pitches!" Luke ignored Roger, just as he ignored the taunts lofted at him by opposing players and their parents during his games.

"Not bad," he congratulated Haley, tipping his head with respect.

"Not bad? Well maybe I should be the one getting the scholarship to LSU instead of you," Haley quipped.

"I try to be nice and look at you, gettin' all smart. Just give me what ya got, girl. Third time's a charm!"

Haley slowed down and patiently concentrated on her form. She desperately wanted to strike him out. "Just one more pitch," she thought, "and the rest will be history." When she released the ball for the third time, it was propelled not only by her physical strength, but also by all the emotions bottled up inside her—all of her dreams about Luke that she surmised would never come true.

The ball blasted over the plate with intense fury and Luke swung with equal power. This time, his bat and the ball met with perfect timing, driving it like a bullet through the air. The moment his bat made contact with the ball, Luke felt its direction and a sinking feeling instinctively filled his gut. "Haley, look out!" But it was too late. In that split-second, that micro-moment in time, the ball struck Haley directly in the temple, just above her left ear. She dropped to the ground like a lead brick.

➤➤ ◄◄

Luke threw down his bat and sprinted to Haley. Behind him, the bleachers emptied as if someone had yelled, "Bomb in the stands!" Everyone ran toward the pitcher's mound. Yet before they reached Haley, she popped up from the ground and was dusting herself off, resilient as always.

Luke pulled her into his arms. "Thank God, Haley. That was some hit you took. You all right?"

"I'm OK. Just a little dizzy."

Luke patted her back and ran his hand down the length of her flaxen hair. Haley leaned into him and placed her head on his shoulder. Even though her head felt disconnected from her body, she enjoyed being held by him. As Luke held her, the aroma of her body swept over him, natural and sweet, a curious blend of sweat and perfume.

Aware of the concerned crowd, Luke broke his embrace with Haley. "She's OK," he shouted.

Dot and Liz, Haley's two best friends, broke through the gathering, smothering her with concern and affection.

"I can't believe the ball actually hit you," said Dot, flipping back her luminous, crimson mane from her fair complexion, her eyes squinting like a cat's as she smiled.

"Yeah, I know. It happened so fast, I didn't have time to get out of the way."

"Come on girls, give her some breathing room," Luke urged. "I'll take her home and make sure she's taken care of." He turned back to the crowd. "OK, folks, game's over."

The group began slowly to disperse. Haley rotated her head back and forth, and then looked up at those still huddled around her. "I'm fine ya'll. Really, just a little shaken up." She turned to Luke with her hands on her waist. "Well, I guess you won the bet."

"It was stupid, Haley. Come on now, you know you're a great pitcher." Luke held up his hand in front of Haley's face. "How many fingers am I holding up?"

"Five."

"No. Four. This one is a thumb," Luke said, cracking a silly grin.

Haley punched him in the arm. "Retard."

"Here, let me look at that bump again."

Haley leaned her head sideways so Luke could examine her. Dot and Liz peered over their shoulders.

"No swelling, good. But man, you're going to have a bruise the size of a grapefruit." He tenderly touched the spot with his finger, causing Haley to flinch back. "Sore, huh?"

"Yeah, a little bit, I guess."

"I think I better get you home."

"No, you don't have to. I told Mama I would ride home with Dot and Liz anyway."

Noticing the obvious chemistry that was happening between Luke and Haley, and fully aware of Haley's infatuation with him, Liz jumped into the conversation. "Don't worry about us. You go ahead with Luke. We're heading over to Ivy's to eat."

"It's settled then," Luke said. "I've been wanting to talk to you alone about something anyway."

"You have?" Haley asked, her mind swimming with the possibilities.

Luke nodded in affirmation. Dot and Liz exchanged glances and smiled. They had both seen the way Luke had almost leaped out of his skin in response to Haley's injury. And neither of them, nor anyone else there for that matter, had missed the warm embrace.

"If you want," Dot suggested, "ya'll go ahead and have your talk and then meet us at Ivy's. But only if you feel up to it, Haley." The two girls couldn't wait to hear all the juicy details of what Luke wanted to talk to Haley about.

"I don't know," Luke said, putting his arm around Haley's shoulder. "I mean she could have a concussion or something. She really needs to rest."

"Oh, I'm all right. Here, look at this." Haley bent over and touched her toes, then she placed her hands on her hips and flipped her hair back. "See, I'm fine. Now let's go to Ivy's. I'll ride with you Luke and you can drop me off at my house later."

"Have it your way, but at least stay here while I go get my car so you won't have to walk."

Luke jogged around the backstop and headed across the grassy field to the church parking lot where his truck was parked—an old, black, and somewhat rusty '51 Ford. It was all his father could afford, but Luke was the type of guy that would be popular no matter what he drove. Still in shock over what had happened, he turned back to glance at Haley who was now talking to a few concerned stragglers. *Why did I ever agree to such a stupid bet?*

"Hey, Luke. You sure showed her, huh?" It was Roger Bridges, who had started the whole thing. He was ambling across the parking lot toward Luke. As he approached, a rage erupted in Luke and he grabbed Roger by the collar and shoved him against a nearby car, his fist cocked back. Roger shook pretty bad while Luke was looking at him, debating what to do, then Luke released his grip and Roger slid to the ground.

➤➤ ◄◄

"I really don't think we should do this," Luke said, opening the passenger door to his truck. The door screeched and whined, refusing to cooperate. Luke gave it a yank, which caused the door to make a popping sound and then to release. "I gotta get some oil on that," he said, rolling down the window. Haley slid onto the worn vinyl seat.

"Oh," she said, lifting her legs up off the seat. "The seat is hot."

"I'm sorry. I forgot how hot those seats could get." Luke yanked off his dress shirt, which was already unbuttoned, leaving him wearing a white tee shirt that revealed his his obvious athletic physique. "Here, this should help," he said as he laid the shirt on the seat so Haley could sit on it.

"Thanks, Luke. You didn't have to do that."

"No problem, Haley." He shut the door firmly behind her; giving it a tug making sure it closed securely, then jogged over to the driver's side and hopped in. She looked absolutely stunning, except for the bright red welt growing on the side of her head. "I still think you ought to let me take you home so you can lie down and rest," he continued, cranking the engine and pulling out onto the road.

Luke glanced over at Haley and she glanced back. Her eyes were an amazing shade of green. Her hair, which had been set free from the constraints of its rubber band, began to flow wildly in the wind as Luke shifted gears and the truck sped down the road.

"Is there too much wind? We can roll up the windows if you want."

"I'm fine, Luke. Just a little dizzy—and a lot embarrassed." Haley tilted her head back and ran her hand through her hair. "The wind feels so good," she said.

When Haley spoke those words, Luke had a flashback.

"Hey, do you remember that time on the fire tower?"

"Oh, I remember all right. How could I ever forget that, you jerk," Haley replied, giving Luke a quick punch in the arm.

"I guess that was pretty stupid of me."

"Yes it was, Luke. And hopefully you have matured some over the years." Haley was serious, though she said it in a joking sort of way.

"I hope so."

CHAPTER 2

THE BRISK SUMMER breeze had felt warm against their faces that long-ago night. A breeze always seemed to be blowing up on the fire tower. It was nice and it kept the mosquitoes at bay.

"Sure is bright out tonight," Haley had said, as the three of them leaned against the guard railing and gazed out over the treetops. The moon hung large and full and looked as if they could have reached out and touched it. "I always feel so special when I'm up here, like I'm on the top of the world." She paused and ran her hand through her hair, then blew away the bangs that were sticking to her forehead. "Being up here makes me think about things. You know, about life and stuff. You ever think about stuff, Luke? Like what you want to be one day?"

"I guess, sometimes," Luke said, while squinting his eyes toward town. About a mile or so away he could just barely make out the glittering lights of the Gordon Theatre on Main Street. From up there you could tell where things were even though you couldn't really see them. Like Ivy's Drive-In; at night all you could see was a big glow coming up around the trees. Of course, the courthouse, the high school, the water tower, and the Bogue Chitto River Bridge were always visible because their tops poked up like monuments through the pines and oaks.

Magnolia Springs had two towers, the water tower that was painted aqua and resembled a giant flying saucer resting on spider legs—until Luke was around seven he was convinced that spacemen had designed it—and the Forest Ranger fire tower located about a mile outside of the city limits in the Bogue Chitto National Forest. The forest started when you crossed over the river bridge. There were several pine-needle-covered trails weaving through the woods up to the fire tower.

Climbing the water tower was out of the question because it stood in the center of town and was lit up at night. Big floodlights illuminated the words, "Magnolia Springs" on one side and "Home of the Mighty Hurricanes" on the other. Sticking out the very top were three antenna-looking things with blinking red lights attached. Plus, it was way too high and had a narrow ladder that went straight up.

The fire tower, however, was a much different story. It had steel stairs that zigzagged their way up to the top instead of a ladder. Stairs were a lot easier and not nearly as dangerous as climbing a ladder straight up. And it wasn't lit up at night either, which made it dark and shadowy. If the ranger's office at the top was closed it didn't matter, because the lookout part was always open. Luke and the other kids went up there all the time. They liked to sit and rest their arms on the guardrail while dangling their feet over the edge. Climbing at night was usually not a problem because they could roam around town until nine or ten o'clock, depending on if it was a school night or not. Parents never worried too much about them, as long as they checked in at suppertime.

Haley nudged Jimmy Pikes, who was sitting on the other side of her. "What about you?"

"What about what?"

"Do you ever think about what you wanna be?"

"Sure, man," replied Jimmy. He stood up and held one of his tennis shoes over the edge of the railing, then dropped it and watched it fall to the ground. Luke pulled off one of his and watched it fall. Then Haley pulled off one of hers and did the same thing.

"All right," Luke said, taking off his other shoe. "See that big anthill down there? Whoever gets the closest to it, wins." Luke painstakingly took aim then released it. His shoe floated and twirled and landed inches from the orange mound. After that Jimmy tried. He was off by about a million miles.

"You guys are pathetic," said Haley. She licked her finger and held it up to the wind. Then, pointed her shoe downward, shifted to a different place on the tower, and dropped it. Her shoe hit the anthill dead center. "I guess that means I won," she said, slapping her hands together like she was dusting them off.

"I'd like to be a pro baseball player and maybe coach one day," Luke said, sitting back down. "If not that, I don't know what I want to be, maybe a cop like Sergeant Friday on Dragnet."

"If anybody can do it, Luke, it's you," Haley said. She always seemed so encouraging. Luke believed if he had said he wanted to be an astronaut and fly to that big silver moon they were looking at or some crazy thing like that, she would have said he could have done it. "Me," Haley continued, "I'm going to be the first lady doctor in Magnolia Springs, but before that I want to make the high school girl's softball team. Coach Brumfield said I could probably make it this year even though I'm only going to the seventh."

"I don't have any doubts about that. The way you pitch and all you could probably make the boys' team. Don't you think so, Jimmy?"

Jimmy silently nodded in agreement.

Luke took off both of his socks and stood back up, then tossed them over one at a time and watched them float down. "Come on, give me your socks," Luke urged, wanting to throw something else down.

In Magnolia Springs there wasn't much entertainment for kids. *The Wizard of Oz* was a big deal because it only came on TV once a year and it really meant something. On that sacred Sunday evening, the streets were vacant early as kids gobbled down their suppers so they could huddle around their black-and-white RCAs. Luke had watched it four years in a row. Once a week, they could go to the movies, but other than that, if they wanted entertainment, they had to create it. Watching stuff fall from the top of a fire tower was kind of neat.

When all of them were barefoot, the three of them started looking for something else to drop down. Luke had his Boy Scout wallet and he chunked it. He still used it even though he wasn't a scout anymore. After reaching the high rank of Tenderfoot, Sarah and James had told him he needed to choose between scouts or sports. Luke chose sports, even though he liked the Scouts. When he was a Cub Scout, he and James had competed in the Pinewood Derby. Together they carved a racecar out of a twelve-inch block of pinewood. They painted it bright orange and wrote the word KOOLAIDE in big black letters on both sides, then drilled holes and attached the plastic wheels. At the father-and-son picnic, they raced their racecar against the others by dropping the cars down this wooden track that looked like a miniature version of the giant super-slide at the State Fair—the kind that you would slide down while sitting on an empty feed sack. James and Luke had won first place and Luke got a trophy with a gold racecar on the top.

Haley had a couple of quarters and she dropped them. Jimmy made a paper airplane out of a wadded-up piece of paper he had picked up off the ground that announced some rally or something for the colored people. The wind took it and they never did see it hit the ground. Finally, Luke pulled his tee shirt over his head and tossed it. Jimmy pulled his off, too. Obviously, Haley couldn't take hers off because of being a girl. When they had exhausted their supply and it appeared that all hope was gone, Luke looked over at Jimmy and dared him to drop his pants off. He stared at Luke and Haley like a cow looking at a new gate. "I ain't crazy, Luke!"

At thirteen years of age, who knows what was going through his mind that night? But in a split second Luke unsnapped his jeans and pulled them off. He wore boxers so he figured they weren't that different from his swimming trunks. Haley and Jimmy were cracking up.

"Captain America, Luke?" Haley giggled. "I figured you for the Superman type."

"Shutuuppp!" Luke said, leaning over the rail. "I wear them because they're comfortable, that's all."

"Sure Luke, anything you say." Haley looked over at Jimmy and they both snickered.

What happened next was one of those quirky twists of life. As Luke's jeans were floating toward the ground, a big gust of wind blew them under the tower where they got hung up on one of the crossbeams. The tower was constructed in such a way that about every fifteen or twenty feet there were these steel beams that made an "X". The "X" beams started at the bottom and continued all the way to the top on four sides. The jeans were stuck on the third "X" up from the bottom—about thirty or so feet in the air. This presented a real dilemma for Luke. You see, they were practically brand-new jeans. If he came home without them, Luke reasoned that his parents wouldn't be too happy and some sort of punishment would be in order. In addition to that, Luke's jeans would be up there in the daytime flapping like a flag. Soon it would be all over town about them being stuck up there. He would never live it down.

"I know you're not thinking what I think you're thinking," Haley had said with her hands on her hips, the moonlight
illuminating her piercing green eyes that were trying to bore a
hole right through Luke.

"I gotta get those jeans," Luke told her, while starting
down the stairs.

"Luuuke!" she shouted. "What if you fall? This ain't
no joke!"

"Come on, Luke. Haley's right you know," said Jimmy.
"Those jeans ain't worth it, man."

The two followed behind Luke as he stubbornly wound
his way down the stairs to get even with the "X" that his jeans
were hanging on. Luke's plan was to climb out on the crossbeam
from the stairs and straddle it, then shimmy up to them. He
would have to pull himself up at an angle because the jeans were
stuck right in the center part of the "X". And that is just what
Luke proceeded to do. The beam was flat on the top, which
wasn't too hard to hold on to.

When he got within reaching distance, Luke stretched
out his arms and caught hold of the very end of one of the pants
legs, then he attempted to pull the jeans to himself. But when he
did, the force of his yank lodged them deep in a crevice between
the two crossbars. They were stuck fast, so he gave them another,
much harder, yank in an attempt to dislodge them. With the
force of his action, his body slipped off the crossbeam and he
started to fall.

Fortunately, he clung to his pants. And to his surprise
and salvation, they held his weight. Luke hung down, dangling

like a piñata. Jimmy and Haley were beside themselves screaming and hollering. As Luke's arms began to burn and he could feel himself starting to slip, it occurred to him how serious a situation he was in. In a split second, he looked down and surmised that if he dropped he would probably hit the next crossbeam down. If lucky he could catch it, but if not, he knew he would most definitely break some bones. So, Luke quickly resolved to pull himself back up on the crossbeam using his jeans as a rope. He was praying that they would continue to hold, because if they didn't, he knew he'd be dead meat. The wiry muscles in Luke's arms and shoulders knotted up as he struggled. Haley was taking notice and Luke knew it. He made it. Once back up on the beam again, he swung the rest of his body over, catching it with his legs.

Luke regained his breath, and he was able finally to dislodge his jeans.

Pulling himself along back to the stairs, Luke was feeling pretty cocky, so he faked like he was slipping off the beam again, letting out a yell for help as he did. Haley screamed in terror. When she did, Luke looked over at her and shot her a stupid grin. At the stairs, Haley was waiting with what appeared to be tears in her eyes, even though she would never have admitted it.

Luke just stood there puffed up like he had done something really impressive. Haley balled up her fist and punched him in the gut so hard that he doubled over coughing and spitting. "You jerk!" she said. "Grow up. Will you?"

CHAPTER 3

"WHEN WE GET to Ivy's at least you can get some ice and put it on your bruise," Luke said tenderly. "It'll help it feel better."

He noticed that Haley was smiling. No, she certainly wasn't the tomboy she used to be. He whipped the truck sharply from the road they were on, onto another road that led to the main part of town and Ivy's. The force of the turn caused Haley to slide over toward Luke. He reached out to steady her with his arm. Touching her brought on a momentary chill. *I ought to say something now.*

"Haley, you sure you're OK?"

"Just kind of tired. Don't feel bad about what happened. It wasn't anyone's fault. I should have ducked is all."

"Haley, I got something to ask you. But if you ain't feelin' right, it can wait."

Haley looked at Luke, puzzled at his tone. "I'm fine, Luke. What do you want to say?"

He pulled the truck to the side of the road, under an oak tree, and he looked down at Haley with a serious expression on his face. "I've been wanting to ask you for a while, but with the baseball playoffs 'n all, it's never been the right time." He inhaled deeply then anxiously brushed his hand through his hair. "You know we've been friends so long, almost like brother and sister." Then he paused and looked away from Haley.

She had never seen him like this, Luke Hatcher, Mr. Control, cool under pressure. His uneasiness made her acutely aware of her femininity and gave her a spark of realization that he just might view her as a woman now and no longer as his "Little Sis."

"Haley, what I'm trying to..." In frustration at his awkwardness, Luke banged the steering wheel with his fists. What he wanted to say to Haley would take as much courage as he imagined it would take to stand up against any opposing pitcher. "I was wondering if you would..." He shifted in his seat. "You know, go out with me?... Maybe we could go down to New Orleans, to the French Quarter, or to Baton Rouge or something? You know, get away from Magnolia Springs."

Haley took Luke's chin in her hand and pointed his face toward hers. She stared into his bright blue eyes for what seemed to Luke like a lifetime. Or maybe it was less than a second. To

Luke, time had stopped. "I would be honored to go out with you, Luke Hatcher."

"You would?" He found himself short of breath, as if he had chased down a long fly ball in right field.

"Yes, I would. And don't look so surprised." She moved her hand behind Luke's right ear and pulled his face close to hers, gently kissing him on the cheek. This was more than two teens agreeing to go out on a date. The two of them connected on a much deeper level. When Haley backed away, her eyes narrowed. "What about Laurie Harrison? I thought you two were hooked up," she joked.

"Laurie and I ain't hooked up. I don't even like her, and I don't know what she thinks of me. I don't care, either."

Haley laughed softly. "Just checking. But Luke, you know you're going to have to ask my Daddy first. You know I can't date until I'm sixteen."

"What do you think he'll say?"

"He'll probably say, `Well, boy, you almost killed her, so you might as well date her.'" Laughing with a little snort, she punched Luke again in the arm.

"That's not funny, Haley. You know how bad I feel about what happened."

Haley looked over at Luke and began laughing hysterically.

"What?" he asked.

"Just remembering that day that you saved my life, Luke, that's all." Now she was coughing she was laughing so hard. "Oh, Luke, you're my hero."

"You just settle down, Miss Smarty Pants, so you don't hurt your head any worse. And please don't remind me about that."

>- -<

There had been six of them on that particular steamy July afternoon—Eli Booty, Roger Simmons, Billy Cain, Jimmy Pikes, Luke, and Haley—five boys and one girl. Haley had stood defiant, with her arms crossed, straddling her bike, a boy's model of course, when Eli suggested that all girls were sissies and that she was chicken to jump from the twenty-foot overpass over the Bogue Chitto river.

"Am not!" she declared.

"Well then prove it, big mouth," taunted Eli.

"OK, I will. Let's go!"

Haley bit the bait, so they pedaled like mad to the river, even though Luke wasn't too thrilled about the idea. That was how Lance Crumholt had broken his neck and he ended up in a wheelchair. But he had been *diving.* Everybody knew you were not supposed to dive from a bridge.

Once they all got to the overpass, Haley just stared down at the bottle-green water flowing below her.

"See, I told you she was chicken," laughed Eli, with the other boys joining in, except for Luke and Jimmy. They weren't laughing.

"Shut up! I ain't no chicken and I ain't no sissy," Haley barked back, inching ever so slowly to the bridge's edge.

"Go ahead then, jump."

"I said I was! I'm making sure there ain't no logs down there." She kicked off her black Converses, rolled up her jeans as far as she could, climbed up on the bridge's steel railing, and wrapped her toes around the overhang.

"You don't have to do it, Haley," Luke had urged. "Eli don't know what he's talking about. You don't have nothing to prove."

She looked over at Luke with this smirky grin on her face, winked, and then dropped feet first off the bridge. The boys all rushed to the railing and looked down. There was a small splash and then silence, except for the constant drone of locusts in the background and Roger wheezing because the strenuous bike ride had caused his asthma to act up. Roger could really work his asthma to his benefit, like whenever he got tagged in kickball or something. All of them kept waiting for Haley's head to pop up, but instead only a flower of bubbles rose to the water's surface and then disappeared. After about thirty-seconds or so Luke knew there should have been some sign of her, but nothing. A nauseating feeling flooded his stomach and when Haley finally did emerge, Luke's emotions went from shock to horror as he saw her floating, face down, moving with the current toward a fallen tree branch that was jutting out from the bank.

"You butthead," Luke had snapped at Eli while jerking off his shirt and shoes. "You just couldn't keep your big mouth shut, could you? Gotta always be proving something."

"I'm sorry, Luke. I didn't mean nothing by it, honest," Eli said.

Just that quickly, Luke was off the bridge and into the river. He surfaced, treading water briefly to get his bearings. Fortunately, Haley's honey-colored hair shone like a beacon when the sun hit it. She was less than ten yards away and Luke swam to her as fast as he could. "Haley? Haley?" Luke hollered, "Can you hear me?" but there was no response.

By now the other boys had raced down the trail to the river's edge. Eli was crying. After grabbing Haley, Luke made sure her head stayed above the water and pulled her to the bank. As he gently lay her limp body on the sand, he couldn't help but notice how pretty she was—and the way the water glistened upon her bronzed skin. But he pushed those thoughts in the back of his head and felt for a pulse. The only CPR he knew came from watching the Buckskin Bill Show on TV after school. Once, two Red Cross volunteers had appeared on the show and had demonstrated on a dummy. Luke remembered some of it, so he tilted Haley's head back. He pinched her nose and began to open her mouth, but before he could, wouldn't you know, Haley spit a stream of water right into Luke's face and started giggling.

"Luke Hatcher, you're my hero," she said, batting her eyelashes.

"Dang it, Haley!" Luke yelled, so mad at her, but at the same time so happy she hadn't drowned. "Don't you ever do that again! You hear me?"

"Why Luke," she continued in an over-exaggerated southern drawl, "I do think you love me!"

"Don't be ridiculous, Haley. You're only eleven and I'm twelve-and-a-half. You're like my little sister. That's all. You know that." That's what he had said, but it didn't explain all the funny feelings he had whenever he was around her, or how he always felt this need to protect her—like he didn't want anything ever to happen to her.

CHAPTER 4

THE PARKING LOT at Ivy's was full, which was not unusual for a Sunday.

Magnolia Springs was what the tourist industry would call "scenic," what those who had lived there long called "peaceful," and what those hoping to escape called "backward." Mixed with the pines were moss-laden oak and magnolia trees, some over three hundred years old, lining the streets like massive umbrellas. Their shade draped all over the lush yards and inviting old homes with off-the-ground front porches. Railroad tracks ran through the middle of town where there was a small train depot. Across from the train station was the courthouse that supposedly flew the largest American flag in the South.

Monday through Saturday, the downtown bustled with activity. There was the Woolworth's five-and-ten-cent store that still had the original wood floors and ceiling fans from when it was built in 1909. Displayed in front of the Western Auto, along the sidewalk, were shiny new bicycles lined up next to the lawn and garden equipment. At J.C. Penney's, the mannequins in the window modeled the latest in summer wear. The Gordon Theater advertised *The Fantastic Voyage*.

Yes, Magnolia Springs bustled with activity on the other six days, but not on this day. It was Sunday, and on Sunday the town virtually shut down, except for Ivy's and The Round Table, the only two restaurants that opened in time for the after-church crowd—Ivy's for teenagers, The Round Table for adults and families. If you had to go to lunch with your parents at The Round Table, you made a straight charge to Ivy's as soon as you were done. The only other place open in Magnolia Springs on Sundays was the new Pac-A-Sac mini grocery store.

Chevys, Fords, Pontiacs, a few Oldsmobiles, and Buicks, and several pickup trucks filled the parking spaces around the drive-in section at Ivy's. Teenagers shouted from car to car and waitresses rushed back and forth carrying trays piled with burgers and shakes. Because the parking lot was full, Luke parked around the corner. He walked to the passenger side of the truck and helped Haley out on the sidewalk. He put his arm around her shoulders for support as they walked up the sidewalk and into the air-conditioned restaurant. Dot and Liz were seated near the front in a red vinyl booth. Haley sat next to Dot and across from Luke. Liz, who was a little on the plump side, was squeezing mayonnaise from a white squeeze bottle onto crackers and popping them whole into her wide mouth.

"That's totally disgusting," said Dot. "I don't see how you can do that."

"I'm hungry," protested her friend. "And you know how slow the service is here on Sundays. It could take an hour for Sue Ellen just to get here with our waters."

Luke said Liz was right for once, excused himself and got up from the table. As he walked toward the kitchen, Dot could hardly contain herself. "What'd he say? What'd he say?"

"You're not going to believe it. He asked me out! He really asked me out... And he was so cute about it, too."

Liz shoved another cracker in her mouth. "Some girls have all the luck."

"That bump looks really bad, Haley. Do you want some makeup to cover it up?" Dot asked.

"No, it'd just look like I was trying to hide something and that would look worse." Haley looked around the dining room, but Luke was nowhere in sight. "His arm really felt nice around my shoulders today."

"He probably just feels sorry for you 'cause he whacked you with that baseball," said Liz.

"I don't think so," said Haley.

About that time, Luke whirled back to the table with a round tray balanced on his left hand. He set down glasses of water in front of each of the girls, then handed Haley a rag full of cubed ice.

"This rag is the best I could come up with," he said. "It looks clean enough. I figured you needed it as soon as possible."

As Haley took the ice from Luke, their fingers touched. Luke looked into Haley's eyes, and then looked down at the table before setting off toward the kitchen again.

"Maybe I'm wrong," said Liz. "Maybe he really does like you." Liz drank her water in one gulp and returned to doctoring crackers with the mayonnaise.

Haley watched as Luke wound his way around tables with the waitress tray.

"Hey, Luke! You make a hip waitress. Can you get me a 7-Up and an Ivy's burger with fries?" While others were laughing at Jimmy Pikes, Luke turned to look at Haley once again. Why did his heart seem to skip when their fingers touched?

When he made it back to the booth, he told the three girls that both Kathy Hebert and Jamie Long had called in sick, so Ivy's was short-handed and it would probably take longer than usual.

"That's OK," Haley said, sounding weary. "I'm not really that hungry."

"Well, I'm taking you home right now—no more waiting. I want your mom and dad to look after you. Maybe you should go to bed or something." As he said this, Luke was already on his feet and helping Haley to hers. She didn't argue, but willingly leaned on his extended arm.

"See ya'll later, Haley. Call me tonight, OK?" Dot watched as they left while Liz reached over for Haley's untouched glass of water.

➤➤ ◄◄ ·

Luke drove slowly out of downtown toward the river and Haley's house. Haley kept her eyes closed and the ice pressed gently against her head. She might have been asleep, except for the way her fingers drummed on the seat to keep time with the Tom Jones song playing on the small truck radio. Luke smiled. As he did, Haley reached out her hand toward him, then suddenly she slumped forward, her head coming to rest on the hard metal dashboard.

Luke covered the remaining mile to Haley's house in less than a minute, startling old Mrs. Stewbacher who was riding her red Schwinn with a basket in the front. She rang her handlebar bell angrily as the old truck spun around her. For a minute, two boys on banana bikes pedaled like mad trying to keep up with Luke, but they quit after about twenty yards or so.

Haley's house was set away from the road with a long gravel driveway that curved past willow trees and a small pond. Luke whipped in a little too fast causing the truck to jostle over the driveway's bumps. Finally, he came to an abrupt stop in front of the house. As they stopped, Haley lethargically lifted her head, looked at Luke, and then at her surroundings.

"You stay right there, Haley. I'll get your dad." Luke bounded from his truck and up the front porch steps toward the screen door shouting all the way, "Mr. Sparks! Mrs. Sparks! Are you here?"

His cries conflicted with the serenity of the porch with its green wooden swing swaying gently, its stained-glass ornaments hanging in the sunlight, casting their own unique art works on the ground, and its three sets of wind chimes harmonizing in the breeze. Harvey Sparks came from the other side of the house, a pair of hedge trimmers in his hands. Virginia Sparks appeared at the door, hands covered with pastry flour that she wiped on her apron.

"Mercy, Luke, what is the matter? Is Haley with you?"

Luke caught his breath before answering. "Yes, ma'am. She's in the truck. But I don't think she's feeling well. She, well, I hit her in the head with a baseball after church."

"You did what?" Harvey Sparks tossed the hedge clippers aside and set out around the porch toward the truck, but his wife beat him to it, barely touching the steps on her way down. Haley was sitting up, but found herself unable to open the truck door.

"Haley, are you all right? Let me get you inside." Virginia Sparks opened the truck door and started to pull Haley by her hand. Her husband pushed her aside, reached his arms under Haley and lifted her out.

"I can walk, Daddy," Haley protested in a weak voice. Her father ignored her protests and carried her into the house, placing her on a couch in the living room. Her mother sat down by her side, a worried expression across her face, and asked where she hurt. But Haley turned her head to find Luke. She smiled, then closed her eyes.

"Go call the doctor, Virginia. Call Doc Spurrier. Tell him to get over here right away." Harvey Sparks was foreman in a lumberyard, with a foreman's voice and a foreman's way of barking orders. But Luke heard the concern in Mr. Sparks' words, the concern only a father can have when he sees his child in pain.

Virginia Sparks returned to the living room with a cold cloth, which she folded and placed on Haley's forehead. "Doc Spurrier said he'd be right over." Then to Luke, "Oh, Luke. What happened?"

"It was a stupid bet, Mrs. Sparks—that Haley could strike me out. Everybody was, you know, all excited 'n all. So I just kinda went along with it. Well, when I hit one of Haley's pitches, the ball hit her in the head. I'm so sorry Mrs. Sparks. It was an accident. I wanted to bring her right home, but she really wanted to go to Ivy's. When I saw she wasn't feeling well, I went ahead and brought her home."

Virginia Sparks looked up at Luke with the concerned eyes of a protective mother. "How could you, Luke? You should have known better. You should have known you could hurt someone like that, especially a girl." She glared at Luke until he shifted his gaze downward.

"C'mon, Son, let's go outside and wait for the doctor." Luke followed Mr. Sparks out the screen door, out onto the driveway and down to the pond. He dared not speak, dared not stir this man's anger.

"Luke, I know you didn't try to hurt my Haley. And I don't see things like her mother does. Haley is, well, we never had a son. And she's our only child. I guess I treat her like a boy in many ways. I pushed her to play sports when other girls were playing dress-up. So when I heard about that bet..."

Luke cut him off in mid-sentence. "What? You knew about it?"

"It was all over the church and I have to tell you, I was proud that Haley was gonna go up against you. I'm sure she'll be fine. But I guess it's time I realize that my Haley's growing up. She's not a tomboy anymore. She's turning into a young woman."

"Mr. Sparks, sir, can I ask you something?"

Slowly, Harvey Sparks lifted his eyes to meet Luke's. He nodded.

"Sir, I know what you mean about Haley being a young woman, 'n all. And I was sort of wondering.... I mean, could I, or would you allow me to take her out sometimes? She's really special—different than the other girls. You know? And I would always be a gentleman with her."

Harvey Sparks looked at Luke long and hard. Whether he was thinking of Luke's shortcomings or his own, only he knew. But Harvey Sparks nodded his head and was about to open his mouth when they both heard a vehicle turning off the road into the long driveway.

➤➤ ◄◄

Fred Spurrier drove a brand-new Ford pickup. He was the oldest of the three doctors in Magnolia Springs and he still made house calls. He had delivered Haley right there in the Sparks' home. Luke, too, had been brought into this world by Fred Spurrier.

Mr. Sparks and Luke met him and led him into the house. Haley was sitting up on the couch, sipping on a glass of water. Her mother was seated next to her, trying to wrap a blanket around Haley's shoulders.

"I don't have a cold, Mama. I just had a fainting spell is all."

Doc Spurrier pulled up a chair next to Haley. He was still dressed in overalls because he had been working in his garden when he got the call and didn't have time to change. By his side, however, was his faithful black bag that told the world "I'm a doctor."

"What have we here?" he inquired at the sight of the bruise on the side of Haley's head. "Looks like you had a run-in with something that didn't give much."

"She was hit in the face by a baseball," said Virginia Sparks, matter-of-factly, trying not to glare at Luke. "It's a wonder she didn't lose an eye."

Doc Spurrier took out an instrument with a pin-light on the front and a set of dials on the back. He used it to look into Haley's left eye, then her right. He went back and forth between the two several times. Then he held the light about eight inches in front of Haley's face and asked her to follow the light with her eyes. After moving the instrument from side to side twice, he turned it off and replaced it in his bag.

"How are her eyes, Doc? Is this gonna affect her vision?" Fear and anger mixed in Virginia Sparks' words.

"Her eyes are fine, Virginia." Then to Haley, "I imagine you have quite a headache, young lady. But how's your stomach? Have you eaten? Can you keep anything down?"

"I haven't had anything to eat yet. Just this water is all. I didn't feel like eating." Luke noticed Haley's voice sounded stronger than when they were talking in his car. "Really, I think I'll be okay if I can just rest a bit."

Doc Spurrier patted her on the shoulder and then nodded with his head for her parents to follow him out onto the porch. Luke stayed behind with Haley, but could hear the doctor's instructions.

"I don't see anything seriously wrong with her right now, but with head trauma, you never know. She's probably going to be just fine, except for a nasty bruise. But to be sure, keep an eye on her this afternoon. If she falls asleep, wake her every half hour. If you have trouble getting her to respond, if she seems really disoriented, or if she starts throwing up, call me right away. Give her some aspirin for her headache."

Inside, Luke was holding Haley's hand. He spoke softly, wanting to get his words out, wanting to sit next to Haley forever, but afraid of stirring up the wrath of her mother. "Haley, I sure am sorry. I never should have done it. I never should have taken Roger's stupid bet."

"Come on Luke, you heard what the doctor said. I'm going to be fine. Besides, it was as much my fault as anybody's. You know there's no way I could pass up the opportunity to strike out the great Luke Hatcher." And it seemed she smiled her words at him in a way that made him feel warm inside.

Harvey and Virginia Sparks walked back in through the screen door, and Luke thought it time to make his way home.

"I guess I better be getting on home now," Luke said to Mr. and Mrs. Sparks as he stepped out through the same door. "I'm really sorry."

"The answer's yes," Harvey said to Luke with a wink, patting him on the back.

"Yes, sir!" responded Luke. "I won't let you down."

Haley lifted her head. "Call me later, okay?"

"Yes, ma'am," was his mocking reply. He could have flown home.

CHAPTER 5

SARAH HATCHER'S FIST came down on the mound of risen dough at precisely the same moment the phone rang. She was making the bread her family would use for sandwiches and as gravy-soppers in the coming week. She felt her bread was better than anything you could buy in the store and spent each Sunday afternoon baking at least three loaves, more if there was a neighbor who had taken sick.

The aroma of a loaf just about ready to come out of the oven met Luke as he strolled in through the screen door that opened directly into the kitchen. His mother's hot, freshly, baked bread with butter was impossible to resist. Luke could practically eat a whole loaf at one time.

"Can you get the phone, Honey? My hands are covered in bread dough," Sarah asked. Everyone always said that Luke was the spitting image of her. Both had thick dark hair, stabbing blue eyes, and russet skin, hinting at their French/Italian roots. Sarah herself was considered one of the prettiest women in Magnolia Springs. In fact, she had won the Miss Tangipahoa Parish beauty contest when she was in high school. James was always telling her how beautiful she was and how blessed he was that she had married him—that he had married above his class. Sarah ate it up. Emily, Luke's six-year-old sister, took more after her father who was quite handsome—fair skin, wavy, sandy hair with hazel eyes, and a lanky build.

Luke pushed through the swinging, saloon-style doors that connected the kitchen to the hallway and grabbed the receiver. He was hoping it was Haley calling, but knew it couldn't be. She was supposed to be resting. But why did his breath come harder just at the possibility? "Hatcher residence."

"May I speak with Luke, please?" The male voice was unfamiliar, but familiar. Could it be another college baseball coach trying to talk him out of his commitment to LSU? Most had given up, but there were a few who still thought they could change Luke's mind.

"This is Luke." *Stay cool. No emotion. I'm not interested.*

"I thought it might be you. My name is Clark, Son, Billy Clark. I want to talk with you about your baseball future."

Sure, you and a hundred others. The coach at LSU had told him he would still get calls like this, but Luke had assured him he wasn't interested in any other team but the Tigers.

"I'm sorry, Mr. Clark, but I'm committed to LSU."

"Son, I'm not with a school." Luke's hand stopped with the phone halfway to its cradle. "I'm with a professional team."

"Professional team?" Luke's voice raised enough that Sarah stopped in mid-knead. "What team you with?"

"The Milwaukee Braves," said Clark. "Or, I should say the Atlanta Braves. It's going to take me some time to get used to that. Atlanta Braves. You know, of course, we moved to Atlanta this year, right?"

Yes, Luke knew they had moved to Atlanta. The Braves had Eddie Mathews at third and the great Hank Aaron in the outfield. Jimmy Pikes didn't like Aaron because he was colored and he had even traded Aaron's baseball card to Luke for Jim Maloney just to keep his card collection all-white. But Luke knew that Henry Aaron was every bit as good as any white player, including Mickey Mantle.

"Yes, sir, the Atlanta Braves. You're with them?"

"Yes, Luke, I'm a scout with the Braves. What they call a 'birddog.' I look for talent that the regular scouts may have missed. Somehow, they missed you. I don't know how, except for the fact you play in a small town. Still, someone should have noticed you. You hit, what, .410 your senior year?"

"Actually, .435 if you count the playoffs. And I pitch, Mr. Clark. I was undefeated this year—10 and 0."

"Yes, Luke, I saw you pitch a couple of times."

"You were at some of my games?"

"Two of them. Including the no-hitter. That was very impressive. But to be honest, I don't think you have big-league material as a pitcher."

"Oh." In that one syllable, Sarah saw excitement drain out of Luke. She was listening to his end of the conversation, trying to figure out who was on the phone. Just then her husband, James walked in the kitchen door. He was tall, over six feet two, slightly graying, and his denim shirt and khaki pants were soiled from working in the garden. He took off his khaki hat and kissed Sarah on the cheek, then reached into the cupboard for a glass and filled it with water from the sink.

"I think Luke's talking to another coach," said Sarah. "I heard something about baseball and the Atlanta Braves." She placed the emphasis on Atlanta, just as Luke had.

"He's probably talking with Jimmy Pikes, trading cards or something. The Atlanta Braves are a pro..." At that point it hit him. *A professional team!* He drained his glass in one long gulp and made a beeline to Luke.

By now, Luke had stretched the phone cord around the corner and down the hall in order to hear the scout better. It was an extra-long cord, that allowed him to take the phone into the bathroom. Luke shut the door and sat on the closed toilet seat. James walked in right after and leaned against the wall listening. Luke lifted his eyes, acknowledging his dad's presence.

"So you don't think I can pitch?" Luke was already penciled in as the number three Pitcher for LSU. The college coach said he would probably be number one by his sophomore year.

"No, Son, not in the big leagues. You have a good fastball, but that's about it. At your level, you can strike a lot of batters out—maybe even in college—for a while. But as soon as you get to the pros, even the low minors, you have to have two or three more pitches or you'll get cooked like a Christmas ham."

"Then you don't think I'll ever make the pros?" Luke's voice rose. He was clearly disturbed by Clark's comments. James had moved to Luke's side. Their dream since Luke was a toddler had been for him to play professional baseball one day. That dream wasn't based on unrealistic expectations. Father and son had worked hard for years and Luke had the tools to work with. He had the raw potential. Now this man had called to tell him his dream was just that—a dream.

"Luke, Son," said Clark, "I said you couldn't ride your pitching to the big leagues. But your hitting, now, that's a different story. Son, I have seen some mighty good players. And I have yet to see a high school player with your skills. You have discipline at the plate that some major league players would love to have. You seem to be able to place a ball just about anywhere you want."

Luke thought about his hit earlier that day—the hit that had knocked Haley to the ground with such force. Is that where he meant to place that ball? No, of course not.

"And your arm, Luke. Well, you may not make it as a pitcher, but as an outfielder, that arm strength is a real gift."

"So are you suggesting I just play outfield in college?"

James was frowning now trying to figure out who the heck his son was talking to, making signs for Luke to give him the phone. Luke held up his finger for his father to hold on.

"No, Luke. I'm saying I would like to talk to you about skipping college all together. I think you are ready for the pros right now."

"What? You're just joshing me, right?"

"I'm as serious as a heart attack, Son."

"So you're saying I could play for the Braves right now?"

James perked up at that. A moment later Sarah made her way into the bathroom to listen.

"Calm down, Son, take it easy. No, not the Braves, but in the Braves' organization. We would start you in the minors-probably. You would have to work your way up, but if I didn't think you could do it, I wouldn't be having this conversation with you."

"Can you hold on a sec, Mr. Clark? You need to talk to my father." Luke took a couple of deep breaths, then handed the phone to James.

"This is James Hatcher. Who is this, please?"

Luke got up from the toilet seat and slid down on the floor with his back against the bathtub. James sat down next to his son, while. Luke and his mother listened to James' half of the conversation.

"Yes. Yes. The Atlanta Braves? Yes. No, just college coaches. He has committed to LSU. Yes. Yes. He starts this fall. You what? What draft?"

At the mention of the draft, Sarah Hatcher groaned.

"No, Luke. That's not the draft board, is it?" Sarah asked her son. "Did you get drafted?"

"No, Mom, that's a pro baseball scout. He wants me to play in the pros right now!"

"You've seen him play?" James continued. There was a long pause. "Not as a pitcher? What about that no-hitter he threw against one of the top teams in Louisiana?" Again a pause. "So you think he can hit big league pitching?... I see. So what about his education? You know his education is important to us?... Oh really? You don't say." The conversation continued this way for several more minutes and then ended with, "Yes sir. I think we can do that. I'm sure Luke is interested. Thank you, too. So, you will call us with the times? Or do you want us to call you? Okay, Mr. Clark. We will. Thanks again." James hung up the phone and looked at Luke.

"Son, do you know who that was? That was Billy Clark, a scout for the Braves! He seems to think you have some talent, and wants to arrange a tryout in front of the coaches for the Braves. If you do well they want to sign you to a contract now."

"What was that about a draft?" Sarah asked. "Does he mean the military? Because, if Luke goes to college, you remember he gets that deferment from Vietnam. I don't want him having to go off to war."

"Sarah, just calm down. It's not the military draft. And Luke would still get his deferment from Vietnam. Baseball teams draft high school and college players now. Whoever drafts you is who you play for, unless you get traded. This guy is with the

Atlanta Braves—they used to be in Milwaukee, but they moved last year. They've already had the draft, so they want to sign Luke as an un-drafted player. He said there would even be some bonus money involved. Maybe as much as $10,000."

"$10,000? That's an awful lot of money," Sarah said, shaking her head. "I don't feel good about this, James. This guy could be a fraud or something." She said that knowing good and well that she had little influence when she saw this type of father-son excitement. She saw it when they were planning a hunting trip, or were working on the '53 Chevy coupe convertible the two were rebuilding under the carport. Sarah did not understand all the ins and outs of baseball, but she knew it was another cord binding her husband and son, so she had learned to love it.

"So, how would Luke play baseball for the Braves when he's going to college?" Sarah continued. "Would they let him just play on the weekends?"

Luke and his father exchanged glances. Luke's look said, "What do I say?" His father's face read, "Let me handle this."

"Sarah, if the boy signs with the Braves, they would want him to start training right away-this summer. His college might have to wait."

"What? Not go to college? But James, he's worked so hard to get that scholarship. You know we can't pay for his schooling. This is the only way he'll get to go. And to just throw it out the window because some charlatan calls offering a chance to play who-knows-where."

"Sarah, the boy is still going to college, he can get his degree on the off-season. Pro players do it all the time.

According to Mr. Clark, if Luke makes the team, they will even pay for his tuition."

"They'd do that?" Sarah asked. "I don't believe it."

"Believe it, Honey. And you have to know, I want Luke to get his education as much as anybody. I don't want him having to work the mills like I had to. But one of the main reasons he's going to college is to train to be a professional baseball player. Now this scout is saying he may be good enough already. If Luke does well in his tryout, he would be getting a head start on what could be a very good career."

In the end, Sarah agreed that Luke could attend this tryout, but insisted that before he sign any contract, that he make a contract with her that he would not let professional baseball stop him from getting his college degree.

"You would be the first man in our family to get a degree, Luke. Forgive me if I have too much pride, but that is something I sure have been looking forward to. Seeing you walk down that aisle and come away with a graduation certificate, well, the only thing I am looking forward to more is the day you get married."

Luke was slowly coming out of his fog. So much had happened, it seemed he had lived a lifetime in this one day. "When do they want me to workout? What do I have to do?"

"Well," James said. "Mr. Clark said we could probably schedule something in two weeks—give you a little time to get ready so you can be in top shape. He would want you and me, Sarah, and even Emily, to fly into Atlanta, and you would workout in their stadium, with the team."

"You mean I'll be working out with Hank Aaron and Eddie Mathews?" Luke's mind was racing.

"I assume the whole team will be there," said James.

"Way out! I can't wait to tell Haley!" With that, Luke remembered his promise to call her. "I gotta call her to see how she's doing and tell her the news. She's not going to believe it."

Sarah and James exchanged glances. What was this with Haley all of a sudden?

Luke gave his mom a kiss, grabbed the phone and sat back down on the toilet seat. James and Sarah left him alone. Luke thought about Haley, how she had looked into his eyes and exchanged thoughts with him, and then the phone call from Mr. Clark. It was only 2:30 in the afternoon, and Luke had already hit two home runs! Nothing could possibly go wrong on a day like this... or could it?

CHAPTER 6

THE PHONE RANG three, four, five times. Where were they? Luke hung up. Maybe he had dialed the wrong number. He tried again. On the fourth ring this time, Mrs. Sparks answered.

"Hello, Doctor? I'm sorry I couldn't get to the phone. Haley was throwin' up again. My husband is holding her right now—but she's shaking real bad."

"Mrs. Sparks? This is Luke. What's going on with Haley?"

"Oh, Luke! I've got to keep this line open for Dr. Spurrier. He's supposed to be calling back." With that, she hung up.

By the sound of her voice alone, Luke knew Mrs. Sparks was worried. Very worried. And it had to do with Haley. Without hesitation he made a beeline out of the house. Lula Yarbrough, the neighborhood gossip and busybody, was just sitting down on the front porch swing to have a Sunday afternoon visit with Sarah when Luke came charging through the screen door, slamming it behind him.

"Luke, Mrs. Yarbrough tells me there was some kind of accident after church today involving you and Haley. Is she all right? Why didn't you say something?"

"I'm going over there right now, Mom." He jumped off the porch without touching the steps and, seeing his truck blocked in the driveway by Mrs. Yarbrough's Oldsmobile, he turned to his left and started running. He ran past the Nelson's house and between the Simmons' camellias and roses, catching his shirt sleeve on a thorn, cut across the Williamson's yard and jumped the drainage ditch into the Thibodeaux's backyard. From there, he was only one house away from the Spark's. And that's when he saw it.

The week before prom, all of the juniors and seniors at Magnolia Springs High School had been bused over to Meek's Funeral Home, where they were shown a hearse, caskets, and the embalming room. This was supposed to scare the death out of the seniors and keep them from driving drunk the night of the prom. (Jimmy Pikes said the trip was a waste because they didn't get to see any dead bodies.) Luke now thought how much the long orange and white Cadillac ambulance in Haley's driveway looked like a hearse. The siren was not going, but the red light on top was rotating around in circles, casting its flashes on the front of the Sparks' house. Dr. Spurrier was directing two men in white uniforms where to go with the stretcher. Luke, out of breath and sweating, grabbed the doctor by the sleeve.

"What's wrong?" he asked anxiously. "Is there something wrong with Haley?" Harvey Sparks came out the door and took Luke aside, freeing the doctor.

"Luke, Haley is very sick. She started shaking and vomiting, then got very sleepy and we couldn't get her to wake up. Dr. Spurrier called for an ambulance. He wants to take her to Mercy Medical to find out what's wrong."

The only time someone from Magnolia Springs would be taken to Mercy Medical in New Orleans is if it were serious. Mercy was equipped to handle big emergencies, unlike the small, fifty-bed hospital in Magnolia Springs.

"Is she going to be all right?"

"Pray for her, Luke. Just pray."

Everyone's movements seemed to be choreographed. The stretcher-bearers wheeled the flat bed across the porch, with Haley strapped semi-conscious in it, and hoisted it in unison to lower it down the porch steps. The ambulance driver, also dressed in a bright white uniform, turned the large vehicle around so it was pointing down the long drive. Dr. Spurrier, stethoscope hanging around his neck, black bag still open in his hand, was talking in low tones to Harvey Sparks. Virginia Sparks pressed a cold cloth on Haley's forehead, keeping pace with the stretcher all the way to the ambulance. She climbed in next to her daughter, ignoring the request that she sit up front, "where you'll be more comfortable, I'm sure, ma'am." Only Luke seemed to be frozen in his place.

"Luke, would you like to go to the hospital with us? I think Haley would like it if you came to see her."

Luke heard Harvey Sparks' voice from far away, as if from a dream. "Yes, sir. I'd like that. But I think I'll drive myself, sir, if you don't mind."

When the ambulance pulled out of the driveway, Luke retraced his path back to his house, this time moving much more slowly, with a trunk full of guilt strapped to his back. Mrs. Yarbrough was gone, but his mom and dad were both sitting on the porch.

"Luke, Son, why didn't you tell us what happened to Haley? Is she okay?" James tried to sound calm. Luke stood; shifting nervously from left foot to right, and told them what had happened that morning. He finished in a hurry, saying he wanted to drive to New Orleans to be with Haley.

"James, I think you ought to drive him there. That's a long way for Luke by himself. And I don't like that road."

"Luke, Son. Why don't you let me drive you in the Chrysler?"

"No, Dad. I want to go by myself. I need to go by myself."

"Well at least take the car."

"No, I'm used to the truck."

"Well, we're going to the hospital, too," Sarah said. "There's no sense in taking two vehicles."

"I need to be alone. Please, Mom."

"The boy will be fine, Sarah," said James. "Luke, call us if you see that Haley has to stay and we'll come up later. okay?"

Luke ran for the truck and spun the wheels as he backed quickly down the gravel drive. He was out to Main and then on Highway 38 before it started to sink in where he was going, and why.

Highway 38 curved and dipped continually, with a bayou on the side as a shoulder. Drive off into that, and chances were you wouldn't be seen again. Luke knew to drive carefully on this stretch, and did so without thinking about the road. His thoughts replayed the events of that day. The bet, the crowd he was playing to, then the hit. He saw the ball again in his mind. He could almost count the stitches on the seams.

He had put all that he had into hitting that pitch. His instincts had taken over; he could not have done otherwise. His obsessive competitiveness and his pride had propelled that ball back at the pitcher—the enemy. Only this time the enemy was the girl he was just beginning to-to what? Love? What did he know about love? He knew that he loved baseball. And, sure, he loved his parents. Who didn't love their parents? What about God? Well, yes, he guessed he loved God, too. His parents had raised him to be good, act polite, to treat others with respect. He went to church and Sunday school and even youth camp in the summer of '63.

But could he love a girl? Could he love Haley? Right now, he believed no matter what the future held for the two of them, he needed to see her. He needed to touch her hand, to hear her voice. He had never felt this way before about a girl. Something had awakened in him today, and he liked it. He also feared it. It seemed to come so easily, and he had always been taught that nothing good came without earning it. He must earn Haley's love—he couldn't just accept it as a gift. And now, after what he had done, now that she was in the hospital because of him, well, he wouldn't blame her if she didn't want to see him.

Luke rounded a corner only to see the back end of a slow-moving gravel-truck. He tried to pass, but couldn't. Hitting his brakes hard, he almost swerved too far to the right toward the bayou. Traffic coming toward him was pretty heavy. *Where's everybody going on a Sunday?* Occasionally, there would be a space between the oncoming cars, but as soon as Luke would pull out to pass, another car would come. It was like they were spaced just perfectly to prevent anyone from passing. Luke was sure they were doing it on purpose. *Why are they going so slow? What's a stupid gravel-truck doing on the road on Sunday?*

He felt it rising in him, that rage that controlled him when he was between the white lines of the baseball diamond, the feeling that pushed him to defeat all foes on the field of battle. The rage that pressed him to throw fastballs under the chins of hitters who dared to get too close to home plate, like the great Bob Gibson did. The rage that made him punish baseballs, hitting them so hard that it seemed they would never come back down. This same rage now rose in him. He had to get past this obstacle, this enemy who was keeping him from his goal.

Despite the double-yellow lines in the middle of the highway and despite all the oncoming the traffic, Luke again nosed his way carefully out from behind the gravel-truck, but quickly pulled back in, narrowly avoiding a collision with an oncoming Buick. He slowed down and again, pulled slightly to his left, but the stream of cars fleeing New Orleans was offering no reprieve.

There was a small shoulder on the right of the highway made of white shale, next to the bayou. Luke slowed again slightly and then eased to the right of the gravel-truck onto the shoulder. He did not think. He just drove. Just like in baseball. "If you think too much," said Larry Brewer, his high school coach, "you'll only mess yourself up. Do your thinking in practice, then, in the game, react." That's what Luke was doing now, reacting. After he drew up even with the gravel-truck, he floorboarded the accelerator. White shale was flying like buckshot from behind his truck. There were only inches separating the left side of his car from the right side of the truck and, he imagined, the same margin keeping him from sliding into the bayou. He increased his speed a little more and pulled even with the front of the truck. All would be lost if there was another car right in front of the gravel-truck. Maybe that is why it was going slow after all. Luke crept forward past the cab enough to see the road in front of the gravel-truck was clear. In that instant he pushed the pedal down and quickly pulled in front of his enemy. The gravel-truck driver blasted his horn in protest. But Luke kept the pedal to the floor, attempting to make up his lost time. His heart raced as if he had just beat out a throw to second. His hands were covered with cold sweat. He was terrified and thrilled at the same time. His parents wouldn't have been too thrilled. That, he knew for certain.

Now why did I do that? His actions had happened without thought. Luke had been no more able to control his actions than he could stop himself from hitting a ball thrown down the middle of the plate. Well, his lack of control had seriously hurt a beautiful, young girl. That surely was a sin against Haley and, he was sure, against God. If he had plunged into the bayou, it would be understandable punishment for what he had done.

His thoughts continued along these lines as he drove South, slowing only when passing through the towns of Ponchatoula and LaPlace. At last, Luke arrived in New Orleans— the Big Easy—enveloped in sin and guilt. Mercy Medical was not hard to find. The large, blond, brick structure was located just inside the city limits, right off the highway. He followed the signs and found an open space in the lot marked "Visitors."

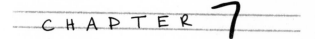

CHAPTER 7

MERCY MEDICAL WAS not the most aesthetically pleasing hospital around. Yellowed tile floors and bare walls made it a cold place. The lobby was empty and strangely quiet. Luke thought maybe he had entered at the wrong door. He looked around for anyone that could help him find Haley. Finally, he saw a sign marked "Registration" with an arrow pointing down a hallway to the left. He followed this to what appeared to be a smaller version of the lobby where a woman sat behind a wooden desk, flanked by two telephones, a typewriter, and a clipboard. By the look she gave him, Luke knew she considered him just one more interruption.

"I'm looking for Haley Sparks," he said, trying not to sound too anxious. Luke was not comfortable here in this hospital, knowing he was the reason Haley had been brought here.

The woman behind the desk looked up at Luke over the top of her glasses, then consulted her clipboard. She ran her finger down the length of the page, then the second page. "Did you say Sparks?" The woman had a deep, raspy voice, as if she were exhaling cigarette smoke instead of words.

"Yes, ma'am—Haley Sparks." Luke repeated the name slowly, like that would help it appear on the papers on the woman's clipboard.

"Don't see no Sparks on here." She reached for the ivory rotary phone on her desk and dialed three numbers. Luke could hear a voice on the other end answer "Emergency."

"Shirley. Do you have a Haley Sparks down there?" The woman said the name as if it would be unbelievable for anyone named Haley Sparks to be in an emergency room. After a few seconds she hung up without saying "thank you" to Shirley.

"She was just admitted to Intensive Care. That's on the fourth floor. But they don't take visitors in the rooms."

"But I've got to see this girl. It's very important."

"Are you family?"

"No, ma'am. But I'm very close to the family."

"Well," said the woman, obviously anxious to be rid of this young man so she could be about her other business, "you can go up and wait in the fourth-floor lobby. Maybe someone up there can help you. There is an elevator just down the hall." With that, she looked back down at her desk.

Luke stepped out of the elevator into a dimly lit lobby cluttered with gray plastic chairs that had been pulled into groups. Only two other people were in the lobby, and they were both asleep. Luke walked up to a window cut in the wall directly in front of him, expecting to find a nurse or at least an orderly to tell him that only family was allowed. But there was no one in sight. He waited at the window for several minutes wondering if he should call for someone to help, but the complete silence on the floor seemed to forbid any noise from rising out of him. He looked at the table on the other side of the window opening and saw a list of what looked like names and room numbers. Reading upside down, he saw the name "Sparks, Haley" and a number— "17." Still no one came to help, so Luke—hesitantly at first, then with a bit of boldness—pushed open the door that led to the patients' rooms and began to walk directly through an area with scattered metal tables, desks, a sink and a large gray cabinet. As he passed the tall cabinet, he saw a nurse seated on the other side writing on a notepad.

"Can I help you with something?" she asked.

"I'm looking for Haley Sparks," said Luke.

"The doctor is in with her right now—and her parents. Are you a member of her family?"

Luke could not lie. His parents taught him lying was a great sin, and never let him get away with even a small fib. A blistering on his backside with a switch from the tree in the backyard had seared this lesson into his mind at an early age.

"No, ma'am."

"Then you can't be back here. You'll have to wait in the lobby." She got up from her desk and escorted Luke back to the plastic chairs. "I'll tell her father she has a visitor."

Luke thanked her, feeling slightly embarrassed for being caught in the act. He went back and sat down in a corner chair, looking at the couple still asleep—an elderly black duo, each with salt-and-pepper hair. He noticed they were holding hands even as they slept. He remembered holding Haley's hand that afternoon, thinking it felt so soft compared with his calloused hand.

"Luke? Luke?"

He shook himself from his daydream to see Harvey Sparks standing at the door the nurse had just sent him through. "Come on back, Son. I told the nurse you were wanted back here."

Luke pushed himself out of his seat and walked with Mr. Sparks, this time down the hallway on the left, to the room with the number 17 above it.

Dr. Spurrier was there, but his black bag was nowhere in sight, nor were his overalls. Dressed casually, he was talking with another doctor who was wearing white and had a stethoscope hanging around his neck. They paid no attention to Luke as he walked toward Haley's bed.

The last time Luke had seen Haley—had it just been that afternoon? Or had it been years?—in his truck, she had been slightly pale but with a sparkle in her eyes when she looked at Luke. Now she was nearly as white as the sheets that covered her. Her left arm was propped up on a table with a needle inserted into it, held there with white tape. The needle was attached to a long tube that ended at a glass bottle full of clear liquid. Haley's eyes were closed; she looked weak and frail, yet peaceful. Almost like she was…No! Luke couldn't go there.

"She's been drifting in and out, Luke. She really doesn't even know where she is. But she's called your name a couple of times. You can talk to her if you want." Mr. Sparks' words were spoken softly, but there was noticeable fear in his voice.

"Thank you, sir." Then, leaning down near Haley, Luke spoke barely above a whisper. "Haley, this here's Luke. You're at Mercy Medical Hospital, Haley. Your dad said it was okay for me to come back and see you." What was he supposed to say? What should he say to a girl that made him feel weak and warm, but was only here in this hospital bed because of what he had done with a baseball bat?

"Dr. Kennedy thinks the best plan is to operate immediately before the pressure builds anymore." Dr. Spurrier was talking to Harvey and Virginia. "He has gone to begin the preparation procedures."

"What is going to happen is this; Dr. Kennedy is going to put what he calls a shunt into Haley's skull. This is going to act like a drain to take away the liquid that is causing the swelling. Until he does this, he can't assess the damage."

"Will that make her better, Doctor?" asked Harvey.

"Dr. Kennedy is afraid the swelling of her brain may have already caused some permanent damage, but he can't tell until after he does this first operation," Dr. Spurrier emphasized. "In cases like this, patients sometimes regain full use of their senses. But others lose their sight, or their hearing. There could be some mental loss. This is a very serious situation."

Virginia Sparks, eyes bloodshot from crying, looked as if she'd aged ten years in one single afternoon. On the brink of collapse, she leaned fully on her husband's wide shoulders in order to remain standing.

Harvey asked the doctor what he knew his wife wanted to ask but was unable to form the words. "What are her chances of not surviving?"

Dr. Spurrier looked at his young patient lying still in the hospital bed, then looked fully into Luke's face, then back to Mr. Sparks. "Chances are definitely in her favor. The truth is; it's just too early to tell, Harvey. We have to pray that her brain returns to its normal size quickly."

This was more than Virginia could take. Her sobs became full-fledged wailing, and Harvey quickly took his wife out of the room. Dr. Spurrier also took this opportunity to exit, leaving Luke alone with Haley. He gazed down at her in her frailty, replaying the doctor's words with disbelief.

Too early to tell...What?...Die? Haley can't die. She just can't. Luke's mind and emotions were numb. Everything seemed surreal. It was all happening too fast. *This can't be true.* Luke felt helpless. He should be doing something. *Pray...Just pray.* That was what Haley's father had told him to do. *Yes, pray.* His mom prayed at times, he knew. Luke had never really heard his father pray, other than at suppertime—never about anything as serious as this. How should he pray? He somehow knew he should kneel, so he sank down next to Haley's bed, folded his hands, and closed his eyes.

"*God, I pray that Haley will get better,*" whispered Luke, "*that this operation will make her better.*" He remembered hearing Dr. Spurrier talk about Haley's brain being swollen, but he didn't really know how he should pray about that. What else should he say in his prayer? He was silent on his knees. Then he spoke from deep within his core, a cry.

"Oh, God, it's my fault Haley is here! I'm so sorry this happened! I'm really sorry I did what I did. If you'll make her better, I'll do anything you want." His cries became louder and panicked. He pleaded, *"Don't let her die, God. Please don't let her die."*

Luke felt a hand on his shoulder and he jolted upright to see the nurse he had met earlier.

"Son, I have to prepare your friend for surgery now. If you'd like, there's a chapel on the second floor. I'm sure you will find it a good place to pray." The calm in her voice transferred to Luke, who nodded and stood to his feet. He started to leave, then turned back to Haley, bent down, and kissed her forehead.

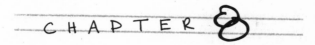

CHAPTER 8

LUKE FOUND THE chapel in a darkened corner of the second floor. He noticed a wooden table at the far end of the room with a large Bible lying open on it. He looked to see what it was open to, and he saw "Psalm 120."

He began reading the text, beginning with the first verse of that chapter.

"In my distress I cried unto the Lord, and he heard me."

It was only one simple line, yet the words seemed to leap off the page, seizing Luke's frayed heart. He stepped back from the table and sat in one of the miniature pews to think about those words. To Luke, his whole religious life had consisted in his involvement with his church. He seldom thought of God outside of its walls. When the services ended on Sundays and he at last stepped out of the church doors into the bright sunshine it made him feel as if he were being released from prison, kind of like when the bell rang at the end of seventh hour in school. Luke always tried to do what was right, and tried to be good to others, but he really never thought about actually talking with God about, well, about regular life. His prayers in Haley's room a few moments before had burst forth from his gut like an oil gusher up from out of the ground. They surprised and, truth be told, frightened him. He had never prayed with such emotion— never cried out to God before. *Could God really hear me? And if He did, would He answer me? What if He didn't?*

"In my distress I cried unto the Lord, and he heard me." Luke recited the verse under his breath, then he stepped forward and reread it out loud in a low voice. Sitting back down, he had a warm sensation inside, thinking that maybe it was true. Maybe God did hear his prayer and would make Haley better. Just to be sure, Luke decided he should pray again. He closed his eyes, folded his hands together, and bowed his head. How loud should he talk? Would it be better to just pray silently? He decided to talk to God in a respectful whisper.

"Dear God, I know I'm just a guy. I really don't know all the right things to say. But I'm asking you, please, please hear me. I'm begging you, God. Please make Haley better. I'm so sorry for what I've done. Please God, if you are up there–if you can hear me–please help her to get better. Amen."

Luke turned around, looking to see who had come into the chapel. He had sensed someone else in the room as he prayed, even though he had not heard the door open. He also felt a strange peace in his heart. Luke stood and walked the ten or so paces to the door, which was shut tight. There was no one there.

The benches were empty, as well as the floor. He was sure there had been someone else in that tiny space with him. Luke shrugged it off as strange and after another couple of minutes, left the chapel and headed back to the fourth floor lobby.

The sleeping couple had awaken, speaking softly with their heads close together. Luke also found his parents sitting there, along with Pastor Taylor of Galilee Baptist.

"Luke, Honey, we wondered where you had gone off to." Sarah had a strain of concern in her voice.

James stood and put his arm around Luke's shoulders, steering him to a chair. "Mr. Sparks called the church to alert the prayer-chain. When we were called to pray, we thought it important that we come. We dropped Emily off at your Aunt Lydia's. How you holding up?"

"I'm fine, but it's not me I'm worried about, Dad. Any news?"

"We spoke with Harvey. They've taken Haley to the operating room. Harvey and Virginia are waiting in her room."

At first, Luke stared at them blankly. Then he rubbed his eyes as his emotions began to rise.

"Oh, Luke," said Sarah, placing her arms around her son. "We all know it was just an unfortunate accident. I'm sure everything's going to be all right and Haley will be fine. She's a tough girl, you know." The sound of his mother's voice, more than the words themselves, brought a calm to Luke's sorrow, just as they had when he had thrown a football into a tree when he was six, knocking a robin's nest to the ground. When he saw the five broken blue eggs on the ground, he ran to his mother, crying that he had killed five birds. His mother's calm words and presence had comforted him then, too.

After a few moments of stillness, Luke excused himself to find a restroom. Once there, he splashed water on his face, cranked down the white cloth from the metal box and wiped himself dry, then stood in front of the mirror examining the creature staring back. With his face only inches from the mirror, Luke peered deeply into his own eyes, remembering something Coach Brewer used to say. If he had said it once, he must have said it a thousand times: "Men, if after losing a game you can look yourself in the mirror and honestly say that you put out 100 percent, then you have no reason to hang your head in shame." Well, Luke was looking in the mirror now. He had put out 100 percent all right. And he was feeling plenty of shame.

Instead of a star athlete, he felt more like a character from one of Hans Christian Andersen's fairy tales that Mrs. Stewart had forced him to read back in his sophomore reading class. It amazed Luke how much of that stuff he actually remembered. In one of his tales, Hans Christian Andersen, this 19th-century Danish poet and author, wrote about an unusual mirror that showed people what they were really like, not just on the surface, but underneath all the masquerade as well. On top of that, every bad and good-for-nothing trait stood out, no matter how much you tried to hide it.

Well, Luke was seeing every bad and good-for-nothing characteristic about himself. It was all so obvious. Though he didn't really want to take on that stupid bet, once at the plate, his pride and ego had taken over. *I should have just let Haley strike me out. Why didn't I just let her? Why did I have to hit the ball so hard? That was totally uncalled-for! I did exactly like I did that night on the fire tower. I had to show off. Haley was right. I am a jerk and I haven't grown up!...*

When he returned, he found his father and Pastor Taylor standing and talking with Dr. Spurrier, who had been in Haley's room. He walked up close to where they were talking. James moved to his left, creating a space for Luke to join them.

"Luke, I was telling your father and the Pastor that Haley has what we call a closed-head injury. The skull is like a box to protect the brain; only right now the brain is swollen, pushing it against the sides of this 'box...' We are going to drain some of the fluid to help the brain tissue return to its normal size." Dr. Spurrier paused for effect before he continued. "After this happens, we can evaluate any damage that has been done."

"Might there be permanent effects?" asked Pastor Taylor.

"Well, as I said earlier, it's too early to tell. In cases like this it is not uncommon for there to be lingering reminders, such as a slight slur in the speech, or blurred vision. In extreme cases, patients have suffered paralysis. But it is my hope that Haley"— here the doctor looked into Luke's eyes for the first time— "comes out of this just fine. I do know she's in good hands with Dr. Kennedy. He's one of the best surgeons around." Dr. Spurrier laid a hand on Luke's shoulder, a warm, comforting touch to match the warmth in his eyes.

With a final glance at Luke, Dr. Spurrier headed around the corner to an elevator and up to surgery.

"I think I'll head down to the cafeteria," said James to Luke. "You want to come with me?"

The two of them found their way to the cafeteria on the first floor. The same yellow tile gave it a cheerless look. The food serving line was closed, so James Hatcher put a few coins into the coffee vending machine.

"When you were just a kid," James said, as the coins dropped in the slot, "around four or five years old, you'd get a real kick out of these cups dropping down. When the coffee would pour into them your eyes would get as big as saucers and you'd laugh. You remember that?"

Luke watched as his father took the first cup. "I remember," he said softly, as the second cup dropped down and began to fill up.

They each took a cup and made their way to a table.

"Dad, what if something really bad happens?" Luke said, pulling a chair out. "I mean, what if she can't walk or something after this? I don't think I could live knowing that I caused it. Or what if she…"

James reached across the small linoleum-covered table and put his large, calloused hand on Luke's arm. His hand was leathery, with only three full fingers, because he had lost one in an accident at the mill. He worked at the same mill as Harvey. A large number of the men in Magnolia Springs worked at the mill. James was struggling, because he was not the best communicator. Having grown up on the farm during the Depression, he had been taught that real men were supposed to be tough and never show too much emotion. Action, to James Hatcher, spoke much louder than words. "Son, when bad things happen, we have to believe that somehow God will help us get through them," he said. "You gotta be strong."

Unresponsive, Luke stared down blankly at his coffee.

James saw he wasn't having much effect on his son, so he tried to steer the conversation into safe territory for both of them. Baseball was the glue that held them together, and it had been for as long as either of them could remember. They could talk for hours about hitting a change up, or pitching a slider. They both agreed that the great Bob Gibson was the best pro pitcher around, although an argument could be made for Sandy Koufax.

"How 'bout that Billy Clark calling? That's some opportunity, yeah? A tryout with the Braves, who woulda thought?" James' eyes lit up. "Mr. Clark said they want to see you in about two weeks. That doesn't give us much time. Starting tomorrow we need to work on your hitting and throwing. Since Mr. Clark said they're thinking about playing you in the outfield, I think we also need to work on catching some deep flies—I want to see you really stretching for those balls. Then we have to get some reps throwing from the outfield to the infield. I want to see some frozen ropes. We gotta run, too. You have to be in the best shape of your life."

Luke swished the coffee around in his cup. "Sure, Dad. Anything you say." No emotion. No feeling.

"Luke, Son," James said with a sense of urgency in his voice. "This is an opportunity of a lifetime. You're gonna need to be focused like never before. I know you're upset about Haley, but I'm sure she's going to be fine. You know doctors. They have to take every precaution just to be on the safe side. Heck, you got nailed in the head with a baseball once and you were okay."

Luke looked at his father, somewhat amazed at his apparent insensitivity to Haley's plight. How easy it was for him to shift away from the crisis at hand. "I was *eight*, dad. The batter was also eight. I don't think that is a fair comparison. That ball didn't have quite the same power as mine did. And you know as well as I do that Coach Brewer is always drilling us on safety—on not doing stupid things. You've heard him say a million times, 'bats and balls are like weapons, so don't horseplay around with them.' And he never let us practice hitting off a pitcher without him being behind the screen."

"Luke," said James, "none of the pitchers you hit off of in games were behind screens. Haley was just a bizarre accident."

"Yes, but it could have been prevented and I should have known better. It was on a softball diamond, Dad—a smaller than regulation softball diamond for that matter! They use that diamond for stupid church games and little league practices."

"Watch it, Son. There's no need to get upset."

"Come on, Dad. Haley was much too close for me to be hitting a hardball like I did! The pitchers in my games are much farther away. You know that, too!" Luke stood up abruptly, obviously frustrated. "I'm going back to the waiting room."

Just as his son had done a couple of minutes ago, James was now the one who was staring blankly into his half-empty coffee cup.

→→ ←←

When both of them had returned to the fourth floor lobby, they found additional visitors. Dot and Liz were there, along with Dot's mother, Nell.

"When we found out what happened, Mama drove us here," said Dot. "We just had to come."

"A nurse told us that Dr. Spurrier is in talking with Haley's mom and dad," reported Liz. "And he would come talk to us after he finishes." Liz had a way of sharing information as if she were a news reporter on the radio.

When Dr. Spurrier came out, it was nearly 9:45 P.M. Haley had been in surgery for over an hour.

"So far, so good," said Dr. Spurrier. "Up to this point, things have gone smoothly. But we are not quite out of the woods yet. Dr. Kennedy has a little more work to do. Probably about another hour before we know for sure. I'm heading back to be with Harvey and Virginia. I know they are glad you all are here. As soon as we know something we'll let you know."

Sure enough, after another hour of forced patience, Harvey Sparks, flanked by both Dr. Spurrier and Dr. Kennedy, came through the gray steel door that led to the patients' rooms. They walked to the center of the small lobby and let the others come to them.

Harvey spoke first, his voice revealed obvious exhaustion. "I know you all are wanting to know about Haley and the

81

operation, so I asked Dr. Kennedy if he would tell you. As you know, he's the one who did the operation."

"Haley is resting in the recovery room right now," Dr. Kennedy started right in. "The operation went just about as I expected. We were able to drain much of the fluid. Hopefully, this will allow her brain to return to its normal size. This could take anywhere from a few hours to several days. We'll take X rays every several hours to monitor the progress."

"Can she come home soon?" Dot asked.

"I'm afraid she'll have to be here for several days—more than likely it will be a week or more. With good friends like you, I'm sure she'll want to get back home as quickly as possible." Luke could tell the good doctor was trying to put them at ease, and he felt the doctor was not telling them something, something that Luke needed to know.

"Will there be any permanent damage?" he blurted out.

Kennedy made eye contact with Haley's father before answering Luke. "It's still too early to tell, Son. But the part of her brain that was most affected by the swelling is the part that controls speech. You may have noticed she was having trouble getting her words out before she was brought to the hospital. We'll have to see how she recovers, but there is nothing I can tell you right now."

A loudspeaker from up in the ceiling came to life just as Luke was about to press further. "Dr. Kennedy to O.R. Recovery—stat! Dr. Kennedy to O.R. Recovery—stat!"

Dr. Kennedy did not take time to say goodbye to the gathering of friends. He bypassed the elevators for the stairwell while Harvey and Dr. Spurrier followed. Liz asked no one in particular, "Where are they going? Why did they leave so fast?"

Dot started to sob. She turned to Pastor Taylor, who stood with a look of confusion on his face, then she went to her mother, who gathered her in her arms tightly.

"What does 'stat' mean, Mr. Hatcher?" Liz pressed. But before James Hatcher could answer, Dot said through her crying, "It means 'fast.' It's what they say when there's an emergency. And it is probably about Haley."

As if to confirm Dot's assessment, the door opened at that moment to allow a nurse, acting as an escort, to take Virginia to the elevators.

"Oh, my!" With that, Pastor Taylor also left the quickly diminishing group for the elevator. Sarah Hatcher opened her arms wide to take Luke in, but he ignored her offer, opting to stand by a window and stare mindlessly into the dark. Liz ran to fill the empty space in Sarah's arms. James sat down and buried his face in his hands.

In the recovery room, without warning, Haley had gone into some sort of seizure. Her body contorted and jerked. Then, after a few seconds, it fell limp. At that same moment, the heart monitor stopped making its short, rhythmic beeping sounds and went into one, long continuous *beeeeeeeeeeep*. The red line that usually jagged up and down had gone flat. Dr. Kennedy and the nurses worked frantically. They jerked the covers back from Haley's chest and placed two shock paddles on her chest.

"Ready. Clear!" Dr. Kennedy yelled. The machine made a loud thud-like sound as the electric shocks went into Haley's heart. Her body arched several inches above the bed.

"She's still not breathing!" a nurse shouted after checking Haley's pulse.

"Again!" Dr. Kennedy yelled. Thud. Haley's body arched once more. "Again!" Thud. Jolt. "Again!"

⇥ ⇤

Fifteen minutes had passed since the loudspeaker had called for Dr. Kennedy, then half an hour. No one dared ask the obvious. However, when the elevator opened and Pastor Taylor stepped out, they had their answer. Pastor Taylor's eyes were red and moist. His hands clenched and unclenched into fists. He spoke in a stage whisper.

"Haley," he said, clearing his throat, "passed away a few minutes ago. She had a brain seizure, and her vital organs just shut down."

CHAPTER 9

SHEER DISBELIEF AND confusion rendered them speechless. Everyone in the room was in a state of shock. Dot was the first to break the frozen tension. She lifted her voice into a howl and buried her face into her mother's blouse. Sarah Hatcher's broken, stammering voice managed, "How can this be?"

Pastor Taylor's pale, stricken expression spoke the words that he couldn't. He simply shook his head in sorrow.

James walked woodenly over to Luke and put his hand on his shoulder. This seemed to arouse Luke out of his daze. He looked at his dad as if not seeing. His expression of shocked disbelief gave way to grief and then to fury. Shaking off his father's hand and violently pushing him away, Luke yelled, "Get away from me! Just get away! Liars. You're all liars!" Then he bolted from the room.

Instead of taking the elevator, he exploded down the four flights of stairs, bursting through the yellow-tiled lobby and out into the humid night air. Under parking lot lights that were swarming with bugs, he searched for his truck. James ran after his son, but he couldn't keep up.

Luke found his truck, jumped in, and sped away into the night, leaving behind a smoking rubber stripe. On Highway 38, he pushed the pedal until the engine produced a high-pitched whine. The whole truck began to vibrate so much that it threatened to fly apart. Mile-posts passed in fast succession; telephone poles whizzed by like pickets in a fence. It had started to drizzle, so Luke flipped on the wipers.

He knew he needed to slow down, to be more cautious, but he couldn't. If he drove off into the bayou—so what, he deserved it. Yet, his own death would be almost too easy—too simple—too fast. He deserved a lifetime of pain and punishment.

By the time James got to his car, Luke was long gone to who-knew-where. So, instead of trying to run him down, James went back into the lobby and placed a call to the State Police telling them to be on the lookout for his son, that he was acting out of his mind and was possibly a danger to himself and others.

Luke drove like a maniac until he was atop the Lake Maurepas Bridge—a tall, steel-framed suspension bridge with a narrow shoulder. Pulling over, he killed the truck's engine, climbed out into the rain, and reached into the truck's bed. Lying there like dual assassins were the baseball and the bat. His glove was with them. He grabbed all three and with strength produced by the storm raging within him, threw them as far as he could into the lake.

"I hate baseball!" he screamed, as if his heart had been ripped from his chest. All of the mounting tension and anguish from what happened was exploding from the depths of his soul. "How could this happen? How could this happen—from base-ball?... I swear to God, I will never play again!"

He climbed back into the truck and slammed the door, which jolted his keys out of the ignition onto the passenger side of the floorboard. As Luke bent down to retrieve them, he noticed for the first time that Haley's crumpled up stockings and heels were on the floorboard as well. In all the commotion at her house, she had forgotten them. Luke picked up and her shoes and held them close to his face absorbing every detail. How Haley hated to wear them. Yet, they were a part of her. By now the rain was beating hard upon the tin roof of the truck and for the first time, Luke began to weep. Like the rain, he wept hard, lamenting from his very depths. "Noooooo!" he wailed, punch-ing the metal dashboard, cutting his knuckles. It didn't matter. Nothing mattered. "Noooooo!" He continued until his voice was hoarse.

From out in the rainstorm, there came a tap on the truck window. It was a state trooper tapping with the butt of his flashlight. Luke sniffed and wiped his nose with his sleeve, then cracked the window. The trooper was standing there in the downpour wearing a blue raincoat, water pouring from the brim of his hat.

"You all right, Son?" he shouted through the rain, but not like he was scolding or anything. He was trying to show some compassion because he thought Luke's truck had broken down in the downpour.

"Yes, sir."

"Did your truck stall?"

"No sir."

"Then what were you thinking?" Now he seemed upset. "You been drinking or something?"

"No, sir."

The trooper shined his flashlight into the truck's window. "I need to see your driver's license, please."

"Yes, sir." Luke reached into his back pocket and retrieved his wallet, then handed over his license. "What'd I do?" he asked, knowing good and well that between there and the hospital he had committed a plethora of violations. Take your pick; speeding, reckless driving, tailgating, stopping on top of a bridge with no shoulder, just to name a few.

The trooper didn't even acknowledge Luke's question. Instead he shone his light down on the license, examining it as if he were expecting Luke to be an escaped convict or something. Without looking up, he walked back to his patrol car; blue lights on top still spinning around and casting flickers of light onto the truck and bridge's railing, and began talking on the two-way radio. After a couple of minutes, he came back to the truck's window.

"I could write you up for several things, being stopped on this bridge with no shoulder for one. Did you know that a car could slam into you, Son—especially in this rain. And you'd be dead, just like that. Not to mention, you could kill someone else—someone innocent!"

"I already did," Luke mumbled incoherently under his voice. *Why don't you just arrest me for murder?*

"What did you say?"

"Nothing."

At that moment, there was an incoming call on the two-way. The trooper again walked to his car and picked it up. While talking, he looked up at Luke then attached the handheld walkie-talkie device back to its radio box and made his way back to the truck.

"There was a call out from your parents for us to be looking for you." The officer's tone turned back to compassion. "I heard you had a pretty rough day. Look, for your own protection, I want to follow you on home, to make sure you arrive safely. All right?"

Luke offered no resistance, no argument. He was devoid of emotion—completely poured out—empty. He drove home in wearied haze with the trooper kindly trailing him.

CHAPTER 10

SLEEP WAS HIS enemy. He would drift off, only to have his mind ripped awake by nightmares that badgered him with the truth that he had killed his beloved Haley, with a baseball of all things. And as much as he felt guilt, he also felt the pain of her absence. He missed her fiercely, with a throbbing in his stomach and a feeling of sandpaper down his throat. He longed for her silly laugh and snort—if he could just once touch her lips to his. A massive hole had been torn out of Luke's gut and nothing could patch it up.

How could something so–so weird, crazy, tragic happen? Things like this don't really happen. Yes, they do. It did. And Haley's not coming back. If only I could turn back the clock.

The nightmares usually began with Luke seeing a ball coming toward him as if in slow motion. He would swing with all his might to kill the ball, then the ball would rocket toward Haley. He would yell, "Noooooo!" Then he'd helplessly watch the ball hit her in the temple. Haley would spin around and drop to the ground. At that point from somewhere above his head he would see Virginia Sparks wagging her finger, saying, "Luke, you should have known better! What have you done? You've deprived me of my only daughter! She's not coming back, Luke. She's gone forever. You should have known better! You should have known better." And that's when he would wake up, shaking, sweating. Sarah had tried to sit up with him, but he made it clear that he did not want anyone near him right now. So she left him alone, but left the door to her room open to be able to hear her son if he called out.

In her room, Sarah would kneel by her bedside and pray until she could no longer stay awake. Once, she ran to Luke's side when he was crying out in his sleep, but instead of receiving her comfort, Luke pushed her out and locked his door in her face.

James and Sarah talked to Dr. Spurrier, who assured them that Luke was going through the normal grieving processes. He prescribed some sleeping pills for him, and he instructed them to give him his space as long as they knew where he was and could keep a watchful eye on him. Dr. Spurrier cautioned them that it could take weeks, possibly months for Luke to be "normal" again—that they would have to be patient.

Luke paced in his room, did sit-ups, push-ups. He went to the bathroom only to relieve himself, never to bathe or brush his teeth. He did everything to stay awake as much as possible. Sarah and James urged him to take the sleeping pills, but he refused. By the third day, Luke had survived on less than a total of eight hours of sleep.

At 3:00 P.M. that day, he could not resist sleep any longer by staying in his room, so he put on his shorts, tee shirt, and canvas sneakers and made his way outside. He ran down White Street to the city park. Luke had run in this park for as long as he could remember. He had worn a trail where he liked to run around a small lake with geese and ducks, through a patch of pine and oak trees, a playground with a high, winding slide and a couple of seesaws and a merry-go-round. He would run past three youth league baseball diamonds before turning back toward his house. As he passed the baseball diamonds, Luke recalled the times his father would take him there on Saturday mornings and during the weekdays after dinner—just him, his father, a bucket of baseballs, and a bat. James would pitch to Luke, who would hit just about everything thrown his way. When the balls were gone, they would both race to the outfield to see who could collect the most. Today, as he ran past the diamonds, Luke thought about how his dad sometimes would laugh as he danced out of the way of balls hit back to the mound.

"That's good, Son," James had shouted back. "Keep those pitchers on their toes!"

Luke stopped cold. The thought of his dad laughing had just turned into a picture of Haley lying face down in the dirt.

Stupid! Stupid! Stupid! I'm such an idiot!... It should have been me!

His stomach began to knot and he felt as if he was going to throw up, but there was no food in his system. Finally, after his stomach settled a bit, Luke turned toward home. Before he could move, he heard a voice calling his name.

"Luke! Luke!" a female called from across the park. "Hey, Luke! It's me, Laurie. Hold on a sec."

Luke turned to see Laurie Harrison waving in his direction. She was wearing white short shorts, white tennis shoes, and a light blue tucked-in blouse with the letter "L" embroidered on one side. Her hair was shoulder length, bleached blonde, hairsprayed perfectly in place. Her makeup was layered like icing on a birthday cake. Laurie Harrison was the only girl in town who would actually get dressed up like that to go the park and she, like so many other girls, had her eyes on Luke. She saw this little surprise meeting as an opportunity to win some points with him, to take him in her arms and comfort him, to give him what she could give him that other girls couldn't.

Luke pretended not to hear her, hoping she would just leave him alone, but no such luck. She raced over, ever determined to catch him.

"How are you doing?" Laurie asked, panting for breath, slightly bent over with her hands on her knees.

Luke said nothing.

"I'm so sorry to hear about Haley and I'm soooo worried about you, Luke," she said, in an over-dramatized manner. "It was just awful what happened 'n all, but you can't be too hard on yourself. It was an accident, you hear? Just an unlucky accident."

This is the exact reason I did not want to leave my room.

Luke still refused to answer back. He merely looked at her like she was an alien from another planet or something.

"Are you sure you're okay? Cause, you don't look so good, darlin'." She brushed up against him ever so slightly, and then awkwardly moved her hands to his shoulders, attempting to massage them. "Oh, my. You're *soooo* tense." She was trying to sound comforting and sexy at the same time.

"You're sick," Luke told her, jerking himself away, obviously irritated. Gnashing his teeth, he could not believe her audacity. He shoved her away, looking at her briefly with an expression of disbelief. Then, shook his head and without saying a word, broke into a dead sprint, leaving Laurie standing there alone in the park.

"Shoot," Laurie mumbled under her breath. Then she yelled out, "I'm sorry, Luke. I'm really sorry."

By the time Luke reached home, he was soaked with sweat. Sarah was in the kitchen, but he never acknowledged her. Instead, he went straight to his bedroom and locked the door behind him. He opened his closet door, pushed through his hanging clothes and began sifting through a pile of stuff—an old basketball, a Frisbee, a half-deflated football, a old electric football set, several dusty trophies, and a stack of board games—feeling around for the leather case leaning in the corner.

Placing the case on the bed, he slowly pulled out his Browning .410 single-barrel shotgun that James had given him for his thirteenth birthday. He fumbled through the top drawer of his dresser for some shells and inserted one into the gun.

Should I leave a note? Why bother? I don't know what I would say. Anyway everyone would know why I had to do this. It had to be done. Luke sat on the edge of the bed and placed the butt of the gun between his feet. Leaning forward he inserted the barrel in his mouth. It was cold and uncomfortable as it pressed against the roof palate.

Luke couldn't remember exactly where, maybe it was in a movie or something, but he had picked up the knowledge that if you ever wanted to shoot yourself, you should put the gun in your mouth. He reasoned that a person with shorter arms would have trouble reaching the trigger, but, alas, he had no such problem.

As he adjusted his position and caressed the trigger with his finger he heard a tender voice from just outside his door. It was Emily—little Emily. Luke startled upright. His hands began to tremble. *Come on, you coward. You can do this. Just pull the blasted trigger! It's not so hard. You don't deserve to live.* Now his hands were clammy.

"Luke, are you in there?" His sister's voice sounded strained. "I just want to tell you that I love you and miss playing with you. Mama didn't tell me to say it either."

A chill went down his spine. Oh, how he loved his baby sister and oh, how she loved him. He remembered the day she was born, how he was so excited that he ran to all the houses on the street, knocking on the doors and announcing to everyone that he had a little sister. *What would his death do to her? What would happen if she were to see me dead and bloody? Would she blame herself like I am doing?*

"Luke, I drew you a picture. I'll just slide it under the door... Maybe we could go to the park later and you could push me on the swing? Maybe?"

Luke set the gun on the floor and retrieved the picture. He studied it like one would study a Monet or a Van Gogh. It was a crude crayon drawing on a piece of Red Chief blue-lined notebook paper, a picture of a house with green grass and a tree in the front yard. The sun was shining down from the top right corner of the page. It had been colored yellow with long streaks shooting out in several directions. In front of the house were four stick figures with big round heads, holding hands and smiling. Two of the figures had hair that flipped up and dresses, to look like Emily and her mother. Emily's figure was much shorter than the other three.

Not wanting to live, but too afraid to die, Luke returned the gun to the closet, stretched his body on his bed and immediately fell sound asleep.

CHAPTER 11

ON THE MORNING of Haley's funeral, Luke's eyes were wide open long before the sun came up. Outside his window, thunder clapped and the wind whipped in an intense furry. Rain began to fall, first pattering, and then pounding upon the tin roof. He lay on his back, staring upward into the darkness, listening to the thunderstorm. Blackness was all around, yet the sorrow that veiled his soul was even blacker. He had thrown heavy blankets over the windows to keep any light from seeping in. His baseball clock radio had been unplugged hours ago. Lying there in the shadows, Luke spiraled deeper into the jagged pit of despair.

He had been locked in his room now for almost four days. His parents had pleaded with him to come out, but Luke had ignored them. He did let them in once, just briefly, to get them off his back. He assured them he would be fine, that he just needed more time. Jimmy Pikes had stopped by, so had Dot, Liz,

Pastor Taylor, and even his high school baseball coach, but Luke refused to see any of them.

By 1:00 P.M., the thunderstorms had stopped. That was a good thing, because the line of mourners waiting to get into Galilee Baptist Church stretched for more than a half block. The whole town of Magnolia Springs was in a state of mourning. White ribbons were hanging from everywhere. They were pinned on shirts and blouses and hung from car antennas and storefronts. The live oak trees that ran down Main Street all had white ribbons tied around them. A huge hand-painted sign in front of the high school read, "Haley's spirit lives with us."

Galilee Baptist had not seen a crowd that large, ever. During the wake, people had to wait for, sometimes, more than thirty minutes just to sign the guest book. And the flowers. The whole back of the church was overflowing with flowers. There were so many arrangements that they had to be stacked on top of each other to make them fit. Around Haley's casket in both directions, flowers reached all the way to the outside walls of the church and behind the casket up into the choir seats. Local florists couldn't keep up, so arrangements were coming in from New Orleans and Baton Rouge. Haley's casket was white with gold trim and it had pink roses on top. Set up beside it was a table with framed pictures that told her life story from infancy. One particular picture was of Haley, Dot, and Liz, making goofy faces, on the beach in Biloxi with their arms slouched around each other. Her softball jersey—number 10—hung down from the table.

At the actual funeral service, the church was so packed that people were standing in the aisles and flowing out into the church corridor. The church windows were opened so those standing outside in the sunshine could peer through and listen to the service. Luke knew he could not face these people, could not answer their questions, could not accept their pity. James and Sarah had insisted that he ride with them to the church, but Luke would have none of it.

"I'm not going," he informed them, pulling his pillow over his head. "Shut the door when you leave."

"You have to do this, Luke, even though you don't want to," James said, standing over his bed. "It's for Haley—your last chance to honor her. I know it's hard, but one day you will be glad you did. You need to at least pay your respects."

"Honor her! Pay my respects! You still don't get it, do you? I killed her, Dad! Haley's dead. Understand? Dead. Never coming back—because of me! How can I honor her? I'm not going and you can't make me."

What could they do? Wrestle him to the ground and physically put him in the car? He was now eighteen, technically an adult and bigger than both of them. James and Sarah could only hope and pray that their son would eventually come around.

Sarah reached down and ran her fingers across Luke's back. "We love you so much, Luke. Can't you please let us help you?"

Luke turned his back to his mother and put the pillow back over his head.

"Sarah, let the boy alone," said James. "There's not much we can do."

"But James, I'm so worried. He won't let us help him through this. Why can't we help our own son?"

"This is his journey; Sarah. This is Luke's passage. He'll come to us when he's ready."

>> <<

During the wake and funeral, the question that everyone was whispering was, "Has anyone seen Luke?" Because he had not shown up at the wake and was still not at the funeral, all kinds of rumors had begun to float around. Laurie Harrison had done a good job of spreading the word of her encounter with Luke in the park—how, in her view, "he had fled into her arms for comfort."

James and Sarah, along with Emily, were sitting on the third row from the front. For the past few days, except for a couple of afternoon visits, Emily had been staying with Sarah's sister Lydia.

At 1:30, the choir began singing *It Is Well With My Soul*, and Pastor Taylor moved slowly to the pulpit. Haley's funeral service was going to be the hardest duty he had ever had to perform during his pastorate. His words of comfort, his counsel, all seemed superficial in the midst of so much pain. As had many others', his faith had been challenged to the core.

When the music finally tapered off, a hollow silence blanketed the sanctuary, save for the sounds of a few muffled sniffs. A toddler's voice echoed across the sanctuary. "Mama, lookie, there's Sleeping Beauty."

"Shhhh!" the mother responded, embarrassed, placing her hand over the toddler's mouth. Sobs increased.

Pastor Taylor gave the congregation a moment to settle down. "It is well with my soul. Yes. This very day, we can say, despite our deep pain and obvious questions that 'It is well with our souls' Why?… Because God's Word assures us that Haley Marie Sparks is in the presence of her King, living in eternal joy."

Pastor Taylor was tall and lean, in his mid-fifties, distinguished-looking, but approachable. Leaning against the pulpit, he scanned the group before him, and in a soft voice he continued his eulogy. "One of the great promises of Scripture is located in 2 Corinthians 1, verses 3 and 4: 'Blessed be God, even the Father of our Lord Jesus Christ, the Father of mercies, and the God of all comfort; Who comforts us in all our tribulations…' As believers in the Lord Jesus Christ, at this time of great need, we stand upon God's promises. Our strength for this moment is not in ourselves, but in Him. We call out to Him for comfort and assurance."

Pastor Taylor stretched his arms out toward Harvey, Virginia, and the rest of the family sitting on the first row. "And this family and all of us are gathered here to recognize Haley's life and home-going into the presence of God."

He backed out of the podium and paced across the stage, slowing directly over Haley's casket. "Though many things in this life are a mystery, we can rely on and trust completely in the clear Word of God, who promises His presence. We can be full of hope today." The pastor cleared his throat and paused to gather his thoughts, and the pause seemed to give more power to his next statement.

"Folks, either Jesus did, in fact, rise from the dead, or He did not. If He did, then we can truly have peace, because Haley is with God in Paradise. Did not the Apostle Paul say, 'To be absent from the body is to be present with the Lord?' Now either we believe that or we don't. If Jesus did not rise, then we might as well go home and never come back to church or pray again, because we've all been swindled. But our spirits bear witness with God that Jesus did in fact rise from the grave. This is the hope and foundation of what we believe.

The Apostle Peter said, 'We did not follow cunningly devised fables when we came to you, but we were eyewitnesses of His majesty.' I ask you today, why did every one of the apostles willingly lay down their lives and allow themselves to be tortured for Christ's sake? A group of men, mind you, that were so afraid for their lives after Jesus' death that they were hiding out, full of fear. What changed them? Where did their sudden burst of courage come from? I'll tell you where it came from, the risen Christ. They came face to face with the resurrected Jesus, and they were never the same. Remember, a man may lay down his life for a cause that he thinks is right, but a man will never lay down his life for something he knows to be a lie. If Jesus did not rise from the dead, then His disciples would have never been able to be martyrs. The same Peter who died for our Lord was also the same Peter who denied him three times. It was the resurrection that gave him his courage. Yes, our faith was founded on something solid."

Turning back toward the podium, he placed his hand on his chin and rubbed it. "In Job 19:25, after his world came apart and he had lost his family, his health, and his fortune, Job made one of the most powerful statements of faith in all of the Bible. It is a statement of praise to God. It is an affirmation of his faith, despite his circumstances."

Now the pastor was again behind the pulpit, gripping both sides with his hands. "Job cried, 'For I know that my Redeemer liveth...and though my body is destroyed, yet shall I see God.'"

He dabbed his brow with a white handkerchief and let the words of Scripture have their full affect.

"Haley's time with us was short, but her life was full. Haley was a precious gift. She was a gift to her family and her friends. To all who knew her, her contagious smile and zest for life affected them. When you left Haley, you were not the same. She had a way of lighting up a dark room. Haley always saw the glass as half-full, not half-empty. And who can forget how she played softball with such a passion? She was a gift to her teammates. Haley was a good person. She was as good as you get. Haley was one of those people who would stop to help a hurting kitten. I remember how she cried when the missionaries from South America came to the church. In fact, Haley confided in me that she would one day like to do some missionary work. But more than all of that, Haley loved God and just last year she made a genuine confession of faith in the risen Christ. The reason we can have peace and hope today is that Haley had settled the issue of her eternal life. Haley Marie Sparks loved God and Haley Marie Sparks is in the presence of the Lord."

"We can not understand why Haley was seemingly snatched from us. None of us have the answers. But you can be sure that God welcomed Haley home. Paul said, 'We see through a glass dimly. Now we know in part, but then we shall know fully.' No, we don't know why things like this happen. That is the grief in all of this. This is a loss. There will be a void that only Haley could fill, and it gives us great grief to say goodbye. Do not think for a moment that we, the family of God, do not experience sorrow. We know pain and sorrow and it is a mistake to tell people not to weep. Yes, there is weeping. The difference is; we do not grieve as those who have no hope. Our hope is in He who grants eternal life for those who believe. And our tears are transformed into a testimony, because somehow God takes our tears and washes our eyes and we are able to see the Lord in his glory and grace. Yes, there are tears, lots of them. There is loss here and there is grief here and it is important that we, as the Body of Christ, put our arms around this family and support them in this time of great need."

Pastor Taylor looked up. To his surprise, he saw Luke standing in the entrance of the sanctuary. Their eyes locked as he continued. "To so many, death is a mystery. What's it all about? To others it is a tragedy. There is no explanation."

Luke started to make his way down the aisle toward the front, but Pastor Taylor held up his hand for him to wait a moment. Luke respected him and stood still. Two hundred pairs of eyes turned upon him. Whispers could be heard filtering through the crowd.

Pastor Taylor continued, aware of the sensitivity of the moment. "But to the Christian, death does not have to be a mystery, nor a tragedy, but a victory. I would like to end by reading 1 Corinthians 15:54-57, 'When the perishable has been clothed with the imperishable, and the mortal with immortality, then the saying that is written will come true: 'Death has been swallowed up in victory... Where, O, death, is your sting?... Thanks be to God! He gives us the victory through our Lord Jesus Christ.'" He closed his Bible and uttered a simple closing prayer. Coach Brumfield, Haley's softball coach, was supposed to speak next, but Pastor Taylor motioned for Luke to come up instead.

The mere actions of showering and shaving himself that morning had been among the most difficult tasks Luke had ever undertaken. Somehow, after his parents had left, despite the depth of sorrow he was experiencing, he managed, for Haley's sake, to push through and put on his best Sunday clothes—blue dress pants, a white button-down shirt, red tie, and his brown sports jacket.

With bloodshot eyes, he slowly made his way down the center aisle of the church toward Haley's casket with what appeared to be some type of garment rolled up under his arms. Stabbed with the pain of seeing her son suffer, Sarah wanted to jump up and take Luke in her arms. She wanted to fix him—to take away the suffering, yet she remained frozen in her seat, clutching her husband's arm.

Luke could feel the myriad of eyes fixed on him. He felt like a criminal on display for the whole world to judge. As he moved closer to the casket, he could see Haley's blonde hair. Then, he could see her face and her hands. Luke staggered under the weight of his emotions. His heart was pounding and he wanted to weep, but he was too numb. Instead, he found the resolve and he leaned forward to gently kiss Haley's forehead. But it didn't feel like her. It was more like kissing a wax figure in a museum. And it didn't smell like Haley either. It smelled like a funeral. The form before him wasn't Haley. It was just her shell. The real Haley was gone. Like a butterfly that had shed its cocoon, her vivacious spirit had flown away.

Luke removed the item of clothing from beneath his arm, his purple and silver Magnolia Springs letterman jacket, one of his most cherished possessions. Sewn on the big M and S were bars for each year he had lettered on the varsity teams. Luke was the only one in Magnolia Springs who had ever lettered in baseball, football, and basketball for all four years. Up and down the sleeves—his collection of award patches—Most Athletic, All State, All District, All American, State Champions '64 and '65. He folded the jacket neatly and with great care he placed it in the casket beside Haley's body. Then, Luke turned toward Harvey and Virginia and said in a respectful voice, "I'm so sorry for taking your daughter from you." His voice echoed off the hardwood floors. Both Harvey and Virginia just stared mechanically into the space directly before them.

Luke looked out over the congregation staring at him. *Who are these people?* He glanced back at Haley's parents, then up to Pastor Taylor, then back to the congregation, then to Haley. Next to him was the communion altar with a large Bible propped on a wooden table. He wanted to just knock it off onto the floor and stomp on it, but because of his mother's presence and out of respect for Haley, he didn't. *That book is full of lies! God promised He would answer me if I called to Him! Well, I called to Him, but Haley died anyway. So, He's a liar! And all you people are hypocrites. You're idiots! Don't tell me God loves us when He lets something like this happen—when He lets me do something so stupid it ends up killing Haley. That doesn't sound like a loving God to me!*

Luke looked directly into the eyes of his parents. James seemed satisfied at his son's effort—it was a sign that he might finally be coming around. He scanned the congregation, seeing the multitude of his friends, Haley's friends—Dot, Liz, Jimmy Pikes, Eli Simmons, and even Laurie Harrison were just a few of the many. He felt as if all of them had some kind of X-ray vision and they could look right through him, reading his thoughts.

He took a quick look back at Haley for one last time and then, with all the composure he could muster, he walked calmly out of the sanctuary knowing full well what he was going to do next. This time, he had used his head. He was being cool and calculating, not wanting his parents to follow him or the cops to come looking. Luke reasoned that by the time the funeral was over and his parents were finally back to the house, he'd be long gone. He just hoped he had the strength to go through with his plan. James left his seat and followed his son into the parking lot.

"You're leaving?" James asked.

Luke turned to face his father. "It took everything I had to do this Dad. I can't do anymore. I'm sorry. I'm going back home and sleep." This was the first time he could remember, since getting that whipping when he was seven, that he had lied to his parents.

"Why don't you let me ride with you? Your mom can bring the car home."

"No, that's okay. I really want to be alone and I would appreciate it if you stayed. It would mean a lot. I feel like you are representing me. Please, Dad." Luke knew that if his father did go home with him, his plan would be spoiled.

"You sure you're fine?"

"I'm very tired. I just want to go home and sleep."

"You're not planning on doing something foolish are you? If you know what I mean?" James asked.

"Dad! Of course, not."

"I had to ask, Luke. Because we are worried about you."

"I'll be fine. I just need time, a lot of time."

"All right, then. I'll see you later, Son."

CHAPTER 12

LUKE HAD TRAVELED fifty-nine miles when Highway 190 widened into Florida Boulevard at the Baton Rouge city limits. It was the main route in and out of Baton Rouge from the southeast and it had been bumper-to-bumper all the way, with several delays. Luke had thought he would never arrive. Because he and James had visited from time to time to watch LSU play ball he was somewhat familiar with the city. Also, he had made a trip when LSU was recruiting him. Now, on his own, he drove up and down the streets trying desperately to find what he was looking for. He was sure that he remembered some time in the past seeing a sign with the tell-tale sleek, gray dog.

Catching a glimpse of a cop car sitting partly hidden in a parking lot, Luke slowed his frenzied pace. He considered asking the policeman for directions, but then realized his parents may have already put out a call to the cops to be on the lookout for a scared young man in a black '51 Ford pickup. Still, asking directions seemed to be the only way he was going to find it. Instead of the cop, though, he opted for the nearest gas station.

"Fill 'er up?" the service station attendant asked, wiping his greasy hands on a red rag and then sticking it into the back pocket of his gray overalls.

"No gas, thanks," Luke said, leaning his head out of the truck's window. "I was just wanting some directions to the Greyhound bus station."

"You on the right road," the attendant answered, spitting a mass of chewing tobacco on the ground, then wiping his mouth with his forearm. "Juss keep goin' up yonder way through two more red lights and you cain't miss it."

Luke nodded politely and was back on the road. Sure enough, after a couple of miles and as many red lights, the bus station was right where the attendant had said. He pulled into a spot toward the back of the parking lot, killed the truck's engine and walked inside.

The main lobby had a group of benches that looked like church pews. People were sitting on these benches and all of them were facing toward the window that looked out onto Florida Boulevard. But there was no preacher standing in front of them telling lies about a God who loved people but let them be killed.

Luke shuffled up to the ticket window.

"Help you?" The woman was about the same age as Luke's mom. He stared at her, wondering what his mom was thinking right now. *Was she crying? Would she be able to take her son leaving like this?*

"I'd like a one-way ticket to...?" Luke knew what he was looking for, and knew why he didn't want to do it in Baton Rouge—it was too close to home and he might change his mind—but he had not thought about where he should go. He studied the listing of destinations behind the ticket agent and their scheduled departures. After a minute or so, he selected a bus that was leaving in half an hour.

"I'd like a one-way ticket to Houston, Texas, please. How much is that?"

"Eight dollars."

Luke handed her a crumpled-up $20 bill that he pulled from his pants pocket.

"The bus will be leaving from Platform B—and they try to leave right on time, so don't fall asleep in the waiting area. You can get something to eat around the corner over there," she said, pointing to a small snack bar down the hallway.

"Uh, ma'am?"

"Yes?"

"Would you happen to have a piece of paper and a pen I could borrow?"

"Just one second." The woman went back to a desk and returned with two pieces of stationary that displayed the bus company's name and address on the top.

"Thank you," Luke said, taking his ticket along with the pen and paper back outside to his truck where he sat down in the driver's seat leaving the door open. Sitting there, he began to write his letter. When finished, he folded the paper, wrote "Mom & Dad" on the outside, and placed it securely on the passenger seat. He glanced at the big clock on the platform wall—fifteen minutes to go. After locking the doors, he grabbed a battered duffel bag and pushed the truck keys into the tailpipe the length of his index finger. There was a pay phone just outside the door to the bus station. He flipped his bag over his shoulders, walked across the parking lot, and dialed "0." The operator asked him to deposit fifteen cents for three minutes, so he dug in his pocket, pulled out the change, and inserted the coins. Luke heard the number he gave being dialed. After two rings someone picked up.

"Pikes residence. Helen speaking."

"Hi, Mrs. Pikes. Is Jimmy there?"

"Luke? Luke, is that you? Where are you? Everybody's lookin' for you!"

"I figured, and I'm fine. Just need to talk to Jimmy and I don't have much time. Get him for me, will ya?"

Luke heard Mrs. Pikes calling for her son, then whispering, "It's Luke."

"Luke? Is that you, buddy?"

"Yeah, Jimmy. Listen. I don't have much time. Can you do me a favor?"

"Sure, Luke. Uh, where you at, man? You doing okay?"

"I'm at the bus station in Baton Rouge, Jimmy. I want you to wait a couple of hours, then call my dad and tell him that the truck is at the Greyhound station in Baton Rouge. The keys are in the tailpipe. But Jimmy, you have to wait at least two hours. You hear? I don't want nobody on my tail." He said this last part with his hand cupped over the mouthpiece so no one else would hear.

"Sure, I can do that. But why can't you just drive, man? Why you taking the bus?"

"It's complicated Jimmy. Please just do this for me. I'll owe you big time."

"I told you I'd do it, buddy. You can count on me."

"All right then. I'm really counting on you—at least two hours. Don't rat on me." Luke heard a man's voice over a loud-speaker announcing that passengers for the bus to Houston could begin boarding. "Look, Jimmy, gotta run. Thanks man. I'm depending on you." After hanging up, he found his way to Platform B, and stepped onto the bus.

"Ticket please?" The bus driver asked. He was a rugged-looking man with a glut of wrinkles on his face who looked as if he had already lived two lifetimes.

"Yes. Where should I sit?"

"Anywhere you like," said the driver—no smile, zero expression.

Luke handed the driver his ticket, then took one last look at the station. Shuffling to his seat, he unexpectedly felt a pang of hunger in his stomach. He had not eaten for quite a while—a couple of days of nothing but small nibbles of the food his mother had brought him in his room. For a brief moment Luke allowed himself to visualize one of her hot bread loaves fresh from the oven. His mouth watered at the thought, yet his mind quickly dismissed the vision. In this new reality, it would be a long, long time before he would ever taste his mother's cooking again.

→← ←←

Luke had never been on a bus like this, though he'd ridden many school buses on his way to play in ball games or on field trips. He remembered when the sixth and seventh graders went on a trip to the art museum in New Orleans. He and Jimmy Pikes had made fun of Haley's new braces until she had tears in her eyes. Jimmy thought that very funny indeed, but later Luke found Haley by herself and told her he was sorry. She told him he was a jerk just like all boys, but on the bus ride back they had sat across the aisle from each other and talked about baseball.

On this bus bound for Houston, Luke did not want to talk with anyone. He found a seat near the back with no one else nearby. Just before the doors closed, however, an elderly woman got on board and slowly made her way to the seat next to Luke. *Now why did she do that? Why couldn't she just sit in the row up front?* The bus was only half full. Luke moved over in his seat and stared out the window.

The bus pulled out from the station and headed west out of Baton Rouge over the newly constructed Mississippi River Bridge. Tug boats pulling long barges moved up and down the river. Luke imagined that he could have hitched a ride on one of them in exchange for labor and been carried down the river to the Gulf of Mexico and then to a foreign country. Looking down from the bridge, he saw how narrow the road was and how far the river ran below. He shuddered as he remembered his stunt driving on the road to Mercy Hospital a few days before.

There was no air conditioning, and most of the passengers had lowered their windows. Luke lowered his too, and he breathed in the hot, sticky air. He closed his eyes and thought maybe sleep would help the time go by faster.

A certain culture accompanies a bus ride. For the first fifteen minutes or so, the bus is mostly quiet. Then, small conversations begin to crop up between those sitting next to each other. These conversations will spread across the aisles and to the seats in front and behind. Then the bus becomes a temporary community. When it stops and admits new riders, these people are treated as strangers, left out of the conversations. After they undergo the unspoken waiting period, however, they are gradually granted full admission into the community.

"I'm going to see my son. He's in the army."

Luke was almost asleep when his neighbor started talking. He opened his eyes and looked in her direction. She wasn't talking to him, but rather to a couple sitting across the aisle.

"He's a sergeant—was wounded in Vietnam, so they sent him to a Veteran's Hospital in Houston. He hasn't told me how serious the injury is, and I'm worried sick."

Luke turned back toward the window. *What am I doing? What is Mom feeling now? She has no idea where I am or where I'm going, or why. What about Dad? Baseball was our lifelong dream. What have I done? It's not too late to turn back? No! I can't turn back. I won't turn back!*

The bus pulled into a station in Lafayette and let off about a third of the passengers, but it let on that many more. Luke stepped out for a couple of minutes to use the restroom. Inside, he splashed water onto his face and stared at himself. As he did, that prowling, slinking, depression that had been haunting him pounced upon him, this time extra-brutal. That's the way it had been these last few days, like waves thrashing a shoreline—sometimes small, sometimes massive and engulfing, but ever-persistent, continually eroding the sands of his soul. His thoughts shifted to the way Haley's eyes had lit up, optimistic and vivacious, when he had asked her out. Then his thoughts turned to the coffin. Now they were closed and still—forever. *Was that just today? It seems like a lifetime ago.* One thing was for sure—because of him, the life that had been once so bright was now gone forever. Luke knew he had to press on. He had to do what he had to do.

Back on the road again, the sun began to set and the bus quieted down. Drops of rain began to patter against the bus window. Through the rain Luke could only see lights and reflections in the distance. With his forehead pressed against the glass, he stared, he contemplated, and he hurt. All Luke wanted was for the pain to go away. The old woman next to him had fallen asleep with her chin on her chest. Luke thought he saw tearstains on her cheeks.

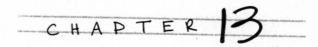

CHAPTER 13

SARAH WAS LYING across the antique bed that had been handed down to her and James from his favorite Aunt Queenie. Her eyes were bloodshot and her nose pink from all the crying. Luke's letter lay unfolded in her hands. She dabbed her eyes with a Kleenex and read it once more, thinking maybe, somehow she'd misread.

Dear Mom, Dad, & Emily,

I know what I am doing. I couldn't tell you because I knew you would try to stop me. Please understand this is something I have to do. I am joining the army. It seems I am good at killing people and that is just what Uncle Sam needs.

I will not be going to LSU or Atlanta. Tell Coach Rogers and Mr. Clark that I appreciate all they've done, but I'm sorry. I will never play baseball again. It's supposed to be a game, something fun. Look what happened.

I'm sorry if I have disappointed you. It's not because I don't love you, because I do. I am going to miss you very much. I know you probably won't understand why I am doing this, but please don't be too angry with me. I will call you or send a card when I get where I'm going. I borrowed $40 from Dad's dresser. I had to have some cash in my pocket. I'll pay you back as soon as I get my first pay. I'm sorry for letting you down.

Love,

Luke

P.S. Give Emily a big hug for me.

James paced back and forth in front of Sarah. "I can't believe this!" he shouted, his sorrow giving way to rage. "He's throwing away his entire future!"

"He's in pain, James! Lord help him honey, look at what the boy's been through," Sarah snapped back. "Haley's dead and he feels responsible."

"I know he's in pain, Honey, but if he would've just talked to us. We're his parents. We could keep him from doing something he'll regret—something stupid."

"Well, I think it's too late for that," Sarah shouted. "Besides, it was you that was telling me to give the boy his space! That he'd come to us when he was ready!"

"You're acting like it's all my fault!"

"There's more to life than baseball, James!"

"What are you trying to say, Sarah?"

"Admit it, James, that's what you're upset about, isn't it? That he's throwing away his future—in baseball." Sarah rubbed her nose with a tissue and sniffed. "Well, I don't blame him for not wanting to play again. Lord knows, every time he picks up a bat or a ball, he's going to think about Haley. At least our son is alive, James. At least he's alive!" She fell back across the bed and began to weep uncontrollably.

Out in the hall, the two of them could hear muffled cries. Emily! Sarah jumped out of bed and rushed into the hallway. Bending down, she squeezed her arms around her daughter. "What's the matter my little angel?"

Emily dropped her saucer-like hazel eyes—the same eyes as her father's. Her lower lip trembled. "Why are you and Daddy mad at each other? I don't like it when you fight."

James stood in the doorway. Now, for the first time, wetness coated his eyelashes. He took a deep breath and put his arms around both of them. He then placed his finger under Sarah's chin and tilted her head gently toward his. "I'm sorry, Sarah. Please forgive me. Neither of us is to blame. We can't let this tragedy tear us apart. One day Luke will come back and we must be here for him when he does. We've got to stand strong for Luke and for Emily. She needs us, too." James kissed Emily on the top of her head. Although his words were calm and reassuring to Sarah and Emily, underneath he was just as deeply disappointed and hurt at what Luke had done.

Sarah embraced her husband. She searched deep into his eyes, stroking the back of his head. "God will help us through this somehow. Won't He?"

"He must," James said. "He must."

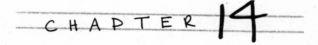

CHAPTER 14

DOWNTOWN HOUSTON AT 7:00 A.M. was a bustling, booming metropolis, the likes of which Luke had never seen. It was like New Orleans times three. Cars and delivery trucks honking echoed off the buildings as if in a deep, shadowy canyon. People on their way to work brushed by with impatience, stopping only at intersections and scurrying across the streets as soon as the red, shiny hand at the traffic light turned to green. These folks didn't have time to stand and stare at the tall buildings blocking out the morning sun.

Luke wandered casually along a sidewalk, looking for a U.S. Army recruiting station but, more immediately, a restaurant. He hadn't eaten since, well, he could hardly remember his last real meal. After paying for the bus ticket he still had more than thirty-two dollars. He didn't know how much money—if any—he would need once he got to wherever the army would send him.

He passed two hotel restaurants that appeared a little too fancy, however, a diner on the other side of the street named "Carl's" looked just right. After entering, he found a booth by a window where he could watch all the activity on the street.

As soon as he scooted into his seat, a waitress made her way over. "Today's Special is two eggs cooked any way with hash browns and coffee, juice, or milk." She was an older woman with a pleasant smile and gray hair bundled up underneath a hair net.

"Uh, yes ma'am, I'll have two Specials, please, with orange juice and a side order of bacon."

"Two Specials?" She asked, more like a mother than a waitress. "You sure you can eat all that?"

"Yes ma'am. I don't really know when I'll be eating again."

"How would you like your eggs?"

"Scrambled, please. And can I have some ketchup with that?"

"Coming right up," she said, placing her pencil securely in her hair.

A scattered copy of the *Houston Chronicle* was lying on the seat next to Luke. He picked it up and began flipping through it. The sports section was gone, so he turned to the front page. Luke had never really read newspapers before, except for the sports. In fact, he hadn't paid much attention to the news in general. Sure, he was aware of the racial tensions across the country. How could he not be? Magnolia Springs was about as segregated as a southern town could get, even though Magnolia Springs High was on the verge of integration. Everybody had been talking about it and they all had their strong opinions. He was aware of the war in Vietnam, because he had registered for the draft. Yet, with his scholarship deferment, he knew he wouldn't have to go, so he had kind of put it out of his mind.

For the most part, Luke's life had been so consumed with sports practices, games every week, hunting with his father, working on the old '53 Chevy he and his dad were rebuilding, and running with his friends, that he never gave much thought to the sufferings of others, nor to the tensions in the world outside of Magnolia Springs. You might say that Luke Hatcher had lived a very sheltered and innocent life. What had happened to Haley, however, had shattered his utopia like a bullet to a plate glass window, leaving him now questioning everything.

Glancing at the paper, his sense of hopelessness was magnified. The six main headlines read:

USSR NUCLEAR TEST IN EASTERN KAZAKH

RACE RIOTS FORCE CLEVELAND STATE
OF EMERGENCY

NATIONAL GUARD MOBILIZES IN MEMPHIS
AFTER 3-NIGHT RIOT

NORTH VIETNAMESE CAPTURE GREEN BERETS
AT ASHAU VALLEY: 16 KILLED, 27 WOUNDED

MAN RAPES, KILLS 8 NURSES IN
CHICAGO DORM

CHOPPER SHOT DOWN IN DA NANG KILLING 5

Death, fighting, unfairness—is that what it's all about? It's not supposed to be this way. It's just not supposed to be this way.

Luke set the paper aside and tried to imagine what the army would be like. Would he be tough enough to make it? What would happen if he were sent to Vietnam? Would he have to kill? Would he be killed? Could he actually kill someone... again? It was not too late to turn back. All he would have to do is pick up the phone and call his folks. They'd be here to get him in less than six hours. Watching the busy people outside, Luke pondered the seriousness of what he was about to do.

Yes, he was hesitant, but for only a moment. An underlying force seemed to propel him along. It was the force of guilt and shame—the notion that he didn't deserve to live in happiness.

The waitress came back with two plates stacked full of eggs, bacon, and hash browns. "I had my husband put some extra food on there to help fill you up," she said. "And I'll get some more juice for you. Anything else?"

"No ma'am, thank you very much." Then Luke thought of something else. "Ma'am? Do you know where there's an army recruiting station around here?"

The waitress thought for a moment. "Hold on, I'll be right back," she said.

Instead of the woman, a burly man of about sixty or so came out, wiping his hands on a soiled apron. He held out his hand. "I'm Carl. You the young man looking for the army?"

"Yes, sir," said Luke, swallowing a bite of egg and sticking out his hand.

"Well," Carl said, his grip like a pair of pliers. "There's a recruiting station not far from here. Go down this street till you get to Main, then turn right. It should be on Main about five blocks down." He looked Luke over, then asked, "Didn't they give you an address on your draft notice?"

"No sir, I mean, I didn't get drafted. I just want to enlist."

Carl nodded. "Yeah, I know how you feel. I joined up myself—served back in World War Two." He rolled up his sleeve revealing a faded tattoo of a shield with a sword and snake on it. "See that? Special Forces," he said proudly.

"My dad was in World War Two," Luke said. "I don't know what unit or nothing. He doesn't talk about it much. I know he was a Marine, though."

When the waitress returned, she patted her husband on the back while filling Luke's juice glass.

"Is that all you need?" Carl asked.

"Yes, sir. You've been real helpful."

After wolfing down his food, Luke stood and walked over to the cash register.

As he was reaching in his pocket for money the waitress hollered, "No charge, darlin'."

"You sure?" Luke replied pleasantly surprised.

By now Carl's wife was at the register. "Son, you must have impressed my husband, 'cause he said 'not to charge you for the breakfast' and Lord knows we need the money. Carl doesn't do that very often."

Luke continued to pull out his money. "Here, I insist. Take this."

"Darlin', you just hold on to that," she said gently, giving him a little wink. "You're going to need it more than us."

Carl came out from the kitchen and stood by his wife. Luke thanked them profusely and then stepped back out onto the city sidewalk. He followed Carl's directions to Main and found the recruiting station just where he had been told it was. The door was locked and a sign gave the hours as eight to five. Luke didn't have a watch, but he figured that 8:00 A.M. couldn't be that far away, so he sat on the curb and watched all the people rush by. He stood up when he saw a black '51 Ford pickup drive by. For a brief moment he thought it might be his father, but then realized it wasn't because the cab was crammed full of Mexicans.

Interrupting his thoughts, a gruff voice bellowed from the open door of the recruiting station. "Hey, you waitin' to come in here?" The uniformed man had entered from the building's back entrance.

Once inside, the man directed Luke to a small wooden school desk and gave him a stack of forms to fill out. A myriad of army posters plastered the walls along with the traditional old man with white hair in a red, white, and blue uniform pointing his finger saying, "Uncle Sam Wants You." Other than that, it was a pretty plain office. One of the questions on the forms asked if Luke had discussed this decision with his parents or guardians, he thought for a moment before leaving it blank. No one ever asked him about it, besides he was eighteen now and could do what he wanted. When done, he placed the forms on the officer's desk and sat back down. For the longest time, the officer never said a word, just methodically went through the paper work. After he finished he put the forms to one side and looked up.

"You'll do your basic training at Fort Wiggins. From there you will be assigned a unit and redeployed. Are you sure you want to waive your ten days?" Volunteers were given ten days to settle all their affairs before beginning their basic training.

"Yes, sir," said Luke. "I want to get started as soon as I can."

The recruiter's brow furrowed. "Son, you know if you're in trouble with the law you can't hide in the United States Army. They will find you. You understand that?"

"Yes, sir. I understand. I'm not in trouble. *At least not the kind of trouble you mean.* I just want to sign up is all. I am eighteen."

"Yes you are. But what you have to understand, and it's my job to make you understand, that once you sign up, that's it. There's no turning back. It's a big decision, young man."

"I know what I'm doing," said Luke. He cleared his throat. "Sir, I don't mean to be disrespectful or anything, but I really want to join and get on with it. I have my reasons."

"All right then. It's your life," said the recruiter and he began stamping Luke's completed forms.

"There'll be a bus this afternoon leaving at 4:00 P.M. for the indoctrination center. From there you'll be transported to Fort Wiggins. I would advise you to be here at least thirty minutes early. If you don't show, we'll find you. You can stow your gear here until then if you want." The recruiter extended his arm out. Luke stood up and the two shook hands firmly. "Welcome to the United States Army. Good luck. You're gonna need it."

CHAPTER 15

AFTER HE FINISHED signing up, it was still only 9:35 in the morning and Luke had nowhere to go until time for the bus. He walked up and down Main for a while, not wanting to get too far away lest he get lost and not return in time.

A theatre down a side street advertised *The Good, The Bad, And The Ugly*, starring Clint Eastwood, first showing at 10:30 A.M. It also advertised "Air-Conditioned Comfort." Luke bought a ticket, walked around a bit more, and then went into the theatre a half hour early. He sat in the back, eating a box of popcorn, observing the type of people who would watch a movie in the morning during a weekday. There weren't many of them. The theatre was virtually empty except for an elderly couple that looked as if they were on a high school date, an extremely obese man who must have had a movie fetish, and a handful of drifter-looking types. The film got underway and

Clint disposed of the bad and the ugly with only a few scratches to show for it.

Yeah, right. Only in the movies. I wonder if Clint could dodge a baseball like he does bullets? Back outside, the heat of the day greeted Luke with a slap. He considered going back into the theatre and watching the other movie that was playing, but decided against it.

After grabbing a burger and some fries and walking in circles for a while, he sat down on a sidewalk bench. There was a sign in front of the Esso Oil building that read, "Observation deck on 61st floor. Open to the public." The highest thing he'd ever been on was the Fire Tower back home in Magnolia Springs and that was maybe ten stories high, if that. Luke bounded up to the elevators and pushed the number "61." His stomach quivered momentarily as the cable pulled the steel box upward. This elevator moved quite a bit faster than the one at Mercy Medical. Each time the car stopped, several important-looking people would get on or off. No one spoke. They just stared ahead like the people who'd been cloned in the movie, *The Invasion of the Body Snatchers.*

Up on the observation deck, one could see for miles—maybe a hundred. The people below moved around like ants and their vehicles resembled the Matchbox cars that Luke had collected as a kid. He'd play in the dirt with them for hours, digging roads and making bridges with sticks. Looking down, Luke followed the route of a dump truck as it made its way down one street and then turned onto another and another and finally went out of sight behind some buildings. The wind whipped forcefully, much more strongly than the breeze on the Fire Tower.

Haley would have loved this. With that thought, sorrow seized him again, wrenching him back to reality and the mission at hand.

You know, you could easily jump off this building, he thought, while scanning the scene below. *You wouldn't feel a thing and it'd be all over.* Luke began to look for an opening in the high guardrail. *Haley's dead and she's not coming back. You killed her! You should have known better. You should have known better....*

Almost as soon as he started to think about jumping, just as he had done in his bedroom, he froze, unable to go any further. *Go ahead, jump. Just get it over with. You know you deserve it.* Wrestling the barrage of thoughts tormenting his mind, he literally shoved himself away from the guardrail and fell onto the concrete floor. He couldn't live with himself, yet he couldn't kill himself either.

Luke leapt up and sprinted back through the double glass doors and down the stairs. Sixty-one floors, times about forty, was a whole lot of steps. Nonetheless, his feet hit every one of them, and he hit the ground floor having only broken a minor sweat. For the next hour he just kept moving, eventually making his way back to the recruiting center.

At about 3:30, Luke joined about a dozen other young recruits who were waiting for the bus. Everyone was quiet for the most part, engaging only in small talk. Luke kept to himself, at a distance.

Soon, they boarded a converted school bus that was painted army green. It had sticky vinyl seats and windows that were hard to lower. The heat was oppressive, and the stench of sweating bodies reminded him of the baseball or football team riding the bus back home after a game. When they reached the indoctrination post about an hour later and the bus doors opened, a tall, thick man in a crisp uniform and a perfectly shaped round-brimmed hat stepped on board.

"Leave your gear in the bus and line up outside!" he shouted, his eyes squinting like slits. "Well, what you waiting for? You think the U.S. Army is going to come to you? Now move!"

The sluggish young men stumbled off the bus and lined up in front of him.

"My name is Sergeant Olsen," he barked. "I will get you through this indoctrination and on the bus for Fort Wiggins. You will do everything I tell you, precisely the way I tell you to. You will not speak unless I give you permission to speak."

"Do you understand?"

"Yes, sir!" the group answered in unison.

"Good. Now form a single file line and walk rapidly to that door straight ahead. The one marked 'A.' Now!"

Luke found himself near the end of the line, right behind a guy who was wearing his hair in a ratty ponytail. As the line moved forward, he felt like a cow being herded into a loading chute. Inside Door A was the main gathering hall, where they were ordered to stop. For some reason, a couple of the recruits thought Sergeant Olsen was a pretty funny fellow. One of them, standing about a foot away from him, started chuckling under his breath. When Sergeant Olsen heard him, he spun around and landed a punch directly in the guy's jaw, knocking him over several chairs. The rattle of chairs hitting the floor echoed off the walls. Looking up from the floor with blood trickling down his chin, the poor guy was in total shock. He didn't know what had hit him. Sergeant Olsen squatted down, his nose so close to the recruit's face that you probably couldn't have slid a piece of paper between the two.

"You think this is funny?" he screamed. "I hope you mess up one more time, Boy! 'Cause when you do, you are *mine!* And it's not going to be a pretty sight. Now get up and get back in line!"

The recruits were stunned. Grins dropped off their faces like anvils from a cliff. It didn't really faze Luke that much, though. He was used to it. His coaches, especially the football coaches, quite often yelled at guys like that, though he had never seen one actually hit someone, without pads, that is. He had a flashback to one time, when the Hurricanes were prancing into the locker room at halftime with a 21 to 0 lead over the Catholic High Bears of Baton Rouge. Luke had thrown two touchdowns and had run for another, so a cocky grin was pasted across his face. But the moment his cleats hit the concrete locker room floor, Coach Klienpeter had slapped Luke on the helmet so hard it knocked his mouthpiece out of his mouth. (Luke always chewed on it, even when he wasn't in the game.) Coach grabbed his facemask, twisted it sideways, and shoved him back against a locker.

"What're you smiling for, Hatcher? You really think you're something special, don't you?"

Luke had been in too much shock to respond. All he could do was stare back at his coach, the cocky grin replaced by a stupid one.

"You ain't done diddly-squat! You better get your head screwed on right or Catholic is going to whip our butts in the second half! You hear?"

Now, as if they were playing in a game of Simon Says, the recruits were commanded to look straight ahead into the back of the person in front of them and not to move until told otherwise. As Sergeant Olsen paced around them, inspecting the lot, he noticed the recruit directly in front of Luke peering at him from the corner of his eyes instead of looking straight ahead. Olsen snatched him by the ponytail and jerked his head back.

"You like me, boy?"

Silence. Shaking. Sweating. It seemed to take all of Luke's self-control to make himself stare straight ahead and not shift his eyes, too—something so simple, yet, under this pressure, so hard.

"Well, answer me!" The sergeant demanded.

"Yes, sir," the recruit replied, trembling, too afraid to say anything else.

"I can't hear you!"

"YES, SIR!"

"Yes sir, what?"

"Yes sir, I like you, sir!"

"You one of them queers?"

"No, sir!"

"Then you don't like me?"

"Yes, sir! I mean, no sir!"

Olsen's voice changed to a softer, more sarcastic tone. "You know what your problem is Boy?"

"No, sir."

"You're too cute!" He pulled out an army pocketknife, opened it slowly, stretched the guy's ponytail and began sawing it right off. Just like that. After completing the task, he handed the hair to the recruit. "Here," he said. "Put this in an envelope and send it home to your girlfriend... or boyfriend."

The Sergeant had most definitely made his point. Like broken horses, the young men were marched smoothly throughout a maze of stations without further incident. The first stop was weight and measurements. Next, it was to the physicians for physicals and inoculations, then through a series of psychological and vocational exams. Along the way, corpsmen toyed with their minds, yelling a creative assortment of obscenities. After the tests were over, the recruits were given a box meal to eat while waiting for their papers to take with them. Finally, they were loaded, this time on a much nicer Greyhound bus, to head for Fort Wiggins about four hours away.

The bus ride offered a temporary reprieve from the verbal onslaught. On the bus, a few of the recruits cried silently. Others stared grimly out of the window, no doubt wondering what in the world they had gotten themselves into. Luke clutched his stomach. For the first time, a longing for home pierced his gut with nauseating reality.

Smelly, sweaty, and exhausted, sleep did come. Luke slept nearly all the way until the bus pulled into the gate at Fort Wiggins around 12:30 A.M. and he was rudely awakened by another drill instructor—one strangely similar to Sergeant Olsen—standing in the bus aisle yelling. As before, the group was once again herded off the bus and marched to an old, wood-framed, barrack where they fell unwashed onto cots, and slept the rest of the short night.

→→ ←←

"Clang! Clang! Clang! Clang!"

Luke jumped up in his bed startled from his sleep—disoriented. It was a deep sleep, too. The deepest he'd experienced in a while—one of those sleeps that you just don't want to wake up from. He grabbed his pillow and covered his head, hoping the noise would go away. Yet, the unbearable sound became even louder.

"Clang! Clang! Clang! Clang!"

Luke sat back up and rubbed his eyes. *What the...?*

"Clang! Clang! Clang! Clang!"

"Wake up you bunch of pond scum! What you think this is—a picnic? It's 4:32! You've overslept two minutes! Now, get up and be in full assembly by 4:37! You've got four minutes and 55...54...53 seconds!" The drill instructor barked his orders while beating an empty jumbo vegetable can with a huge stainless steel spoon.

"Clang! Clang! Clang! Clang!"

When what was going on finally sank into their groggy heads, the new recruits began leaping around as if they thought the building was going to collapse on top of them. It was a hectic scene, but nevertheless, the twenty-nine young men somehow made it. They looked like anything but promising solders. Their shirts were un-tucked and unevenly buttoned. Their long hair was disheveled. Their eyes were crusty. Their shoes were untied and some of them were not wearing socks. Luke's white dress shirt hung wrinkled over his blue dress pants. He was still wearing the same clothes he had worn to the funeral.

The first thing the drill instructor did when he saw them was burst out laughing. Then suddenly his face shriveled up like a raisin. "I've never seen such a group of losers. I tell you what; the United States is in big trouble if they can't do any better than this!" He looked over them once more critically before giving them the order to follow him out of the barracks.

The group was marched directly to another building. Inside, taking short turns in about ten barber chairs that were lined up side by side, their heads were shaven unmercifully. Now, with their new crew cuts, everyone looked the same. For a while, all the recruits were walking around pointing and laughing at each other.

"Hey Julio, is that you, man?" one guy asked Luke.

"No, man. I'm Luke."

"This is way out, man," said his fellow recruit. "You look funky without your hair."

"*You* looked in the mirror lately?" Luke shot back.

From there, they were marched to another building, given big duffel bags and issued military uniforms, socks, underwear, boots, and toiletries. All their civilian articles were taken away to be placed in storage.

Luke now looked like a soldier. By breakfast that first morning, he had been officially assigned to the F3 Platoon with forty-six other recruits. Things were happening so fast that Luke hardly had time to think. His brain was running on autopilot. He was numb to everything that was going on around him. The lack of feeling, good or bad, was comforting to him.

In the months to come, Uncle Sam would provide his food, clothes, and transportation. In return they would tell him how to dress, walk, talk, and think. For the past five or six years, Luke's goals had been well defined and clearly focused. He had felt in control of his destiny. Now, he turned the controls over to a higher power—the United States Army. Whether it was the right choice or not, the United States Army now owned Luke Hatcher.

CHAPTER 16

STARING BACK AT Luke coldly, without emotion, was a clump of pallid, watery, scrambled eggs, a mass of something that resembled sausage, although he wasn't entirely sure, a huge mound of potatoes, and two pieces of unbuttered toast. He sprinkled pepper on the eggs just to give them some color. *Now I know why they call this place the Mess Hall,* he thought to himself. The food wasn't nearly as good as Carl's and most certainly not as good as his mother's. Luke thought about his mom's breakfasts. Why did her scrambled eggs always look and taste so much better? Maybe it was the loving touch of cheese she blended in so perfectly with the grits and eggs. It was more than merely mixing everything together. Making breakfast was a finely tuned work of art that Sarah took seriously. Luke could eat a couple of pounds of his mother's grits and eggs, but this stuff...it just turned his stomach. *I'm definitely not in Magnolia Springs anymore.* Luke ached for the comfort of his family.

Fortunately for him and the other recruits, the military knew exactly how to deal with the problem of homesickness— don't give the men too much time to mope around. The army kept them going at a rapid pace from dawn till dusk, so that by the time the bugle played Taps in the evening, they were too exhausted to do anything but sleep.

Refocusing on the cold aluminum plate before him, Luke tried to push his sentimental thoughts aside and get some nourishment into his system. For the next couple of years, the army would be his family. *Besides, this is what I deserve. I'll get used to it. At least I won't go hungry.*

Immediately following breakfast the group was marched to a large field in the center of the compound. Once there, they met with several other sets of new recruits, were assigned their platoons, split up accordingly, and marched to their permanent barracks, where they were assigned bunks. The F3 barrack housed a platoon of between forty and sixty men. Bunks were arranged perpendicularly alongside the two walls, one right after another, with an aisle down the middle. At the end of each bunk was a footlocker. Near the head of each bunk, against the wall was an upright locker for storing uniforms. There was no plumbing in the platoon barracks. Each morning, the men of the platoon gathered in the latrine building to shower, shave, and do their personal business.

Upon arrival to the F3 Platoon barrack, the drill instructor introduced the recruits to their permanent platoon sergeant. He wasted little time getting down to business.

"All right, men. Listen up. My name is Sergeant Millhouse." He paced back and forth in front of them. "For the next eight weeks, I will be your Mama. I will be your Papa. I will be your sweetheart. I will be everything to you. You exist to please me. Do you understand?"

"Yes, sir!" The group responded in a vain attempt at unison.

"Don't call me sir! I work for a living. You will address me as Sergeant."

"Yes, Sergeant!" They screamed, veins protruding from necks.

"Now, this is the way it is going to be. My job is to turn you bunch of pansies into lean, mean, fighting machines. When you look good, I look good. When you look bad, I look bad." He stopped pacing in front of Luke, glaring at him. "And I don't like to look bad!" A wad of spit flew out of his mouth and landed on Luke's shoulder. Luke could feel the heat of Sergeant Millhouse's breath bearing down upon him. "Don't make me look bad. Don't ever, ever make me look bad."

Luke's eyes were fixed straight ahead, afraid to flinch, his legs shaking. Sergeant Millhouse started pacing again as he continued his introduction.

"Every morning you will have exactly three minutes to get dressed, make your rack, and fall out. If you don't pass inspection you will pay the price. Do you understand?"

"Yes, Sergeant!"

"Good." He moved to the center of the room, but never stopped his lecture. "The military has four main objectives in basic training. Number one is to teach you how things work in the United States Army and where you, as soldiers, fit in. Number two; to condition you to follow orders without question. An officer on the battlefield does not have the time, inclination, or opportunity to explain to the members of his company his decisions. Remember this little saying and you will do fine: "Slow obedience is no obedience." Not following orders rapidly could cause the death of yourself or one of your fellow soldiers. Stupidity and not thinking can cause people to die! I'll say that again. Stupidity and not thinking can cause people to die!"

The Sergeant's words catapulted Haley's death and Luke's own stupidity front and center in his mind. He might as well have been punching Luke in the gut with his fists. The guilt and shame surged over him yet again. Though it seemed a lifetime away, in reality, it hadn't even been three complete days since he'd kissed her lifeless forehead. Luke fought to push back his tears, but they stubbornly filled his eyes anyway. A single drop trickled down his cheek. Millhouse didn't miss the opportunity to exploit the situation.

"What's this?" the Sergeant interrogated, taking his index finger and flipping the tear off Luke's cheek, "Are you crying, boy?"

"No, Sergeant!"

"You want to run back home to your Mommy? Is that what you want?"

"No, Sergeant!"

"Well you better not be crying, cause you ain't had nothing to cry about yet. Now hit the floor and give me forty push ups."

Luke dropped to the floor.

"One-two-one-two-one-two-one-two," the sergeant counted out.

Pushups were a breeze for Luke. On any given day, he could whip out fifty. On this day, he was fueled additionally by that inner rage he'd become so accustomed to. With each rep, his anger boiled a little more until he was doing pushups like a madman and finished his last five one-armed just to show the Sergeant up.

"Are you mocking me son?" Millhouse shouted. "I know you are not mocking me. Certainly you are not that stupid." Sergeant Millhouse was taken aback. He hadn't expected Luke to be in such good shape.

"No, Sergeant!"

"Looks like we got us a little smart-aleck here. Well, I'm going to teach you a lesson, Son. Do ten more—with one arm. And if you can't do them, everybody will do pushups till they drop. And I mean until they drop!"

Luke hit the floor, more resolute than ever, but after the fifth one, his arm began to burn and tremble. For a moment he paused, breathing heavily. Doing one-armed push-ups was tough, even for Luke.

"Get going soldier—five more!"

He struggled through the next two and on the eighth one it appeared he was going to collapse. But instead of caving in, he glared at his leader even more determined, and to the Sergeant's amazement, he completed the task. Inner rage was a tool that Luke was learning how to exploit for his personal advantage.

"All right Hatcher, fall back in line."

Luke jumped back in line next to the other men who had watched the exhibition with marvel and new respect.

"Now where was I?" said Millhouse. "Number three, to build teamwork. From now on, you are a team. You will act as one! If one person messes up, everybody suffers. If one person wins, everybody wins. And number four, to get you in the best physical shape of your life. When I am finished with you, you will be as tough as a Texas rodeo steer. Now fall out to the latrine, get showered, shaved, unload your bags, and be back here in full marching gear at ten hundred hours sharp."

➼ ⤙

As one might imagine, the F3 Platoon was about as diverse a bunch of guys as you could get. Julio Rodriguez was a short and stocky Mexican-American fellow from El Paso who spoke broken English. His gift for becoming a citizen had been a draft notice. His family had come across the Rio Grande just five years prior. Dennis Stanley was a dairy farmer from Poplar Bluff, Missouri. Alton Baker, Jr., a tall lanky fellow from Los Angeles, who felt he had something to prove because his father had been a colonel in World War II. The rest of them represented cross-cultural America in a similar way.

Bunked on one side of Luke was Howard Spivak, a thin, peppery Italian from Brooklyn, New York, who spoke in sharp, fast, sentences. On a couple of occasions, Luke had to ask him to slow down and repeat himself. He was loud and liked to poke fun at the "slow-tawlkin'" Southern boys.

Bunking on the other side of Luke was Samuel Williams, who hailed from a place called Kentwood, Louisiana, not forty miles from Magnolia Springs. Samuel, at twenty-four, was the oldest of the new recruits, and he was at least six feet, four inches tall and two hundred forty pounds. He wasn't fat, but he was built as solid as the wood walls the barracks were made of. His chest was broad and thick and it chiseled down to a small, flat stomach. His great white eyes illuminated a boxy, black face with a jaw set firm. Yet, the most spectacular feature about Samuel Williams was not his stalwart build, nor the noticeable scars adorning his arms and chest, but his warm and tranquil personality. He was the quintessence of cool. Not cool in the stylish sense, but cool in that he never seemed to become undone. Sergeant Millhouse, whose forehead was about even with his chin, would get so close to his face, looking up as if to Goliath, and scream till the veins looked like they were going to pop out of his neck and forehead, but Samuel always stayed impermeable. It just didn't bother him. Nothing seemed to bother him. He was solid, inside and out.

➤＊ ＊◀

"It is well...with my soul..." Samuel sang in a low, soothing, almost hypnotic rhythm—a natural bass, his voice pitch spot on. He lay in his bunk facing upward toward the ceiling with an old, worn looking Bible in his hands.

Everybody was settling down just before Taps played and the lights went off. Spivak lay on his stomach writing a letter, while Luke sat on the edge of his bunk polishing his boots.

"It is well with my soul, ummm, ummm. It is well, ummm. It is well, with my soul."

"Okay," Luke snapped. "That's enough." He buffed his boot that much harder. "Do you have to sing?"

Samuel calmly turned his head toward Luke. "Sorry, man. Didn't mean to upset you."

"I can't believe this," Luke mumbled to himself. "Of all people, I'm bunked next to a preacher."

"Hey, leave him be," Stanley shot back from the bunk on the other side of Samuel. The rest of the guy's heads popped up with curiosity. "I like his singing," continued Stanley. "It make's me feel good. Anyway, it's a free country. He can sing if he wants."

A balled up pair of socks flew out of nowhere, popping Luke on the side of the head. "What are you, some kind of atheist or something?" someone else yelled out.

"Well, it doesn't make me feel good and I don't know what I am and I don't want to talk about it, all right," said Luke in a firm voice.

Luke wasn't an atheist, but he wasn't lying either. He didn't want to talk about it. Every time he saw Samuel reading his Bible or heard him sing one of his songs, it stung; causing him to remember things—things that he wanted to forget—things he joined the army to get away from. The mere sight of the Bible brought back scenes from the hospital chapel, "In my distress I cried unto the Lord, and he heard me." Or Pastor Taylor's words at the funeral, *"We have to stand on God's promises."*

Well I tried and Haley's dead! Luke had thoughts like that a lot when he was around Samuel. It was as if Samuel was rubbing salt into a deep wound. Yet, strangely, at the same time, in a peculiar sort of way, Luke found something within himself being drawn toward this brown-skinned leviathan of a man. Deep down inside, underneath all the layers of questions, anguish, and bitterness, Luke wanted desperately to believe that God was there and Haley was with Him. But if God was real, Luke reasoned, what kind of Supreme Being could stand idly by and allow such tragedies? So much conflict, yet Luke could not deny the peace—the irritating peace—that radiated from Samuel Williams. The other reason why it was impossible for Luke to distance himself from Samuel was because he would be bunked next to him for eight weeks.

"It's cool, Luke. I understand, man," Samuel said. "I'll stop singing if it bothers you. Ain't no big thang."

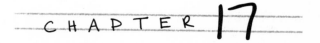

CHAPTER 17

LUKE COULDN'T HELP but feel bad after the way he had treated Samuel. Feelings of remorse were happening more and more, it seemed. Luke figured that if his parents knew about his rebellion toward God, they would be devastated. He had always been a kind-hearted human being. At least he used to be. Something, however, had changed, snapped, and taken root in him since Haley's death. It was like a trap door had been opened that allowed all this hate and bitterness to come up from a pit and literally take him over.

With this sort of a load, his heart was heavy as he picked up a pen to begin writing his first letter home. It was Sunday afternoon. Luke didn't have the courage to make a telephone call and actually talk with his family. Letters were clean and safe and he could choose his words carefully. When he finished, he placed a stamp on the envelope and dropped it off in the mailbox on the way to dinner.

A sea of green fatigues covered the mess hall like a moving camouflage blanket. The rumble of male voices combined with the sound of utensils clinking together as the men wolfed down the food the army had set before them. The longer they were in training, the better the food looked and tasted. Samuel plopped his tray down in the space across from Luke.

"What I'd give for a piece of my mama's sweet 'tater pie. Know what I mean?"

Luke nodded in affirmation, surprised to see how friendly Samuel was being.

"But thank God for them beans, you know? Beans be filled with protein?" Samuel looked up at Luke with a huge grin across his face as he shoved a heaping spoonful into his mouth.

"Look, Samuel," said Luke, shamefacedly. "I'm sorry about the other night, coming down on you about your singing 'n all. It's just that I've been through a lot lately and sometimes it gets the best of me."

Samuel shook his head. "Hey, man. Don't sweat it. I'm sorry, too. You know I wasn't being too thoughtful. Sometimes I forget that I'm sharing a room with thirty other guys. And you can call me Sammy. That's what my friends call me."

"Okay, Sammy, and it's really no big deal. If you want to sing, go ahead and sing."

"I'll try to tone it down. It's just my soul's at peace. Sometimes I just can't keep it in, you know?"

Luke stopped chewing and sat his fork down, his eyebrows lifted as if puzzled. "You see? That's what I'm talking about. How can you be at peace, man? Really, Sam, Sammy, I'm not trying to be smart or nothing, but can't you see what's going on around you? Can't you see all the junk in this world? We're in the middle of a war. People are getting killed every day and you act like everything is wonderful, but it's not wonderful, at least not for a lot of people. There's pain in the world, man. Real pain and I've seen it up close."

"Now hold on a second. I never said there ain't no pain in the world. I've seen pain up close myself, too. In fact, I've lived most of my life in anger and hate until God reached down and took it out of me. It was a real miracle 'cause it was something only He could do. Now, I don't live all torn up inside. It's just that simple. I hurt, man. I hurt just like you. You don't even know what all I been through. I'll have to tell you about it someday. But I can tell you this right now; God is faithful, man. If you reach out for Him, He'll be there for you."

Luke dangled his fork toward Sam's face, getting a little edgy. "It's easy for you to say that you hurt like me, but you never ki..." Luke caught himself and changed in mid-sentence. "Look, I hear you. I did all that Sunday School garbage, and that's what it is—garbage. As I see it, God ain't never done nothin' to help me." The moment those venomous words slipped out, another pang of regret pierced Luke's gut. He had never said anything like that out loud before. Sure, he had thought it, but he had never actually verbalized it.

"It ain't about Sunday School, Luke. It goes way deeper than that."

"Well, it may work for you, but it didn't work for me. It's all a fairy tale. You know? Santa Claus, the Easter Bunny. It's all the same stuff."

"I'm sorry you feel that way, Luke. Real sorry." Sammy slowly stood. "You carry on like you done swallowed a piece of barbed wire or somethin'. Watch out, Luke, it's gonna eat you alive—eat you alive. I'll be prayin' for you, man."

"Don't bother," Luke said as he stood. "Praying doesn't work." The two walked silently side by side and placed their trays on the dishwashing belt, then went back to the barracks.

➤➤ ◄◄

Walking back from the mailbox, Sarah was sorting through the usual bills and junk when her eyes caught the return address of Fort Wiggins, Texas. Her heart began to race as she realized for certain that it was her beloved Luke's handwriting. In a fit of excitement, she ran into the house, brushed everything off the kitchen table, sat down and read the letter. After reading it, she wept. It was after 5 P.M. and James would be home soon so Sarah put the letter back in the envelope, set it on the table, pulled up a chair and waited.

At 5:33 James stepped through the kitchen door, ragged and wiped out from an honest day's work. The moment he saw Sarah, he could tell she'd been crying.

"What's wrong, Honey?" he asked.

Sarah simply lifted her arm and pointed to the letter. James rushed to the table, picked it up, and tore the letter out. Unfolding it, he observed the return address of Fort Wiggins, Texas and sighed with disappointment. He was well aware of what that meant. "So, he definitely went through with it." A part of James was still holding on to the hope that Luke had not gone through with it and would return home soon.

Sarah gave James one of her "Don't go there" looks.

James cleared his throat and started to read.

Dear Dad, Mom, & Emily,...

But before he got any further, a knock came at the kitchen door. "Yoo-hoo! Anybody home?" It was Mrs. Yarbrough.

"Not now," Sarah moaned.

James rolled his eyes back in disbelief. By now Mrs. Yarbrough was already halfway through the door. She was wearing a long flowery dress and a sun hat. In her hands were a couple of jars of homemade pickles.

"I just finished a batch of my special dill pickles," she said enthusiastically.

"That's wonderful, Mrs. Yarbrough, but something important has come up and you're going to have to go now." James gently took her arm and escorted her back to the door. "Thanks for the pickles. I'm sure we're going to enjoy them."

"Oh my, is everything all right?"

"Everything's just fine, Mrs. Yarbrough. Just fine," Sarah said. "We'll have some of these pickles for supper tonight."

Being the ever-observant person that she was, all for the good of the community, of course, Mrs. Yarbrough did notice the letter in James' hand before she was quite out the door.

"Oh, a letter. Is that a letter from Luke?" she asked inquisitively. "You finally heard from Luke?"

Sarah placed her hands on her hips. "Yes, Mrs. Yarbrough. It's a letter from Luke."

Mrs. Yarbrough just stood in the door waiting for James to read it. Then it dawned on her. "Oh, oh my. Am I intruding? Well, I'll be off now. Let me know how Luke is doing. Bye now." And she was out the door.

Both James and Sarah breathed a sigh of relief and focused their attention back on the letter.

Dear Dad, Mom, & Emily,

I am doing as fine as can be expected. Things are hard here, but I am staying busy which keeps me from thinking about you know what. I miss you so much (especially Mom's cooking, Ha, Ha). The food here is not the best, but it's three squares. As you have probably guessed, I'm stationed at Fort Wiggins, Texas. It's a lot different than Louisiana. Not as many trees and more desert. It's dry and hot. I'm learning a lot of stuff.

Sergeant Millhouse is our Platoon Sergeant. He's tough. Every morning he wakes us up at 4:30 by clanging a steel spoon against an empty vegetable can. We only have three minutes to make

our bed and get dressed. Remember how long it used to take me to
get ready for school? Ha.

James started to choke up and stopped reading for a moment. Dabbing her eyes with a dishtowel, Sarah walked over and placed her arm around his shoulder and James resumed reading.

Before breakfast each morning we go on a five-mile road march and then we clean the barracks. I sure am glad Mom taught me to clean my room, Ha... We're good and hungry by breakfast. Each day we do different training exercises. Grenade-launching, rifle range, rappelling. Stuff like that. It's pretty fun. I had to go through the gas chamber without a gas mask. That was not fun. I threw up. My favorite thing is the "Confidence Course." It's an obstacle course with poles, rope ladders, walls to jump, tires to run through, and all sorts of other difficulties. It's kind of like football and baseball practice. I beat the course record that was set all the way back during World War II. Sergeant Millhouse said he's never seen anyone do it as well as me. He yells a lot, but I think he likes me. Other than that, it's mostly following orders, running here and there, scrubbing toilets and stuff. I've met some new friends. I think you'd like them. Don't worry about me. I'm fine. Still not ready to call yet. We can only call on Sundays. I will call soon. I hope you are not too disappointed in me. I did what I had to do. Tell Emily that I miss her so much and that I will see her soon.

Love,
Luke

James set the letter on the table and silently walked to a cabinet over the refrigerator. On his tiptoes, he reached in the back and pulled out a pack of Lucky Strike cigarettes, grabbed a couple of matches, then walked to the front porch and sat on the swing. Sarah watched her husband from a distance as he struck the match, lit the cigarette, and took in a long pull. He held it in for a while then blew out the smoke. Smoking went against everything Sarah had believed in. James had not smoked for more than five years, except on rare occasions. On this occasion, she let him be.

＊＊ ＊＊

It might have been that Luke was getting used to the whole army routine. Maybe his system was starting to catch up with him and he was beginning to settle down. Whatever the reason, for the first time in three weeks, Luke had trouble sleeping again; the nightmares had returned. Night after night, he would toss and turn.

On this night, Haley was dressed in her Magnolia Springs softball uniform. Her legs and arms were sleek and tan, but she wasn't on the softball diamond. Instead, she was hovering in the air. Her golden hair was flowing in the wind with a radiant light illuminating around her. She looked angelic, heavenly. Haley never spoke, rather, she smiled, warm and inviting, while reaching her arms out toward Luke. He stretched in her direction, straining to make contact, but found he was inches short. When they couldn't quite touch, Haley's smile turned to despair and they started drifting apart. Haley became smaller and smaller as she floated away in the distance. "Haley, come back. Haley come back," Luke cried. He tried to force himself toward her, but felt paralyzed, like he couldn't move, like he was strangling. "Haley, don't go!" he screamed. She disappeared and Luke's eyes snapped open. Breathing rapidly, he sat up in bed, his hands trembling and his throat dry. When he did, he noticed two shadowy figures standing over him. Chills ran up his spine and fear filled his soul as one of the shadowy figures reached out and grabbed him. Luke let out another screech.

"Luke, man, you all right?" It was Sammy. He was standing on one side of Luke's bed. Spivak was standing on the other.

"I'm fine. Just a bad dream."

"Who's Haley, man?" Spivak smirked. "She must be some chick. I bet you can't wait to get home to *her!*"

It didn't take Luke very long to acclimate himself. He jumped up, grabbing Spivak by the throat. "Don't you ever speak Haley's name again! You hear me?" Luke shoved him back onto his own bed, causing Spivak's bunk to scratch against the floor and bang into his locker.

Spivak recoiled like a snake and punched Luke in the jaw. At that, Luke was all over him, pounding Spivak until blood was flowing from his nose. By then, the whole barrack was awake in the semi-darkness and had gathered around yelling and chanting as the two rolled onto the floor, knocking into the bunks and metal lockers. Sammy stepped between the two and tried to separate them, both Luke and Spivak still trying to swing at each other. As he was holding them apart, Sergeant Millhouse stormed in wearing nothing but a tee-shirt and boxers and flipped the lights on.

"Fall in!" he shouted.

The men were an emotional mob and continued with their taunting, so he grabbed a nearby wooden stool and banged the side of a medal locker with it. "I said, *fall in!*"

That got the guys' attention, and they began to disperse and trickle into their individual positions. Luke and Spivak continued to lunge at each other, but couldn't because Sammy had hold of both of them by their shirts. He shoved them into their positions.

Sergeant Millhouse glanced at his watch. "I see. You men like to get up *real* early. You must not have gotten enough action during the day. Well, since you seem so awake, we're going on a little run—a five-mile run—in full gear. Now fall out and get dressed!"

Luke stepped forward. "Sergeant, it was my fault. It's not fair for them to run. I'll run ten miles—five for them and five for me."

"That's mighty big of you, Hatcher." Sergeant Millhouse put his face inches from Luke's nose and then lowered his voice to an almost-whisper. "You are correct. It was your fault. And you are correct. It's not fair. But guess what?" Then he screamed, "Life is not fair! Now fall out. All of you."

Hatcher and Spivak were not especially popular that morning with the rest of the platoon. All through the run, the men murmured and shot cutting glances at the two. By 3:45 A.M., the platoon was finally back in their bunks, but forty-five minutes later, at 4:30 A.M., Sergeant Millhouse came in clanging the vegetable can as if nothing had ever happened.

"Rise and shine boys! Clang! Clang! Clang! It's a beautiful day for a road march. Let's go! Clang! Clang! Clang!"

CHAPTER 18

ON EACH OF the previous Sundays, Luke had entertained the idea of calling home. A couple of times he actually began dialing, but somewhere between the first and last numbers, he would back out. On this fifth Sunday, however, after several letter exchanges, Luke felt he finally had the courage to actually make the call. So, he bravely placed his fingers in the rotary, dialed the numbers, and waited. One, two, three, four rings—no answer. *Where would they be? Surely they're home from church by now. Maybe they went out for lunch at The Round Table or something.* Luke started to place the receiver on the hook when, on the sixth ring, someone picked up.

"Hello," Sarah answered.

"Mom?"

For a few seconds there was silence on the other end. The sound of Luke's voice had caught Sarah off guard. While she was desperately hoping for his call, it had been so long that she had not expected it.

"Mom?" Still more silence. "Hello... Mom? You there?"

Regaining her composure, Sarah spoke up softly. "Luke, Honey? Is...Is it really you?" Her eyes were overflowing.

"Yes, Mom, it's me." He didn't know what to say at such an awkward moment. "Are you okay? How you been doing?"

"As well as can be expected, I guess. It's hard not having you around." Sarah's voice quivered, "I miss you so much, Honey."

"I miss you too, Mom. Hey, thanks for the letters and the Polaroids. Sometimes I get so homesick and they really help. Ya'll must've gotten a new camera?"

"Yeah. It was your father's idea. We wanted to send you pictures regularly and with the Polaroid we don't have to wait for them to get developed. We can just snap them and send them."

"That's great. So," Luke vacillated a moment, "how is Dad?"

"He's fine. But like me, he misses you, Luke. We all miss you so very much." Sarah had to sit down on a kitchen stool. "It's so good to hear your voice. I...I don't know what to say."

"It's okay, Mom. You don't have to say anything special. I just wanted to hear your voice too and let you know that I love you and I'm thinking about you." Again, there was a long silence on the other end.

"Mom? You still with me?"

"Oh, I'm here, Honey. I'm sorry. It's, I just can't believe it. Everyday I wait and hope to get a call from you and now I'm actually talking to you. It's been over five weeks now, but it seems like five years."

"I know. It'll get better though, I promise. Now, tell me the truth. How is Dad?"

"Well, he's not showing too much emotion these days and mopes around a lot. It's like something in him died when you left."

The comment stung. While Luke was aware of how much pain he had caused his family, hearing the reality of it made his heart ache even more.

"And he's been smoking again. You know how that bother's me, but I haven't nagged him about it because I know how hard all of this has been on him. He's hurt, Luke and it's going to take some time for him to get over this."

"I'm really sorry," Luke moaned. "But it was something I had to do. I can't explain it and I don't expect ya'll to understand."

"You'd be surprised how much I understand. After all, I am your mother. I brought you into this world, you know."

"Can I talk to him?"

"He's not here. Neither is Emily. They're going to be upset that they missed you. They went fishing."

Luke sighed. He loved it when he and his father went fishing. "Where'd they go?"

"The usual, over to Lake Maurepas."

"Did they take Little Darlin'?"

"Luke, you know the answer to that question. Of course they did. Your father loves that old boat." Little Darlin' was a wooden flat-bottomed fishing boat that Luke and James had built together when Emily was just a baby. After they painted it forest green, Luke was given the honor of naming it. At first, he wanted to call the boat "The Green Hornet," after his favorite super-hero, but James informed him that boats usually had female names. That's when Luke came up with Little Darlin'. James brushed the name on the front in bold white paint.

"All right, but tell them I love them and miss them." Luke started to say goodbye, but he had one more thing on his mind. "Ah, Mom," he said a little uneasily. "How are, you know, Mr. And Mrs. Sparks?"

"Well, Honey, it's hard to say. Mr. Sparks seems better than his wife does. He has spoken to us and is friendly. He's back at work with your father. James says he doesn't seem to be holding a grudge. Harvey told your father that he had to get back into the routine or he was going to go crazy. Virginia, on the other hand stays in the house all the time. Never comes out. We haven't seen her since the funeral. She hasn't been to church, the store, or anywhere. There have been rumors that Dr. Spurrier has her on some pretty heavy medication and that Harvey is carrying the load right now. He's doing everything—working, cleaning house, cooking, shopping, while Virginia recovers. We send them food pretty regularly, but haven't heard a word. I guess that means we need to keep our distance for now."

Luke was now trying to keep from choking up and he sniffed a couple of times. Sarah could tell the report was hard on her son.

"Luke, Honey, you have to know that it was an accident. You can't blame yourself for the rest of your life. You just can't. You have too much to live for."

What about Haley? Nobody thinks about Haley. She had much to live for, too.

"Look, I have to go now, Mom," Luke said trying to be a little more distant. "It's a pay phone and there's a long line of guys waiting."

"Not yet. Can't we talk a little longer? I don't want it to end like this."

"Mom, I'm fine, really. Don't worry, okay?"

"Well can you can call back later? James and Emily will be home this evening."

"I will if I can, but they only let us call on Sundays." It was time to hang up and it was hard. How do you hang up on your loving mother? "I love you Mom. I really do."

"I love you, too, Honey."

"Bye, now. I have to go. Give Emily a big hug from me." More silence—then the sound of muffled crying. "Mom, please don't cry."

"Oh, Baby. I feel so helpless. I wish I could make your hurt go away."

"No, Mom, don't torture yourself. This was my decision—something I had to do."

"When do we get to see you again? I want to hold you in my arms."

"I get a two week leave after Basic is over. I'd like to come home then. Or meet ya'll somewhere. I'll let you know more about it later okay? Bye, now."

"How long till Basic is over?"

"Three weeks, but now I have to go…I love you." Luke sat the receiver on its handle. Click.

Sarah held the phone in her hands, listening to the dial tone. "Bye."

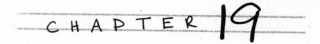

CHAPTER 19

SERGEANT MILLHOUSE FLIPPED
the bulging canvas duffel bag off of his shoulders and onto the
wooden floor. "Men," he said, "here at Fort Wiggins, we take
pride in our operation. We work you hard because we want you
to be the best you can be. But we also do things a little differently
here than some of the other basic training facilities. You've given
your all for seven weeks and will continue to do so this final week,
but we think you are due a little fun—not too much fun, mind
you, just a little. So, this final Saturday, the F3 along with the other
platoons will be participating in a little competition. We're having
a recreational field day. There'll be the usual military events, but in
addition we'll be having my favorite activity." Out of the duffel
bag, he pulled a long, wooden bat. "Softball! Fast pitch!"

Cheers rang out from the men.

"All right, now that's what I'm talkin' about," Sammy exclaimed, slapping Luke on the back, who was standing frozen, not believing his ears.

"Oh yeah, that's really great," Luke, mumbled incoherently.

A stern expression moved across the Sergeant's face. His eyes became like bullets. After giving the men a moment to settle down, he continued. "You men will learn to cherish this game. It's an American game! Like apple pie, hot rods, and beautiful dames!" Then, his mood abruptly changed and he became strangely calm, gazing at the bat in his hands and shaking his head as if in deep reflection. He pulled up a nearby stool and sat down on it. When he spoke, his voice was softer. "Gather around." The soldiers scooted into a tight circle. "Men, most of you are going to 'Nam and it's gonna get tough over there. The stench of death and burning dung will be all around you. If the enemy doesn't get you, the blood-suckin' bugs will. After a while, your mind starts to crack. I can't explain it. You'll have to find out for yourselves, but I'll tell you what, this game has helped a lot of soldiers maintain their sanity over there, me included."

"While under 'hold-up' orders at Camp Baxter in Da Nang, it was those softball and baseball games and roasted pig barbeques that helped to keep our morale." He bent over, picked up an old, battered, glove and slid it onto his hand, popping the palm with his fist. "Games got pretty wild over there. What we lacked in facilities and equipment, we more than made up for in guts. Sometimes, the games were not just called because of rain or darkness, but from incoming 60mm mortar rounds. I'm telling you guys, it was strange over there." Sergeant Millhouse stood up, grabbed the bat again, and resumed his pacing, tapping the bat into his open hand.

Luke could hardly concentrate on what the sergeant was saying. All he could see was the bat tapping back and forth, only a couple of feet from him. Each tap into the Sergeant's hands was like a dagger jabbing at Luke's heart. It was all coming back, not in trickles, but in waves—tidal waves that threatened to break his fragile hold on sanity. Tap—his bat slamming into the ball. Tap— the ball flying toward Haley. Tap—the ball pounding into her head, sending her to the ground. Tap—Mrs. Virginia saying, "Luke, you should have known better." Tap—the open casket with Haley's lifeless body. Tap—part of his father dying when he left. *Haley's dead because of me. I should have known better. I should have known better. So much pain because of me.*

"And in case you are wondering," Sergeant Millhouse continued, "even though it is recreation, everyone is required to participate. No exceptions. Any questions before you fall out?"

Luke raised his hand. "May I speak with you in private, Sergeant?"

"Yes, Private Hatcher."

"Thank you, Sergeant."

"Everybody, fall out! Private Hatcher, see me in my office." Sergeant Millhouse turned his back away from the men and walked with authority down a little hall with the bat resting on his shoulders. He stepped into his office closing the door behind him. A few seconds later, Luke knocked lightly.

"Come in Private." The stern invitation came from behind a heavy duty, green, metal desk.

"Yes, Sergeant," Luke responded, standing in full attention.

"At ease."

Luke removed his hat and locked his hands behind his back, his legs spread slightly.

"What can I do for you?"

"Sergeant, I'm unable to participate in the softball games this weekend."

A look of surprise crossed Millhouse's face. "And why would that be?"

"Sir, it's a personal matter, but I'd be willing to do anything you want to compensate—clean the barracks, or the latrine, whatever you wish, sir."

Sergeant Millhouse leaned back in his chair, arms folded across his chest, his hat sitting on the desk in front of him. The top of his head was completely bald and the hair around the sides had been closely shaven. He could see that Luke was greatly distressed.

"I thought I made myself clear. Everyone will participate, no exceptions, especially you, Hatcher. You and Williams are the two best athletes we've got. I can't afford for you not to play. I want that trophy. You see; the F4 Platoon has won it the last three times. But with you and Williams, I really have a shot at getting it back."

"I'm begging you Sergeant, please reconsider."

"Private Hatcher, you surprise me. You're probably the most athletic man on this whole base. What's the problem here? Just tell me why you feel you can't play in a little softball game? It doesn't make a whole lot of sense."

"With all due respect, Sergeant, it's kind of hard to explain."

"I've got a couple of hours," he said, looking at his watch.

Luke simply dropped his head, defeated.

"Private Hatcher, this is the United States Army and we do things differently here. If you can't explain to me why, then I'll expect you to be on that field giving it your absolute best. Do you understand?"

Luke's eyes shifted around the room, onto the awards and plaques hanging on the wall, onto the bookshelves, and out the window, everywhere except into the Sergeant's eyes.

"Do you understand?"

Luke finally looked up. "Yes, Sergeant!"

"Dismissed."

Sergeant Millhouse had seen a lot of men come and go under his command. It was his duty to push these boys past the limits they had set for themselves and realize their full potential.

Luke gave the Sergeant a firm salute, pivoted his body around, and marched out, a perfect soldier on the surface, but inwardly he boiled. The rage was there again—the rage that had now become so commonplace. *Idiot! He can't do this! He can't force me to play a stupid game of softball. This is a free country. It's not prison.* Luke became increasingly agitated with each step. By the time he caught up with the others on assignment, he was a stuffed powder keg about to ignite.

>> <<

"What's got you all chapped?" Spivak barked out the moment Luke walked in the door. Ten or so of the platoon were sitting in an instruction room, about to begin a session on military map-reading. The instructor had not yet arrived. Luke glared at Spivak before plopping down hard in the small wooden writing desk.

"You look like a hissing mad 'possum that's been cornered by one of them blue tick hounds," Sammy chuckled in his deep voice.

"I'll tell you what he looks like. He looks like he just found out that his best buddy and Haley have been getting it on back in Podunk," Spivak said, grabbing his stomach he was laughing so hard. More laughter peppered through the room.

The powder keg once again exploded and Luke bounded pell-mell toward Spivak, knocking over several of the small wooden desks in the process, but before reaching him, Sammy caught Luke and locked his arms around him.

Luke twisted and kicked, trying to break free of Sammy's grasp. "Let me go!"

"Calm down, man!" Sammy ordered, as he tightened his grip. He knew something was awry. In the barracks a few weeks prior, Luke had been upset by the nightmare, and Spivak, but today, he wasn't just angry, his eyes were crazed. He was a madman—out of control. Sammy knew that look. He'd seen it before, back when he was...

"And Spivak, when you gonna learn to shut your mouth?" Sammy said. "You'd think you'd learn it the first time."

"Hey, it's not my fault Hatcher can't take a joke," said Spivack. "Besides, you're not my boss, Buckwheat!"

Sammy dropped Luke and swung around. He gripped Spivak's shirt, tightening his fist and lifting him up in the air. Sweat pellets formed across his forehead, his heart beat rapidly. "What'd you call me?" Sammy demanded. This was a side of Sammy no one had seen before. There was little doubt that he could have snapped Spivak like a toothpick. He took several quick shallow breaths, then with one long exhale, as if reaching some inner decision, Sammy set Spivak down and turned back toward Luke.

Spivak slapped the wrinkles out of his shirt and backed away, stumbling into his desk, the thin line of his mouth twitching. He was shaken up. Trying to save face in front of his peers, he mumbled under his breath, "stupid nig..."

Before he could finish, Sammy turned and glared, his eyes piercing. "You walkin' on thin ice, Spivak."

Luke, however, not nearly as forgiving, lunged over Sammy to get at Spivak again. "If you ever mention Haley or insult my friend again, I'll kill you! You hear me!"

"Aaaah zip it, redneck."

Luke tried one more time to leap toward him, but Sammy shoved him back down in his desk and held him there. "Calm down, now. Get a grip on yourself. If we all have to march again because of you two, you'll have to fight this whole platoon."

"He can't keep his mouth shut, can he?" Luke spat, his hands trembling. "Well, I'll shut it for him!"

"Whoa, Bro. Where's all this fury coming from? Whatever's eatin' you, you gotta let it go, man, before it destroys you or makes you do something you'll be sorry for. And, Lord knows, Spivak sho ain't worth all the trouble his mouth's been causin'."

Spivak snarled at Sammy's comment.

"Shhhh! Lieutenant's coming!" Several of the other men announced as they looked out the window.

Everybody jumped in their seats like junior high kids that had been acting up before their teacher entered the room. When the lieutenant arrived the guys looked as if nothing had happened. Luke somehow made it through the map-reading session and the remainder of the week. He was on edge, talked little, and stayed disconnected. All he wanted to do was immerse himself in the daily regimen of army training. He wanted to throw hand grenades and shoot things and crawl around on his belly, anything but think. Whoever heard of softball and baseball in the army, anyway? It was crazy, but somehow, some way, he'd have to muster up the courage to make it through this. If the mere sight of that bat in his sergeant's hands had sent graphic images through his mind, what would happen when he actually picked one up and stepped up to the plate, forced to hit again?

CHAPTER 20

SATURDAY ARRIVED, HOT and dry, the sun beating down without mercy. A thermometer in the shade underneath a breezeway outside the barracks read ninety-seven degrees. Rain had not fallen for quite some time, so the ground was hard and parched. Little puffs of dust followed the softball as it bounced across the grass in warm-ups. Luke had to admit, the sounds of the ball popping in the gloves along with the players calling back and forth to one another brought back sweet memories. Deep in his heart, he knew that he still loved the game, but he sure didn't know what do to with these other emotions. He hadn't expected to feel this way.

For a brief moment, he thought maybe he'd made a mistake by running away like he did. *I wonder how my tryout with the Braves would have gone? I could have been signed to a pro team by now, or at least starting school at LSU.* With those thoughts, depression crept over him again. *You have no life now. Haley loved the game too, but now she's buried under the damp Louisiana clay and you put her there. You don't deserve to play, let alone enjoy life. Where do you get off feeling sorry for yourself? Your life is over and you deserve it. If you don't have the guts to kill yourself at least you can live in misery.* Yes, if Luke was going to live, then he would have to pay for his stupidity. Like the good sergeant had said, "Stupidity and not thinking causes people to die."

Luke knew for certain that he could pitch and hit better than anyone of those guys, that if he got up to bat he could send that cowhide over the outfielders' heads or anywhere else he wanted.

➤➤ ◄◄

Two softball diamonds were set up on one of the five gigantic parade/marching grounds, one on one end of the grounds and the other on the opposite end. A cluster of trees grew between them. The trees actually made a nice buffer separating the diamonds. Each diamond was far enough away from the other as to ensure that games played at the same time would not interfere with each other. Backstops were erected out of two-by-fours and chicken wire and the boards were painted the usual army green. Baselines had been marked on the heat-singed grass with white paint. White canvas base bags and other equipment had been borrowed from the PE department at the local high school. There was no pitcher's mound, only a circle painted on the ground. Wooden benches made do for dugouts, and for spectators a small set of bleachers used for military cere-monies had been hauled over from another parade ground. Though it was raw, the diamonds were constructed in a neat, military fashion. Because there were twelve teams representing eight platoons, each playing double elimination, the games were going to be only five innings long, with two games at a time being played on the two diamonds.

➤➤ ◄◄

The bat looked like a miniature toy in Sammy's mammoth hands. His arms and shoulders were thick with taut muscles bulging through his black flesh. He could feel the sweat on his palm and wiped it on his fatigues. It was the top of the first inning and already the bases were loaded, with only one out. It was going to be a high-scoring affair.

Sammy gripped the bat tighter and waited for his pitch.

"Strike one!" Lieutenant Calloway, one of the volunteer Umpires shouted.

Sammy took a militant practice swing and let out one of his famous grins. The F2 pitcher backed up, exhaled slowly, and adjusted his cap. He and his platoon were dressed in green fatigues, white tee-shirts, green caps, and black army boots. F3 wore white tee-shirts with camouflage fatigues and caps.

Sammy's eyes squinted from the sun, but when he swung, the ball detonated with explosive power, blasting like a missile right between the second and first basemen. It bounced across the unyielding turf to the far edge of the outfield, rolling and rolling onto and down the blacktop road that wound through the middle of the base. The hit wasn't pretty, but it was powerful. By the time the outfielder had chased the ball down, Bobby Hall had already scored, followed by Cart Davis, then Alton Baker. Sammy rounded third, slowed to a jog, and then to a walk as he crossed home plate well before the ball was finally lobbed in from the outfield. It was four to zip with only one out. Sergeant Millhouse was going berserk. Luke shook his head, sweat rolling down his face and back. It was going to be a long day.

The next batter up was Sergeant Millhouse. His short, stocky build, and bald head with wrinkles across his forehead sort of reminded you of a bulldog. When he stepped up to home plate, the soldiers let out jeers, claps, and whistles. It only took one swing for him to connect. He knocked the ball clean over the outfield for another home run. Jogging around the bases, he waved and bowed to the guys as they cheered him on.

When Millhouse had touched home plate and moved to the dugout, Spivak ambled up to the plate slipshod, jawing violently on a wad of bubble gum. When the first pitch whizzed by, he swung with every bit of his one hundred and forty-five gaunt pounds, and missed. The momentum of the bat jerked around his body, almost knocking him over.

"Everybody, move up! Easy out!" The pitcher shouted to his outfielders.

"Yeah, yeah, I hear ya. I hear ya," Spivak yelled back.

Spivak swung at all the balls thrown, missing every one, giving F3 their second out. The score was five to zero and Luke was up.

>- -<

Except for the nicks and scuffs, the flaxen hickory was almost gleaming. Luke appeared to be in some sort of trance as he inspected the object lying at his feet. He stared at the thirty-four inches of precision crafted lumber, a Talbot Chesapeake Thunder. It was one of the top softball bats out there, one that Haley would have surely used.

"Luke, what you think this is, Son—a picnic?" shouted Sergeant Millhouse. "You're up!"

Luke didn't move. Instead, remained seated, head down, watching the bat lying at his feet.

"Luke, I said you're up! Now get moving!" This time, the Sergeant was in his face.

Luke bent over and reluctantly picked up the bat. It was the first time he had actually touched one since he threw his off the Lake Maurepas Bridge. A piercing pain shot through his chest as he walked at a snail's pace to home plate. His heart pounded erratically. The next couple of steps were wobbly.

"Stop dragging your butt, Luke!" Sergeant Millhouse barked again. "I'm not getting any younger you know!"

The guys on the bench began clapping and cheering him on. Spivak, bored with the whole event, just blew a huge bubble until it popped.

As if he'd just walked the plank on a pirate ship, the young private stepped up to the plate. He squeezed his hands tightly around the pine-tar handle and crouched in his hitting position. Still, Luke had not made eye contact with the pitcher. In a way, the scene was much like the one at Galilee Baptist—that backyard-game kind of feeling. Waves of guilt surged through him. It was all coming back now. The pain was so deep, so cutting. He felt like dropping the bat and running. Luke looked up, squinting into the sun. His heart rate accelerated more, causing him to pant with breathlessness. He felt flushed and weak. His hands started to tingle, and then they became numb. *What is happening to me? Am I dying? Am I going insane?*

The F2 pitcher completed his windup and flung the ball. It zipped right past Luke, a perfect pitch. On any other day, Luke would have wasted it—knocked it clean over the fence, but that was on another day. Today, he didn't even swing. Instead he stood frozen.

"Aw, come on, Hatcher," someone yelled out.

Millhouse pounded his fist in his hand. "You can do better than that!"

"Get a grip, Luke," He said to himself. *"You can do this."* He crouched and waited for the next pitch. Now, his hands were trembling uncontrollably. All the guys could see what was going on and began speculating to each other.

"Hey man, you all right?" the Umpire asked.

"I'm fine," said Luke. To the pitcher he shouted, "Come on just give me what you got." That was the way Luke always responded to pitchers, but this time, as soon as the words left his mouth, he realized that was exactly what he had said to Haley only seconds before...

"You don't look fine," the Umpire said.

"I said I'm fine."

"Okay, then. Play ball!"

When the pitcher released the ball for the second time, Luke could see it flying through the light of the sun—could see its parallel shadow moving on the grass. It was like slow motion and again, he didn't swing.

"Strike two!"

Luke now felt nauseated, as if the softball was lodged in his throat. Then it happened. He collapsed to his knees, his stomach constricting, and threw up. He heaved, but they were dry heaves, ripping, like pieces of swallowed glass, at his throat. Quickly stepping to his side, the Umpire, Lieutenant Calloway, quickly felt Luke's pulse. It was rapid. His face was white as a sheet and his skin clammy. He then looked into Luke's languid eyes, the pupils dilated. "Get this man to the infirmary!"

Lieutenant Calloway helped walk Luke to one of the nearby trees and instructed him to sit there until someone from the infirmary came to help transport him. While he was waiting, Sergeant Millhouse walked over to him. "This better be good, Hatcher. It better be real good," he said.

CHAPTER 21

"WHAT HAPPENED TO me out there?" asked Luke, sitting on the padded vinyl table as the infirmary doctor shone a pin-light in his eyes—the same kind that Doc Spurrier had used on Haley. This doctor was not nearly as compassionate as the old Doc back home. No, he was unquestionably the no-nonsense, by-the-book, military type.

"Don't know. Might have been heat stroke, but that seems highly unlikely because you've been acclimated to the heat for seven weeks. Seems to me if you were going to have heat stroke you would have had it before now when you were doing a higher-risk exercise. Open your mouth please."

Luke opened his mouth in compliance as the doctor stuck a thermometer right in as if he were an accomplished spear fisherman.

"Close your mouth until I say to open it."

"Okay," Luke mumbled through closed lips.

The doctor then wrapped the blood pressure cuff around Luke's arm and began pumping. After checking his blood pressure and listening to his heart with a stethoscope, he took out the thermometer and held it up to the light.

"Well, you don't have any fever and your vitals are all fine. Your eyes were somewhat dilated but have returned back to normal. Evidently you had some sort of reaction but since your vitals are fine now, I don't think it was too serious. I'm going to give you some medication that should help calm you down. Lie down on your back and hold out your left arm."

Luke reclined and rested his head on the hard pillow that was connected to the table and held his arm out limp. "You're not going to give me a shot are you?" asked Luke a bit anxiously.

"No, not a shot—just going to prick you and take some blood for a test. After that, you're going to move to one of the infirmary beds and I'll connect an IV tube to the same needle. It'll pump you with some fluids that will help strengthen your system."

After the doctor finished drawing the blood, Luke was sent down the hall to a room that had several beds in it. There the IV was connected and he was ordered to rest for a couple hours while receiving the fluids. When Luke's body returned to normal, he was sent back to his platoon. It was after dark, and the moment his feet stepped inside the barracks, he heard the dreaded call.

"Private Hatcher, in my office." Though the sergeant's voice was loud, it lacked the harshness that it usually held.

Luke rolled his eyes back as he followed his orders, for he knew an explanation was expected.

"Private, what happened? And like I told you out there, this better be good." Sergeant Millhouse was standing behind his desk. Luke was at full attention.

"It was the heat or something, sir."

"Or something? Yeah, it was 'or something' all right."

Luke squirmed.

"You know what I think?"

"No, Sergeant."

"I think the heat is just an excuse. You men work in that heat everyday. Yes, it is most definitely something else. Did the doctor say it was the heat?"

Luke lowered his head, "Well, not exactly. He said he didn't know what happened." Luke shifted anxiously before continuing his manner, that of a whipped athlete being inter- viewed after losing a championship game. "Sergeant, if you don't mind, I really don't want to talk about it."

For a moment, the sergeant's eyes softened—the harsh- ness gone. "Maybe you should, Son," he said, walking around his desk, placing his hand on Luke's shoulder. "Maybe I would be a good one to unload on. Whatever you say stays in this room. You have my word on it."

"With all due respect, Sergeant, but I really don't think you would understand."

"Sit down," Millhouse instructed, his hand stretched out toward the chair in an inviting manner.

Luke reluctantly followed his order and sat down in the chair facing the desk, while Millhouse sat on the desktop, his arms folded.

"You know, I've been around the block a few times and seen some things and done some things that would make you cringe. Private Hatcher, you don't have much time left here. Next week you ship out to your AIT and you may never see me again. But it is my job as your trainer and leader to see to it that you are ready." He peered deep into Luke's eyes. "Now you listen to me good. You hear? You can't be having those kind of attacks, or whatever that was, when in combat situations. Your comrades will be depending on you. You act like that out there and you'll get yourself killed or you'll get someone else killed."

He stood and walked over to an open window. Luke shifted in his seat in order to follow him. "I've been thinking about you and some things just don't add up. It never really occurred to me until this softball incident." He paused and glanced out the window. Thousands of bugs hovered and circled around the light poles outside. Beetles banged against the window screen. The night air was heavy with humidity, but a slow revolving ceiling fan above them offered a slight relief. "You're extremely athletic," Millhouse continued. "You're only eighteen. You're good-looking, not to mention very intelligent, and you're not wanted for grand theft. You're a sergeant's dream. The problem is; most kids like you are in college on deferment. What I can't figure out is why someone like you would join the army instead of being deferred? You know as well as I do that you probably wouldn't have had to join at all. It just doesn't make sense," Millhouse scratched his head. "Unless, maybe you're here out of guilt or something—had a brother wounded or killed, or your father. I do know something happened that made you enlist. Guys like you don't just join up without a good reason."

The words shot at Luke like poison darts. He stiffened in his seat. "I wanted to serve my country is all."

"Sure, that's it," Millhouse said with sarcasm. "You're such a bloody hero. Why don't we just go ahead and have a Medal of Honor ceremony right now?"

Luke didn't respond to the harsh remark, but stared straight ahead.

"You know what I really think, Hatcher? I think there is another reason why you joined. You're running. I don't know from what, but you're definitely running. Now that I think about it, I've seen it before, the mannerisms and the attitude. I just can't figure out what happened on that softball diamond today, but I know it has something to do with you running."

It was like the Sergeant was psychic. He had hit a nerve and Luke's expression telegraphed it. Luke took a deep breath. "May I go now, Sergeant?"

"I'm only trying to help you, Private. Simply trying to help."

"Look, I appreciate it, but you can't help me, okay. Nobody can help me."

"Well then, I guess I'll be seeing you on that softball diamond tomorrow ready to go. We have two more games to win. And private, don't chicken out this time. You hear me?" Sergeant Millhouse pointed to the door. "You are dismissed."

Luke stood, saluted, and started walking out. Then, he stopped in mid-stride, let out a sigh and turned back around. "I killed Haley," he said slightly above a whisper.

Millhouse raised his head, "Son?"

Luke looked up at his Sergeant, now a friend, maybe a father, or a coach, and it all came out, surging—a dam of emotion cracking, then bursting forth. "I killed Haley," he said again, only this time a little louder. "I killed Haley! I killed Haley!" Luke shouted out forcefully. The men in the barracks could hear his mournful cries, though they couldn't make out any words. The iron-tough sergeant was taken back. He knew Luke had a problem, but he hadn't expected this. *Did Private Hatcher mean murder?* Millhouse pondered. *Surely not. A car accident, maybe?* His mind was reeling with the possibilities. He placed his hand on Luke's shoulders and then sat back down on his desktop. "Sit, Private Hatcher. Let's talk. I'm listening."

"Haley was beautiful," Luke said, taking a seat in the chair again. "She was the most wonderful person I've ever known. I loved her. And…and I killed her. It's just that simple. I don't deserve to live. I mean, why should God let me live when she couldn't? It's not right."

Sergeant Millhouse leaned forward, rubbing his chin. "How did she die, Private?"

"She was pitching a baseball to me, trying to strike me out...all because of a stupid bet." Luke stared down at the floor, shaking his head. He lifted his hat and ran his hand through his hair. "When I hit the ball, it hit her in the head, right on her temple. That night she went to the hospital and the next morning she was dead."

Again, the Sergeant was taken back. He paused not sure how to respond to such a bizarre set of circumstances. But now things were starting to make sense—the tears, the fights, not wanting to play in the game, the anxiety attack. He put his hands behind his head. "How can you say that you're responsible?" the sergeant's voice was deep and solid. "You had no way of knowing?"

"Come on, Sergeant, you're a baseball guy. You know as well as I do that I should have never been hitting off someone like that. Especially as hard as I hit it, and without a pitcher's screen?"

"You tell me how you could have known? It's not like you're a pro."

Luke punched the side of the metal desk. "That's just it! I've been playing baseball for years. I even signed a scholarship to LSU and the very night before Haley died I had gotten a call from the Atlanta Braves! Don't tell me I shouldn't have known better. I knew better than anyone what playing around like that could cause. I was trained Sergeant. I was trained!"

"Wow, the Braves. I'm impressed," Millhouse said, standing to his feet. He placed his hand on Luke's shoulders. "Son, all I can tell you is you have to be strong. You're a young man with a whole lifetime ahead of you. You can't let this setback destroy your life. You have to suck it up and be a man."

Luke remained quiet, chewing over what had just been said. *Be strong? Suck it up? A setback? Haley's death was not a setback. It was a tragedy.* The more Luke pondered, the more the sergeant's words disappointed him. This is not what he expected. *Is this all you have to offer? I knew I shouldn't have opened up.* Luke wanted to jump up and leave the room, but Sergeant Millhouse was on a roll.

"Believe it or not, I can relate to what you are going through. I don't like to talk about it much, but in your case, I'll make an exception."

How gracious of you, Luke simmered.

"I've been in the military going on twenty-one years now. I've fought in two wars, Korea and Vietnam. And I've seen some pretty nasty stuff—been a part of some pretty nasty stuff. I still have dreams about it. I tell you, Private Hatcher, it never leaves you. It sticks with you for your whole life."

Right in front of Luke, the Sergeant's demeanor physically changed to that of bitterness and resentment. It was like a spirit suddenly possessed him. "It was Korea, 1950, I was fighting with the 27th Wolfhound Regiment along the 38th parallel between North and South Korea. The Chinese and North Koreans had captured Seoul and were launching a massive offensive. It was cold. Ice and snow were everywhere. I arrived at the mobile unit around 0300 hours. Our ship had hit the shores of Korea that night and the Red Cross was there to meet us. They gave each of us a cup of coffee and a donut. Then we were loaded on this rickety old train with wooden seats and no heat.

We rode almost all night. When it stopped, we hiked over an hour in knee-deep snow to camp. I could hear machine guns and bombs in the distance. I knew I was going to die, if not by the enemy, then by frostbite."

Millhouse's eyes shifted away from Luke's and back out the screened window. A beetle had made it inside and was crawling up the screen. Millhouse took his index finger and as if the beetle was an enemy from his past, flicked it through the air. "By dawn it was not only bitterly cold, but there was a thick fog. We were moving down a dirt road and couldn't see ten feet in front of our faces. For about a quarter of a mile, the road cut between these rock embankments that were about fifty-feet or so. Colonel Grey had made radio contact with units ahead of us and they radioed back that the way seemed clear."

The flicked beetle had crawled across the floor and was heading up the wall, back toward the window. This time, Sergeant Millhouse took a sharpened pencil off his desk and meticulously drove it through the beetle's back. The beetle twitched and squirmed, fighting for its life before finally becoming still. Craze filled Millhouse's eyes. "That bug never saw it coming, did it? The little innocent creature was just going about its business, and wham, it's history. Well, I've seen people die just like that bug there. Life's just a cruel game, Private Hatcher, a cruel game."

He carried the pencil and the beetle over to the trashcan and dropped them both in. "I've seen people buried like that bug too—bodies just thrown away in dumps."

Luke nodded.

"All of a sudden, orange streaks blazed from the rocks surrounding us. We dove into the ditches for cover. The hills were crawling with Chinese. Fire was exchanged for about an hour. When it ceased, wounded men were everywhere, flopping around and groaning, their bodies going into spasms. Both of the men on my right and left were in the ditch dead. Then there was this eerie silence. I knew the enemy was out there watching us. After a few minutes, gunfire started up again, moving closer. Most of my regiment had been wounded or killed. The Chinese were going to sweep through and finish us off. I knew I was going to die. I was sure of it. So I took out a grenade and held it in my hands, debating whether or not to just pull the pin and end it all right there. Private Hatcher, I was seconds from pulling that pin when the flyboys streamed over in full fury, dropping napalm everywhere. In the end, I was the only one in my regiment that wasn't killed or severely wounded."

Sergeant Millhouse sat back down in his chair and heaved a sigh. "Why me? Why did I get to survive? Why does anybody die? Why does war happen? Why do accidents happen? Who chooses who lives and who dies? Blast it, Private, I don't know why your girlfriend...what's her name?"

"Haley, her name was Haley," Luke replied, his hands clenched in a fist hanging by his side.

"I don't know why Haley had to die. But I do know that life is cold. It's very, very cold." He threw his hands up in the air as if bewildered. "So, what's a man to do?"

Luke shrugged his shoulders.

"Listen to me, Private, and listen to me good," the Sergeant continued, his mouth straight, eyes blank. "Life is nasty and the weak don't survive. If you're going to make it, you gotta get tough, get strong. And all that religion stuff that Private Williams talks about is for cowards. They create all that nonsense because they can't handle reality. You want truth? You want reality? Seeing all your buddies shot up with their guts hanging out, that's reality. Bulldozing hundreds of dead gooks into common graves, I ask you, where's God in that? There is no God, Private. If there were, surely he wouldn't allow all the things I've seen. If you're going to make it in this world, you're going to have to be strong, Private Hatcher, strong! And I'm gonna tell you something else, too. For your own sake and for the sake of the United States Army, I can't afford to be soft on you. So, I'm still counting on you to play tomorrow. You hear me? You're going to suck up all those worthless emotions you're having and you're going to help us win! And remember this; I have the power to make recommendations that can make your little visit in the military miserable. You may think that I'm being too hard on you, but trust me, Private Hatcher, it's for your own good."

Luke absorbed the sergeant's words fully, measuring them in a way that made his shoulders fall, as though he'd been taken advantage of and beaten up with his own sorrow. While Sergeant Millhouse might have meant well, his counsel had missed the mark. Luke didn't need someone to tell him how brutal life was, he was well aware of that fact. The truth was; Sergeant Millhouse was in the same fix as Luke. Only he was much further along in his journey of bitterness.

By the time Luke made it back to his bunk, the lights were out and the barracks quiet. Those that were awake kept to themselves. Luke lay down on his back, facing the ceiling.

"God feels your pain, Luke," a deep, soothing voice came from the bunk next to him. "He understands because he hung on that cross, man."

Luke closed his eyes and rolled over.

CHAPTER 22

KNOWING THAT HE had to play in the last two games caused Luke to toss and turn all through the night. Even the extra sleep on Sunday morning didn't help. He simply lay in his bunk looking up at the ceiling, in a way strangely similar to the way he had looked up at the ceiling of his room back home. The Sergeant's words had crushed what little spirit he had left. Haley almost seemed like someone from another life. In a way, he was starting to forget—not the event, but *her*, if that was possible? It was becoming more and more difficult for him to hold an image of Haley in his mind. And that disturbed him. Oh how he hated what he had done, but oh, how he didn't want to forget. He determined never to let Haley go. Lying there, Luke played out several different potential scenarios of the games in his mind. What would he do? How would he react? Would he have another anxiety attack? Was it out of his control or would rage take over this time?

The questions were still running through Luke's mind when Sergeant Millhouse addressed the platoon that morning. To everyone's surprise, the Sergeant had some unexpected news. "Men, as much as it pains me to say this, there will be no softball games today. I know that will come as good news to at least one of you," he said sarcastically, yet not looking in Luke's direction. "As you know," he continued, "AIT orders were to be handed down this Tuesday and then you would have your ten days of leave. However, things have been heating up overseas and President Johnson is calling for more troop strength immediately."

At that, the group began murmuring loudly.

"All right, now," Sergeant Millhouse said, holding his hand up in the air, palm out, "just settle down and let me finish...Johnson wants to build the overseas number up from 120,000 troops to 400,000. That means Uncle Sam needs you as quickly as possible. Unfortunately, that also means most of you will not get to take your leave and you'll be shipping out as soon as tomorrow. I'm real sorry, men, but this is not my call. Now, I want you to go to breakfast and report back here for your AIT orders at 0700."

➤➤ ◄◄

"It's hard to believe that this is actually it," Luke said to Sammy as they found their regular spot in the mess hall. "You know, we may not see each other again after tomorrow."

"If we get separated, I'll look you up after I get back home," Sammy said, setting his tray down. "After all, Kentwood is only a stone's throw from Magnolia Springs."

"If I'm there. I may not be going back home to live. Don't know where I'm going to end up."

Once they got settled and began eating, Luke looked up at Sammy with a serious expression. "Sam, man, you're all right. I just wanted to tell you that. I know I've been a pretty tough guy to live with 'n all. You've been a good friend the last eight weeks. I mean, I feel like I've known you all my life."

"You're all right too, Luke," said Sammy, gnawing on a piece of ham. "And I don't know what you been going through, but whatever it is, you're gonna make it. You know the offer still stands if you want to talk about it? I'm here for you, man."

"Maybe later today or tomorrow. I don't want to talk about it right now." Sergeant Millhouse was the only person Luke had opened up to and what a mistake that had been. Now he was pretty sure he was not going to expose himself like that again.

"No, problem, man. It's your life."

Luke looked up, dangling his fork. "Hey, you're not exactly an open book, you know. You never told me about those scars on your arms. You're holding back on me. I know you are."

Sammy looked surprised at Luke's comeback. "Maybe later today," he said, "or tomorrow. I don't want to talk about it either."

After breakfast the two made their way back to the barracks and when the whole platoon had made it, Sergeant Millhouse began handing out the AIT orders.

"Baker!" the Sergeant shouted.

Private Baker reached forward, taking his brown envelope, and ripped it open.

Millhouse never looked up, going right down the line of all the names, each Private responding in like manner as the first. "Brady, Clark, Davis,...Hatcher...Riley, Rodriquez, Spivak, Williams."

After tearing his envelope open, Luke pulled out the slip of paper inside, and scanned it.

Advanced Individual Training Orders

Hatcher, Marion, Luke

Rank: Private, 1st Class

Serial #: RA54214365

Occupational Specialty: Infantry

Training Location: Fort Clements, Florida

Report Date: 09-03-66

Report Time: 1700 Hours

Luke carefully examined his orders. *An infantryman?* He understood what that meant. It meant rifles, machine guns, pistols, mines, grenades, and rocket launchers. It also meant that in all likelihood, he would be shipped to Vietnam and dropped right into the heat of the battle. He sat down on the end of his bunk and reread the orders. September third was Tuesday, that meant he would ship out Monday—tomorrow. To be honest, he actually wasn't all that upset. In fact, part of him was relieved. Though he knew his parents would be disappointed, he also knew that he was not ready to go home—not yet.

Everybody was mingling around, chatting and comparing orders when Spivak loudly announced his. "Combat Medic, now that's what I'm talking about!" he said, plopping backwards onto his bunk. "That's got a nice ring to it. I can just see me now, stationed at some base hospital, gorgeous nurses all around. Yeah, this is right down my alley."

"Hey, idiot!" somebody hollered back. "You know what the word combat means?"

"Whut?" Spivak muttered.

"It means you ain't going to no hospital, man," the guy laughed. "You're going to the front lines. You'll see some action all right, but it ain't gonna be with no good-looking nurses."

Spivak slapped his forehead and moaned.

One bunk over, Sammy was looking down at Luke. "What's yours say?"

"Infantry—Fort Clements, in two days."

"Hey, let me look at that," Sammy asked, snatching the paper out of Luke's hands. Luke stood and hung his arm around Sammy's burly shoulders, looking down.

"They're the same," Sammy said with excitement in his voice. "We both got the same orders. That means we're staying together." Sammy slapped Luke on the back and shook his head, another one of his grins covering his face. "We're staying together, man. Ain't that cool?"

A smile curled up on Luke's lips. *Who woulda thought I'd be so glad to be stayin' with this Sammy fellow?*

→► ◄←

Later that afternoon Luke made his way to the phone booth to make the dreaded phone call to his parents about him not coming home for leave. He considered writing a letter, but then reasoned that, that would just be too low.

"Hello, Emily? Is that you, girl?" Luke asked.

"Luuuke!" Emily shouted back. "Mama! Daddy! It's Luke! It's Luke!"

"Hey, my little pumpkin 'tater pie. I sure do miss you."

"I miss you too, Luke! When you coming? You coming home today? Are you gonna bring me something? You gonna come see my play at school? Mom says you'll be home then and can come."

The excitement in Emily's voice brought sadness to his heart. "We'll see, Squirt. We'll see. Hey, is Mom or Dad home?"

"Oooookaaay," Emily said with a pout.

"Hey, I love you squirt. You know I can see right through this phone, don't ya? Now, I want to see that great big smile of yours." Luke waited a few seconds. "There...There...There it is."

"I love you, Luke," Emily giggled. "Here's Daddy."

"Dad, it's me, Luke."

James took a moment to gather his emotions. Though he had been preparing himself for Luke's return home and expected a call on Sunday, actually hearing his son's voice again still took him by surprise. This was only the second time Luke had spoken to his father, the first being one week earlier. Their conversation then had seemed forced and calculated, like they were reading from a script. "Hello, Son." said James.

Luke was not prepared either. It was an awkward moment for both of them. "Hey."

"So, how you doing?"

"Fine, you know, just hanging in there."

"Yeah, life's tough sometimes. We have to do the best we can." James wanted to weep. He wanted to hold his son and tell him how much he too was hurting over everything—that he was worried sick about him—that he'd lost nearly ten pounds, not from dieting, but from stress—that he'd started smoking again. It may have been the way he was raised. It might have been the era he lived in, but James either refused or was unable to show his emotions and continued with the small talk. "When will you be here?"

"Well, that's why I called...I...I'm not coming."

James was taken aback. "What?"

"It's not that I don't want to, Dad. Today I received my AIT orders and I have to report on Tuesday. President Johnson is beefing up the troops, so they're speeding everything up."

"I know. I heard it on the news, but didn't think it would affect you. Where they sending you?"

"Fort Clements, Florida—Infantry."

"Infantry?"

"Yeah. I think I'll be pretty good at it."

"Your Mom and Emily are going to be very disappointed."

Luke was silent for a moment before he spoke. "What about you?" he said delicately. "Are you disappointed?" Luke couldn't believe he had actually said that.

Though spoken softly, the question smacked James broadsided. "Yes Son, of course I'm disappointed." James stuttered on. "It's just that, this has been hard on me too, you know. It's not all about you. I spent over fourteen years working with you on your baseball and you just threw it all away, flushed it down the drain, like it was nothing."

There was a long silence on the other end of the line.

"Luke? You there?"

"I'm here, Dad."

"Look, I'm sorry. It's just that you're my son and I want what's best for you."

"You mean what's best for yourself, right Dad?"

"That's not true! I don't like seeing you throwing your life away...here...here's your Mother." James handed the phone to Sarah and stormed out of the room.

"Mom?"

"Luke, Honey, I'm sorry about your father. He means well. He's just hurting a lot these days. He's a good man."

"I love him, too, but I can't live my life to please him anymore."

"He knows that, but you have to realize that this has been so difficult on him. He's afraid for you. Your father wants you to have a better life than he had—having to work his fingers to the bone and scratch for everything we have. And he doesn't like to see you in so much pain."

"He has a funny way of showing it...Look, Mom, I have to go now. I love you."

"Luke, don't go yet. Did I hear your father right? You're not coming home?"

"Yes. I'm so sorry, but it is out of my control—a last minute change. Dad will tell you. But I'll be in touch. I'm sure I'll get to come home for Christmas."

Sarah was crying again. Tears were becoming common-place in the Hatcher family. "Oh, Luke. I was so looking forward to seeing you. And Emily is going to be heartbroken. I just know she is."

Luke could hardly take the pain he knew he was causing and had caused. It was getting the best of him, so he decided to end the conversation abruptly.

"I'll call you soon, Mom. Love ya. But I have to go, now. Bye." Luke placed the receiver back on its hook and walked out of the booth.

CHAPTER 23

THE UNITED STATES Army had been experimenting with a program called the "Buddy System." This was when soldiers were kept together, sometimes in units and sometimes in twos, for the entire duration of their duty. They would meet in basic training, attend AIT together, and stay together until discharge or death. Since Luke and Sammy had spent Basic together and had the same AIT orders, neither was too surprised when they were assigned as long term "Buddies."

Instead of a Greyhound, this time, Uncle Sam flew Luke, Sammy, and several other sets of "Buddies" via commercial jet to Victoria, Florida which was located about ten miles north of Fort Clements in the northern panhandle. An army vehicle would pick them up at the airport in Victoria and take them to the base. The soldiers were dressed in full uniforms when they loaded the DC9 aircraft and found their seats. Neither Luke nor Sammy had flown before.

"You want the window?" asked Luke while cramming his canvas army satchel in the overhead compartment.

"No, you're cool," replied Sammy. "I may need the aisle so I can stretch my legs out if I need to."

Luke slid into his seat, leaned his head back and watched the airport workers as they ran to and fro on the runway. He reached up, adjusted the airflow above his head, then glanced over at Sammy, who had already stretched out with his eyes closed as if he were an experienced traveler; a folded newspaper lay in his lap.

The plane lurched forward and taxied onto the runway. Luke closed his eyes also, feeling a mild wooziness as the jet approached its critical speed elevating over the treetops. When it leveled off at its cruising altitude, Luke relaxed.

"Hey, Sam, man, check it out."

"What?" Sammy answered, one eye squinting, the other still shut. "I'm trying to get some shut-eye here."

Luke pointed out the window. "Beautiful, isn't it?"

Sammy unbuckled his seatbelt and leaned over into Luke's space and looked. "No doubt." As far as the eye could see were waves of white clouds presenting and array of contours and textures. "Looks soft, like cotton—like you could jump right out in it and roll around."

For a while, the two soldiers pondered the wonders stretching before them. Occasionally, a break in the clouds offered views of roads and small towns that intersected through the checkerboard patterns of farmland.

"Whoa, what was that?" Luke said, clutching his stomach when the plane bumped and dipped a couple times because of a stretch of turbulence.

"I don't know, man," said Sammy, his eyes big and round as saucers.

"Please return to your seat and observe the fasten-seat-belt sign," the stewardess announced over the intercom. "We're experiencing a bit of rough weather."

Sammy slid back in his seat, buckled up and began flipping through the newspaper.

Soon the flight became smooth again and when Luke turned Sammy's way, he noticed that the big guy's eyes were moist with what appeared to be tears. "You all right?" Luke asked, touching Sammy's shoulder.

"I'll be fine," he answered, wiping his eyes. Then, he slammed the newspaper shut and shoved it violently into the pocket on the seat in front of him. "I need to pray, is all. I just need to pray." Sammy rubbed his nose with his thumb and index finger then closed his eyes as if in deep reflection.

Luke pulled out the newspaper to read. It was creased at the place where Sammy had been reading. Luke's eyes fell upon the page's main headlines:

BOMB EXPLODES AT JACKSON,
MISSISSIPPI CHURCH

3 YOUNG COLORED FEMALES KILLED

Laying the paper down, Luke realized that it wasn't the turbulence that had upset Sammy, but the article.

"Sam, man, I'm sorry. It's terrible what's going on 'n all. It really is." Luke talked with as much concern as he could.

The eight weeks of basic training had sealed Sammy off from the outside world, in a way. He knew what was going on, but was too busy to actually stop and think about it.

"Yeah, it is," said Sammy, his head down, pain in his voice. "Those little girls didn't hurt nobody. They didn't do anything wrong. Pure evil is what it is. Pure evil."

"Hey, you know all white people are not like that? I'm not like that, right? I mean you're my friend, 'n all."

"I know you're not like them, Luke. I knew that from our first week at Basic. And don't go thinking I hate all white people, 'cause I don't."

Their eyes met for a moment, then Luke broke from Sammy's to look back out the window. Sammy continued, "There's evil in my people too, you know. There's evil everywhere. We're in these uniforms because of an evil war."

Luke said nothing, just listened.

"But I don't hate anymore, Luke. I can't explain it all eloquently. I only know that God took my hate out." Sammy slowed his speech and gently caressed one of the visible scars running across his forearm. "No, brother, I'm not hating anymore. Don't get me wrong. I do get angry and I do hurt. I hurt for the injustice to my people. Think about it, man. I'm going off to fight for my country, to maybe get myself killed, and back home in Tangipahoa Parish I'm treated like a third-class citizen. In some places, the dogs get better treatment than Negroes. My mama served a white man in order to feed us kids. Spent her whole life on her knees scrubbing floors and cleaning toilets, but she never complained. Not once did I hear her say a negative word. Not one time. I'd question Mama about her life from time to time and she'd always say something funny like, 'The undertaker may be smiling, Sammy, but God ain't finished with me yet!' And then she'd go right back to working on whatever she was doing...and my daddy he'd..." Sammy stopped abruptly and closed his eyes shut.

"What about your daddy?" Luke asked.

"I can't talk about it now."

Luke frowned and drew his eyebrows up. "I don't know what to say, man."

"You don't have to say a darn thing, just listen to me. You're a great guy, but back in Magnolia Springs you've lived in a sheltered world. You only saw and heard what they wanted you to. Pretty soon you gonna see what the world's really like."

Luke didn't respond, choosing to remain silent, wondering about Sammy's scars and about his past. The plane tilted in the air, turning toward their destination. Something had turned in Luke as well. He felt he could trust Sammy. Again Luke pondered his friend's scars and the hate he'd been freed from.

CHAPTER 24

"YOU HAVE BEEN trained in the basics and you have passed. Congratulations." The Green Beret Ranger stood on a platform in camouflage fatigues, his face unyielding, as he addressed the newest members of the 2nd Rifle Brigade. "Now... get over it! Today you begin your Advanced Training. You're going to be infantrymen. In short, that means your next stop, after your leave time, if you get any, is 'Nam. And if you don't get with the program, you will die in 'Nam. That, I guarantee. So you had better get your head screwed on straight. Those that do, have a much higher survival rate. Those that don't will get shipped home in body bags."

Luke swallowed hard, his mouth dry like cotton. Though he was convinced in his mind that he didn't deserve to live, he was still afraid to die, his mind flashing back to his bedroom nine weeks before—lips wrapped around the shotgun's barrel and coming within a breath of pulling the trigger. He shivered at the recollection.

Luke and Sammy were assigned to the 2nd Rifle Brigade of the 37th Infantry Regiment known as "The Cobras." The members who made it through the training wore arm patches of a military shield on which a coiled Cobra snake was imprinted over two crossed bolts of lighting. The members of the Cobras were highly trained in the art of ground combat with M16 rifles and .45-caliber pistols. They were the guys that did the dirty work, pushing back the enemy lines and establishing new U.S. perimeters.

No question, Advanced Training was going to be tough, the toughest training Luke had ever gone through. Baseball and football, not even his basic training at Fort Wiggins would come close. Yet, there was a silver lining. Training was Monday through Friday, with the weekends off and soldiers were allowed to leave base. Passes were handed out on Friday evenings after Recall and ended on Sundays at 2000 hours. These passes were not a right, but rather a privilege. They could be cancelled for unruly behavior. Soldiers could not travel further than a 75-mile radius or they would be considered AWOL and would be arrested. Usually, they would head a few miles up the road to Victoria, a town of about 50,000, or they would go for the white sandy beaches of the Gulf of Mexico less than twenty miles in the opposite direction. POVs (Privately Owned Vehicles) were still not allowed, for the new recruits anyway, but because the military base was so close, city buses and small-town taxis ran back and forth on a fairly regular basis.

On that first Saturday, Luke and Sammy laid claim to their weekend privilege and decided on town. It had been over ten weeks since they'd set foot outside of a military base except when on a bus or plane. Sammy wasn't too keen on riding the city bus, so they opted to share a taxi ride into town.

➤➤ ◄◄

"I feel like I've just been released from prison," said Sammy, stepping out of the taxi, stretching his arms and taking in a big swallow of fresh air. "You know what?"

"What?" said Luke.

"It's been an awful long time since I've had a big ol' cheeseburger and a chocolate malt. What do you say?"

"Sounds like a plan to me." He ran his fingers through his dark hair, his hat folded neatly and tucked inside his belt with the bronze buckle gleaming in the sunshine. "It's been a long time for me, too."

The two walked down Victoria's main street and around the town square. Victoria, Florida was a place like many other medium-sized college and military towns, too big to be a small town, but not large enough to be considered metropolitan. It was a town in transition. Like a teenager groaning through adolescence, part of the town struggled to stay small, holding on to its past, while another part pushed for modernization and progress.

They walked another block and stepped across the street to the *Frosty Top Downtown Café*, which was squeezed between the Florida State Bank and Woolworth's. At the city park, about a block away, a crowd seemed to be gathering on one side.

The rumble of loud conversation hit them like a gust of wind when they opened the door of the café. Forks and plates clinked against each other. Waitresses walked briskly from one table to the next. Locals and students from Victoria State University filled almost every available space. Luke spotted one vacant booth near the front plate glass window that looked out on Main Street. So they slid in and waited...and waited.

"Did you see that?" Luke asked. "That waitress looked over here and then just ignored us. Now she's waiting on those people. We were here way before them."

Sammy looked at his watch. "Yeah, man. We've been in here almost ten minutes."

Another waitress sped by the table. Luke attempted to get her attention but she too, seemed to ignore him. Finally, when the waitress was looking directly at him, Luke said in a frustrated tone, "Excuse me, miss can we get some service? We've been here awhile."

She didn't move, instead four brawny college guys, each with flat-top haircuts and tight-fitting tee-shirts stepped up to their booth.

"Well, would you look at this," one of them said to his buddies, chewing on a toothpick. "We got us a nigger and one of them nigger-lovers here."

"Hey Jake," another one said. "Can I touch him? I've never seen a real live nigger-lover before."

"I don't know if I'd touch him, Jake. No telling what you might catch. You never know, they might be queer too?" At that, they all cracked up laughing, slapping each other on their backs.

Sammy never even looked up, just sat quietly, staring out the window.

"Hey, what's your problem?" Luke shot back. "We ain't done nothing to you."

"You got some mouth on you, Soldier Boy." Then he turned to Sammy. "You see that sign over there, boy? Can't you read?... Oh, I forgot, you probably can't." Again, they slapped each other, laughing.

Sammy remained quiet, but now his fist clenched.

"What sign?" Luke asked.

"That sign." Jake, the leader of the pack, pointed to the wall at the front entrance.

Sure enough, there in bold black letters was a poster-sized sign that read:

WHITES ONLY

NO NEGROES ALLOWED

The cashier, who was standing in front of it, had obstructed the view.

"Look, I'm sorry," said Sammy, politely. "We didn't see the sign and we don't want no trouble. We'll be on our way."

Sammy attempted to slide out of the booth, but Jake slammed his fist down on the table.

"Well, it looks like you just found yourself some trouble, didn't you, boy?"

Luke made a move toward Jake, fists cocked, but Sammy stretched his long arms across the table and held him in check. "Calm down, Luke. Think this thing through," Sammy reasoned, though he knew that he and Luke could dust those guys without breaking a sweat. He also knew that no matter how justified his actions; he would be the one ending up in trouble with the law.

"You best listen to your nigger friend," Jake addressed Luke, then moved his hate-filled eyes back to Sammy. "You think cause that Martin Luther King fella is coming to town you can just do anything you want?"

By now, everyone in the café had turned their attention to the scuffle.

"Like I said, we're not looking for any trouble," said Sammy. "We just want to leave in peace."

About that time, two Deputy Sheriffs moseyed up to the table. One was tall and skinny with red hair, the other one was also tall, but heavy set and balding, with a huge potbelly hanging over his belt. The big one spoke while the skinny one stood by his side with his arms crossed. "Jake, don't you young men have a game tonight?"

"Yes, sir. Playing Eastern Virginia."

"You best get rested up, all right? Now go on."

Jake and his boys fired Luke and Sammy looks that said, "You haven't seen the last of us." Then they slowly and defiantly shuffled out.

"Now why you boys want to come in here making all kinds of trouble?" said the deputy, to Luke and Sammy, while adjusting his pants.

"But we didn't do anything wrong," Luke said, remembering all the times he had sat in Ivy's, where Negroes were not allowed, and never gave it a second thought.

Sammy looked up at the deputies. "We didn't see the sign and we won't come back again."

"You better not, because if I see you in here again, I'll have to arrest you. And you don't want me to do that, do you?"

"No sir," said Sammy through a clinched jaw.

Sammy rose slow and solid, like a deeply rooted oak tree, towering a full three inches above both deputies. The balding one nervously tapped his pistol as he watched the two soldiers make their exit. Outside, Luke was livid.

"I don't get it, man!" said Luke. "You just let those punks walk all over you. We could have cleaned them out! You know we could have, too!"

"Have to choose your battles wisely, Luke," said Sammy, patting him on the shoulder. "Say we did pound on those guys. Say we whipped up on them real good. What you think would have been the result?"

"We'd have a couple of busted lips and got kicked out of the café, but they would have learned their lesson, not to mess with us again."

"We'd be nursing sore lips all right, but from jail, while those white boys would limp back home, scott-free. You think they'd let a black man go without pinning something on him? I'd get slapped for assault and battery or for unlawful entry. Just a little afternoon brawl to you, Luke, could put me back in the pen. You saw the way those deputies treated us. And they only treated you that way because you were with me. Trust me, Luke. I know what I'm talking about…And then, on top of that, our weekend passes would be revoked. So we're better off just keeping our mouths shut and walking away."

"Back in the pen?" What did that mean? "Yeah, I guess you're right," Luke said, seeing the pain in Sammy's eyes. "It must be tough on you, having to take that kind of stuff all the time."

"It's the most humiliating thing a man can go through— to be treated like an animal when I was created by God, just like everybody else. And Jesus Christ went to the Cross for me, just like everybody else."

"Hey Sammy," Luke said. "You never told me you went to jail before."

"Didn't see the need."

Luke picked up his pace, passing Sammy up, then turned around in his face. "Well?"

"Well what?" Sammy walked faster, his head fixed straight ahead, ignoring Luke. Now, both were striding side by side.

"Jail, man? That's what. I can't picture you in jail." Luke tripped when the sidewalk dipped.

"Watch your step, Soldier. You gonna go and get yourself wounded before you leave the States."

Luke picked up his pace, almost jogging, trying to keep up with Sammy's long-legged steps. Both were now sweating in the afternoon heat and their shirts were spotted with perspiration. When they reached the City Park's edge Sammy stopped and dropped down on a bench under some trees. Luke followed.

"It wasn't jail, Luke. It was prison. Two years of my life, man." He picked up a handful of acorns and tossed them one by one, as he spoke. "Angola State Penitentiary."

"You were in Angola?" Luke asked, amazed.

"Like I said, two years."

"Is that where the scars come from?"

Sam looked down at his arms with sadness in his eyes. "Yep—was cut up pretty bad when I refused to do what some lifer was telling me to do. God spared me, no doubt about that."

"But how could you have gone to prison? I would have never guessed it. You're so...so..."

"Christian?"

"Yeah, that's it. You must have changed in prison or after, right?"

"I thought I was a Christian before I went in." Sammy leaned over to pick up more acorns. "But I'll tell you this; I found God like never before in prison. Was the best thing ever that happened to me. Made me desperate, man, desperate for God."

Luke's eyes widened. Sam's words had amplified his curiosity even more. "Come on. Now that don't make any sense at all. How can prison be the best thing that ever happened to you?"

"Makes perfect sense to me. It's one thing to go to church and do all those churchy things, saying you believe in God, but it's another thing when God is all you have. Prison made me search for God like never before. And when I found Him, I had to cling to Him to survive. Right there in prison God became real to me like never before."

There was a quiet as Sammy paused to gather his thoughts. Kids were playing at a nearby playground. Couples were walking hand-in-hand under the trees. On the other side of the park, a rally of some sort seemed to be taking place. "You ever been desperate for God, Luke?"

The question pierced Luke like a guided missile. He didn't answer. Instead, he sidestepped the question with another question. "What'd you do? You know, to wind up in prison."

Sammy placed his hand on Luke's shoulder. "I'm only telling you this because you're a real friend and I appreciate you sticking up for me like you did."

"It was nothing. You'd do the same."

"In 1961, after I had just turned eighteen, Mama had sent me up to the Sunflower grocer to pick up a few things. All we had was an old, beat up '47 Ford pickup, but we weren't ashamed of it and made out the best we could. I knew of a dirt road that cut through the woods to Highway 39, so I took it." As Sammy talked, a stray Frisbee floated in front of them, landing on the sidewalk. Luke picked it up and tossed it back to its owners. The college couple waved thank you, and Sammy continued.

"I was just driving along, with the windows down. I remember how I was enjoying the fall breeze blowing in my face. All of a sudden, just when I crossed the Black Creek Bridge, I heard a girl screaming from underneath it. I slammed on my brakes and pulled over. I hopped out of the truck and sprinted the trail that curved down to the creek. There was a brand new Buick convertible parked underneath the bridge, with two white guys and one black girl. I knew the girl, Ida Mae Jackson. The doors to the car were open and the two guys were holding Ida Mae down, trying to rape her. She was kicking and screaming. I yelled for them to let her be and both guys turned around with these shocked looks on their faces. When they looked over at me, Ida Mae jumped out of the car and took off running like an Olympic athlete. I hollered for her to get in my truck and lock the doors. I had picked up a hand full of rocks on the way down to the creek and threw them at the two guys, smacking both of them. Knocked one down. I sprinted to my truck and jumped in. It took them a while to get that big Buick up the path because of all the potholes and also how it twisted up to the top of the bridge. By the time they got up, we were out of sight, but they knew who I was."

"But how did you end up in prison? You were helping the girl out."

"When I dropped Ida Mae off at her house, we sat in the living room with her parents, deciding on what to do. We didn't know if we should talk to the police or what. Fortunately, I had gotten to Ida Mae before those boys had a chance to do any damage, if you know what I mean. We all figured it would be their word against ours and we knew who the police would believe. The two white boys were from a couple of well-to-do families. So, as hard as it was, we didn't say anything. The boys, however, were scared to death that we'd talk. And that very night, Ida Mae got a brick thrown through her window with a note attached. Said they'd string her up and torch her house if anybody went to the police. Same thing happened to me."

Luke and Sammy had started walking around the park's sidewalk. Soon, they came upon the crowd of black folks that had gathered. The crowd had a few whites spotted among them. On a wooden platform, a black man had just begun to speak. He appeared to be a preacher. The meeting was a small peaceful group of around a hundred or so. Sammy and Luke stopped to listen. Luke started to feel a little uncomfortable because he had never been in a situation like this, but he tried not to let Sammy see his uneasiness. The preacher stood behind a podium, dressed in a black suit, with a white priest collar around his neck. He held a neatly folded handkerchief in his hand, dabbing his face in rhythm with his melodic words.

"I've been doing a whole lot of praying," he shouted, waving his handkerchief in the air. "Amen. That's right" and a couple of "Hallelujahs" rippled through the crowd. "Yes, I been a praying...and it is time, my brothers and sisters... The day is far spent... We must step forward in faith that a merciful God will protect us as we, His black children, claim our rights under the United States Constitution and enjoy His beautiful world along with all of His children." He paused to catch his breath and wipe his brow. "And the God I serve... Hear me people... The God I serve is a peaceful God, who does not approve of the violence that some of our very own have used... When we march, we must march in peace."

Sammy remembered what the guys back in the café had said about Martin Luther King coming to town. These folks must be getting ready. This probably had a lot to do with the way he and Luke had been treated. There was tension in the air. Tension or no tension, it didn't feel right, to Sammy and he knew that as a soldier and a convicted felon, he couldn't get involved.

"I don't know about you, but I'm still hungry," said Sammy. "We never ate, man. We need to find us some food. Plus, I have to take a wiz."

"Over and out. I hear you loud and clear," Luke responded, relieved that they were leaving. They walked away from the rally, searching again for somewhere to eat—somewhere that would serve both blacks and whites.

Luke put his arm around his friend's shoulder. "Finish your story."

"Okay. Two days later, the ACE Appliance store in town was robbed and four TV sets were taken along with some other stuff. That night, the police got an anonymous phone tip that they thought they saw my pickup truck leaving the crime scene. The police whipped in our driveway at around 3:00 A.M., their lights and sirens blaring. We didn't know what was going on. They busted in the house with their pistols drawn and started searching around real rough-like, knocking furniture over and breaking things. I told them I hadn't done anything, that they were looking in the wrong house. Then, one of the other sheriffs yelled from out in the yard, saying he'd found all four of the stolen TV sets in my truck. I plead with them saying, 'If I did steal them, I sure wouldn't have left them out for you to find them.' They just laughed while putting handcuffs on me, saying how stupid us niggers were, thinking we could get away with such. Mama and my three sisters were crying. My seven-year-old brother was so scared, he peed on himself right there in the living room."

"But you didn't do it!" Luke raised his voice in anger. "You didn't do it!"

"Don't you see, Luke? It didn't matter. It was my word against them. And ain't no way they'd believe me over those white boys, and the evidence was in my truck. And they didn't know it was the boys who called the police. There was no way of proving that I wasn't making the whole thing up just to save my hide. Fact was, those TVs were in my truck. Even though they were planted, I couldn't prove anything."

Luke had to sit back down on a nearby bench, as the implications of Sammy's words set in. "Heavy-duty stuff, man" he said, shaking his head.

"It's reality. We live in a messed-up world."

"What about your dad? I never hear you talking about him."

"My dad is dead, Luke. I'll tell you about that someday, okay. When the time is right."

"I'm really sorry, Sam," Luke said, thinking how glad he was that his dad was alive.

Both walked in silence for a while, each in their own world of reflection. Luke had been amazed at Sammy's story. Not just that he'd been falsely accused, but even after spending two years in prison, and his dad being dead, he wasn't bitter. Somehow, someway, the misfortunes in his life had not consumed him. That, to Luke, was a miracle.

"Hey, Luke," Sammy said, his eyes narrowing.

"Yeah, man."

"Now that I told you most of my story, it's your turn?"

"Somehow I knew that was coming," Luke said, dropping his shoulders.

"It'll be fine, my friend. I think it's time you unload on someone who actually cares."

CHAPTER 25

"YOU WILL BE captured and you will be tortured," the instructor explained, standing before the room full of soon-to-be Cobras, blackboard at his back and a long pointer in his hand. "For the last ten days you have received the best possible classroom instruction available on how to survive in the event you are stranded alone in the wilderness or taken as a POW in Vietnam. Now, we're taking your training to the next level. You must understand, this will be the most strenuous, the most mind-wrenching, the most painful ordeal you will go through during your training. You will be dropped from a helicopter in the wilderness without a weapon and only one MRE food packet to last you for the three days of evasion and the three days of capture. You will take what we've taught you and apply it for your own survival. In addition to survival, your goal is to evade the enemy as long as possible. The longer you evade, the more points you score. But eventually you will be captured and taken to the mock prisoner of war camp for a minimum of twenty-four hours. The POW camp is designed to provide the most realistic conditions possible and to create the maximum anxiety possible without inflicting long-term harm."

"When you are captured, you will hate us. You will curse us. You will want to kill us. But understand again, we will be hard on you for your own survival. The ultimate test of your survival skills will be if, God forbid, you find yourself alone in enemy territory where the next person you encounter desires you dead or captured. The main reason you would be kept alive, after capture, is for the information they could get out of you. So, we will be brutal to you when you are apprehended. The torture will consist of inflicting pain and mental duress without causing permanent damage to your body. After you survive this exercise of Escape and Evade, you will be part of an elite group and will be able to endure almost any situation."

He turned to the blackboard and pulled down a military map of the area. "At 2200 hours you will be dropped off at point A, somewhere in the middle of this swampy, wooded area. The terrain is similar to what you will encounter in Vietnam. The area encompasses over ten thousand acres." He circled a dark green area on the map with his pointer. "Your goal will be to stay undetectable to the enemy and to make it to point B, over here by the end of day three," he said, circling another area on the map, "You will be dropped off with your group, but will be individually staggered apart. It will be every man for himself. This is not a team exercise."

The instructor collapsed his pointer, slid it into his pocket, and walked between the desks. "The woods will be full of 'aggressors'—Green Berets from the permanent unit here at Fort Clements. They will try to capture you by using a variety of tactics, and take you to the POW camp set up in the woods. After capture you will be interrogated. As I stated, your goal will be to evade and hide from the aggressors by whatever means possible. This, men, will be the most serious game of Hide & Seek you've ever played. The longer you evade the aggressors and make it past our entrapments, the greater your reward. After capture, if you make it through interrogation without yielding the information we want, you will also be rewarded…Are you ready?"

"Yes, sir!" the men shouted in unison.

"Good. Group One will be picked up tomorrow at 2100 hours at your barracks. The chopper will drop you off at point A. Enjoy the ride soldiers and best of luck. You will need it. Dismissed."

→► ◄←

Luke lay on his belly motionless with grass shoots sticking out from his helmet. Black paint was smeared all over his face. It was the second night. Hanging out in the woods for forty-eight hours, fighting mosquitoes, fatigue, hunger, and sleep deprivation was now taking its toll. Beneath the grass, Luke covered himself with his poncho and stretched out on the damp ground in an attempt to grab a couple hours of sleep. The mosquitoes were so bad; he made sure his face was covered, leaving only his nose exposed.

Luke began to doze off, but then, to his chagrin, he heard noises from nearby aggressors. They were crunching through the grass only feet away. His breathing slowed, but his heart raced. Luke stayed frozen, and waited. Sleep would have to be put on hold, again.

Eventually, the crunching sounds became lighter, slowly fading in the distance. Luke sighed in relief. He gently pulled the tall grass apart and peered out. He was at the edge of a wide field filled with palmettos that was surrounded by thick swampy terrain. The moon illuminated the sky, causing the trees to cast eerie shadows. On the other side of the field, a muddy trail meandered through the landscape—the path home to point B. Luke had made it this far with only a couple of close calls. He had seen or heard a few aggressors but they had been fairly easy to evade. At first, he started to follow the trail by staying in the woods that ran alongside it, but quickly reasoned that that's where he would most likely go and the more unimaginative aggressors would be lurking. So, instead of the trail, he blended back into the swamp, choosing a long, damp, and much more difficult route.

Battling to stay awake, Luke trudged on. He moved like a whisper over the terrain. It was natural to him. He was comfortable in the woods. Many weekends during hunting season, he and his father had camped in the Louisiana swamps. Stopping a moment to catch his breath, he rolled onto his back and gazed up at the moonlit sky, reminiscing about the night after killing his first deer. Luke's dad, along with two uncles, Scott and Fred, had smeared the deer's blood over his face as an initiation for shooting his first one. Sitting around the campfire that night, Luke had felt like a man, like he had made his father proud. But now he was sure that his father was disappointed, maybe even ashamed.

At this time of the night, the forest was alive with the sounds of crickets chirping, bullfrogs croaking, and owls hooting. For the remainder of the night he clung to the low-lying, boggy parts of the swamp making steady progress. He saw an occasional snake and once, he thought he saw an alligator, but it turned out to be a log. Movement in the bushes startled him so he darted behind a tree and froze. After Luke's arms and legs began getting numb from standing in the same position so long, an armadillo at last came waddling out like a 90-year-old, snooping around like it owned the place. It sniffed around Luke's feet, moseying along until it finally moved on. Luke slid into a sitting position, leaning his back against the tree. He casually plucked up a long blade of grass from the ground and stuck it in his mouth. That caused him to think about how his father used to always say, "When things don't make sense, Son, sometimes you need a long blade of grass to chew on before you know what to do next."

Luke chewed and thought. Fatigue and hunger started to jump on him again causing his mind to weaken. This time, he allowed himself to be lulled into a semi-trance. As the rays from the moonlight filtered down through the treetops, Luke's thoughts now shifted back to Mama Rose's Soul Food Restaurant, a couple weeks earlier in Victoria and him spilling his story to Sammy. Some of the words that Sammy spoke had stubbornly stuck in Luke's mind. No matter how much he tried, he couldn't shake them.

"There's a lot of men in prison, Luke, though they are not behind bars," he had said.

Luke pounded the butt of his rifle against the ground. *I'm in control of my life. I'm not in prison!*

"The Bible promises that God will work 'all' things in your life around for good, if you let Him," Sammy had added with compassion. "Know what that word 'all' means? It means 'all'—even the things we don't understand. And it's not that God causes bad things to happen, it's that we have a big God. What is meant for evil, God will turn around for good. And God has a purpose for you—a destiny He has carved out just for you, but you have to trust Him, Luke, trust Him."

What about Haley? What plan did God have for her life? It's not fair for me to have a purpose when Haley's gone. It ain't right. It just ain't right. Again, Luke banged his rifle butt against the ground in frustration.

Something else moved in a nearby bush, jolting him back to the present. He shook himself out of the trance and glanced at his watch. It was time to get moving. The sun would be coming up in less than two hours. Standing up, he stretched and took about four steps when three Green Beret aggressors dropped out of the trees, snagging him. Luke kicked one aggressor in the mouth, slamming him to the ground. He twisted and contorted his body, rolling in defiance as the three aggressors held him down. He bit another as they attempted to tie his hands. Luke's elbow caught another one in the jaw, but the three of them were too much to overpower. They shoved Luke to the ground, grinding his face in the muddy soil, binding his feet and hands. Blindfolded, he was marched at gunpoint to the mock POW camp, where he was thrown in the "Box"—a dark, damp, room, with a hole in the floor for a toilet. Neither was there toilet paper or running water—just the room and a hole.

In the corner, Luke curled up in the fetal position but for the whole night the aggressors refused to let Luke sleep. Their first agenda was to wear down the prisoner's mind through sleep deprivation. Every thirty minutes throughout the night, someone would poke Luke with a stick or throw cold water on him. He was also deprived of any food, but he was given water periodically. After the first eight hours in the "box," disorientation usually begins to occur. By the second day and into the third, the treatment was the same—no food, no sleep, total darkness, and a little water. On the third morning of the POW camp, the sixth day overall, Luke was dragged out of the "Box" and tied to a chair. He had not slept more than an hour at a time for the entire six days.

"Where were you going, soldier?" the aggressor barked, inches from his face.

Luke sat in defiance, though he was weak and his speech slow. "My name is Luke, Marion, Hatcher. Private 1st Class. Serial number, RA54214365."

Slap! The back of a hand slammed across Luke's face, knocking the chair over backward. Two other aggressors picked it back up.

"Where were you going, soldier?"

"My name is Luke, Marion, Hatcher! Private 1st Class! Serial number, RA54214365!"

The aggressor cocked his forearm back and again released it on Luke, causing blood to splatter from his nose. "Throw him in the 'Pit'!"

They pulled Luke from the chair and tossed him into a specifically prepared mud pit, where the aggressors took turns stomping his head into the sludge with their boots. Sopping wet, covered with muck, they pulled him from the pit and placed him back in the chair. Again his face was slapped and Luke's face fell limp to one side.

"Where were you going, soldier?"

Luke could barely lift his head. "My...name...Luke... Marion...Hatcher." His words came out sluggish, in a whisper. "Private...Serial number, R...A...5...4...2...1...4...3...6...5."

"Throw him in the drum!"

Luke tried to resist, kicking and punching, but his strength was gone and his motions flaccid. He was forced to the ground and stripped to his undergarments, then placed in a huge, steel, drum filled with ice-cold water. Once inside, the top was clamped on and Luke had only a few inches to stick his nose up out of the water to breathe. That was fine, until the barrel was turned sideways and rolled. When they finally let Luke out, he was coughing, spitting out water, shivering, and almost uncon-scious. Nonetheless, they strapped him back in the chair.

"Where were you going soldier?"

Luke's eyes rolled back in his head, his lips barely moving. "My na...na...mm Lu, Hat, Marr. 1st Priii. Serrr, R...5...1...." His head rolled on his shoulders, "4...1..."

"Prepare, the wires!" A military electric stun machine had been devised that worked off a small car battery.

"Where were you going?" the aggressor shouted, touching Luke on the chest with a hot wire that sent volts of electricity through his body—enough to inflict pain, yet not do any long-term, permanent damage.

"Lu...Mar...4...R..." Luke refused to give up any more information.

"Release him! Congratulations, Private Hatcher. You have passed the test. Now, get this man taken care of!"

CHAPTER 26

ONCE AGAIN, LUKE found himself back in sickbay, but this time it was to get his bruises and gashes doctored and his ears flushed. Mud from the "Pit" was packed in his ear canal and he had acquired several dreadful looking purple marks, two with deep cuts. One underneath his left eye needed a few stitches, and another along his neck where an aggressor's boot had come down on him. Other than that, all Luke needed was some rest and to have his body fluids replenished. For the remainder of the afternoon and night he stayed in the infirmary to rest. Because of his spectacular performance, Luke was awarded a steak dinner served to him in bed in the infirmary and a special three-day weekend pass that started on Thursday instead of the traditional Friday.

He had looked forward to this particular weekend with a combination of apprehension and excitement. His family was driving over to spend the weekend with him. Victoria was only about an eight-hour drive from Magnolia Springs.

James had taken Friday off. He and Sarah loaded up the family Chrysler and left with a sleepy Emily at 4:00 A.M. James figured if he hit the road that early, they'd be in Victoria somewhere around noon. Emily had covered the backseat with blankets and a pillow. She carried along some of her favorite books and her Barbie suitcase that was overflowing with Barbie dolls and clothes. Sarah had purchased a travel puzzle/game magazine for Emily and a hardcover copy of *The Valley Of The Dolls* for herself. She wanted to find out first-hand what all the hoopla was about. Eight hours in the car would give her plenty of time to read.

The Chrysler didn't have air conditioning, so all four windows were rolled down, and the still-humid, late September air whipped through the car. Sarah wore a white cotton sundress, sandals, and a matching white scarf in her hair. After a couple of hours into the trip, Emily's bangs were pasted to her forehead. Every now and then, she would dangle her bare feet out the window.

Most of the Interstates were either under construction or still on the drawing boards, so James decided to head East on Highway 90 along the Gulf Coast, through Gulfport and Biloxi, to Mobile. After Mobile they caught Highway 98 that took them into Pensacola. Passing through Navarre Beach outside of Pensacola, they couldn't believe how pretty the water was. In Biloxi, it had been brown, but here the Gulf was a beautiful aqua color and the beach was snow white. They stopped to stretch their legs and let Emily play on the beach awhile. Because it was September, the sand was not too hot for bare feet. Sarah took off her sandals and James his shoes and they walked hand-in-hand behind Emily, who was trying to find as many seashells as she could in the 30 minutes her father had allowed.

"Do you remember when Luke was her age?" Sarah asked James, as they strolled along, the tide slapping at their feet and wind whipping their hair.

"Yeah, I do, even though it's hard to believe he was ever that little."

"He was a good kid, James," said Sarah, her hand gently stroking the back of her husband's head, "and still is."

"I know, Sarah. I've never doubted that," a slight smile came across James face. "You remember that time when he was three or four and we almost lost him? Thank God you were there, Sarah."

"How could I ever forget that day? We have a lot to be thankful for, James. I can't imagine what Harvey and Virginia are going through. It could have easily have been Luke. I still believe it was a miracle. I know it was God that spoke to me."

"It was pretty amazing. I have to admit that."

The incident, or miracle as Sarah would argue, occurred between Luke's third and fourth year of age. Sarah and Luke had returned home from grocery-shopping at the Sunflower. Before she unloaded the car, Sarah took Luke to play in the backyard, where James had fenced in an area specifically so Luke could play and they would not have to worry about him running into the road. Inside the fence were a sandbox under a huge oak tree and a small swing set, around which were a dozen or so of Luke's toys. A lock had been placed on the gate so Luke could not get out.

As Sarah was putting away the groceries she suddenly and unexplainably stopped dead in her tracks. A voice in her head said, "Go check on Luke." It was so distinct that it seemed almost audible. Sarah even looked around to see if someone else had entered the room. The voice came again: "Go check on Luke." She set the groceries down, didn't even put the milk in the refrigerator, and rushed to the backyard. Luke was on the ground, his face purple; he appeared to be dead.

Sarah screamed at the top of her lungs, running to her son's side. She set him upright and began shaking him, trying to see if he was alive. He was, but he couldn't breathe and had nearly passed out. Sarah opened Luke's mouth and saw something lodged in his throat. Her motherly instinct took over and without thinking, she grabbed Luke by the ankles, held him upside-down and slapped his back. After the third slap, a round, red-and-white fishing bobber popped out onto the ground. Apparently, it had dropped out of James' tackle box by accident the last time he had walked to his shed to put it away.

"Mommy," Luke coughed.

"I'm here Baby Boy. Mama's here." She squeezed Luke tight, realizing that if she hadn't paid attention to that voice, she would have been holding a dead baby. "Thank you Jesus," Sarah whispered.

When James, Sarah, and Emily got back to the car, it was on to Fort Walton and then North on Highway 285 into

Victoria, where they arrived at about 1:30 P.M.—about one hour behind what James had originally calculated.

Instead of picking Luke up at the base, they had decided to meet at the newly constructed, bright orange and blue Howard Johnson's Inn. It was Luke's idea. He didn't want an emotional display in front of his peers, but he did want his parents to meet Sammy and some of the guys. His parents would take him back to the base on Sunday afternoon.

→→ ←←

Room number 201 was upstairs and at the complete opposite of the building from the front office. The motel was nearly full because of a Victoria State football game on Saturday. There were a lot of college kids and alumni hanging out of rooms with their doors open, drinking, hooting, and carrying on. The Hatchers were waiting in their room for Luke, rather than meeting him in the motel lobby.

Luke's ride dropped him off. The walk to the room from the parking lot was less than a hundred yards, yet to Luke, it seemed like a hundred miles.

He stood tall and lean, his shoulders square and his uniform neatly tucked, the perfect image of a soldier. He could have posed for the United States Army poster. No longer a high school boy, Luke was now a man, transformed by his sufferings and the disciplines of military life. Yes, his decision to join had been an impulsive one. It had ruined his chances for college or a baseball career, but overall, the military had been good for him. Without the army making him get up in the mornings and forcing him to push through the days of structured activity, he would have certainly bogged down in the pits of depression and despair from which some never return.

As he walked past the college kids who were loitering outside the rooms, some mockingly saluted him. Others showed respect, stepping aside politely. More than a few girls drooled over him.

"Hey Babe! I just love a tall, dark, handsome man in uniform," one yelled out as he walked past. "I'll help you shoot your rifle if you want me to."

But Luke's eyes were set like flint straight ahead. He was a man on a mission with no time for such nonsense. By the time he arrived at the room, his palms were sweaty and his heart felt as if it would leap out of his chest. He stood before the door waiting, trying to muster the courage to knock. *What if they hate me? No...stupid, they don't hate you. They wouldn't have driven all this way if they did... They love me. But I've hurt them and they're angry. I know I've let them down. I know they're disappointed in me. My dad... I've probably ruined his life... I can't do this... I don't want to do this.*

Luke started to knock, but just before his knuckles touched the door, he pulled away, and walked around the breezeway one more time. He leaned over the railing, taking in the afternoon air and the rustling sounds of the small city, trying to gather up his courage.

Back at his family's door again, he took a deep breath, lifted his hand and this time felt it hit the door. The hollow sound of knocking echoed down the breezeway. Luke heard movement inside, then a giggle from Emily. He knocked again. *What's taking them so long?* The knob began to slowly turn. The door creaked on its hinges...then, it flew open. There were his parents and sister, all three. The four of them were together again. For the first few seconds there were no words, just hugs, lots and lots of hugs.

Sarah stepped back, sniffling. She placed her hands on both of Luke's cheeks. "Here," she said, sniffing again "let me look at you." She took a Kleenex and dabbed the cut under his eye. Luke flinched back. "What happened, Baby?"

"It's nothing. Just a cut from a training exercise."

"My, you are so handsome. And you've grown into such a man."

"I love you, Mom. I'm sorry if..."

Sarah touched his mouth gently with her finger. "Shhh. Don't say it. You did what you thought you had to do."

The whole time, Emily was locked around Luke's waist, squeezing him. He picked her up, lifting her above his head. "What have we here? A little pumpkin 'tater pie." Luke swung her around and dropped her on the bed, tickling her. She kicked and giggled and squirmed. He held her down and started blowing on her tummy, then picked her up again and hugged her tight. Setting Emily down, Luke turned to his father. "Dad," he said, holding out his hand.

James extended his hand out and the two shook, strong and firm. Then, James pulled Luke to himself for a solid embrace. "Son, it's good to see you."

"It's good to see you too, Dad."

"So, tell me about the army," James said, adjusting his gold-rimmed glasses. "How'd you get that nasty cut?"

"I am not supposed to talk about it. Was given strict orders, but we can talk about everything else over lunch. I think I could eat a horse. Because I knew ya'll were coming, I didn't eat lunch yet."

"Well, let's do it," said James.

CHAPTER 27

SWAMP MAMA'S FAMILY Restaurant served breakfast, hot plate lunches, and steak 'n seafood dinners. It was an old shack-like building with a rusty tin roof, but the parking lot was always overflowing with cars. A solid mix of college kids, military personnel, and locals loved the place. Swamp Mama's had a reputation for having the best home-cooked food in the panhandle. It was only a block from the motel, and because of all he'd heard, Luke highly recommended it. As soon as Sarah touched up her makeup and ran a brush through Emily's hair, they were off. Since the restaurant was close and the afternoon pleasant, they decided to walk. Luke held Sarah's hand and rode Emily on his shoulders. For the first time in a while, Luke truly smiled. The Hatcher family strolled, engaging in small talk, simply enjoying the blessing of being together once again.

"So how'd you get those gashes?" James asked.

"Oh, it was nothing, just a secret training exercise. I told you I'm not supposed to talk about it."

"Must have been Escape and Evade, right?"

Wrinkles formed on Luke's brow. "How did you know?"

James slapped him on the back, laughing. "Don't forget, your ol' pops was in World War II. Things haven't changed that much. How did you do?"

"I'm on a three-day pass aren't I?"

"You're a chip off the ol' block," said James, sucking in his stomach with pride.

"It was tough, Dad, but they say its nothing like Vietnam's going to be. We're working double-time to be ready. I'm surprised they gave me this three-day pass."

"You must have deserved it, or believe me, they wouldn't have given it to you."

"I guess so," said Luke.

Sarah squeezed Luke's hand and hugged his arm tightly. "I'm so glad to see you. I just wanted to say that again."

"Me too, Mom. I'm really glad to see all of you. It's been a tough couple of months."

James stopped walking and looked at Luke seriously. "Son, don't you take any chances over there, you hear? If you follow orders and do everything by the book, you should come out of this thing okay. The odds are in your favor, you know."

"Thanks, Dad. You sound like one of my sergeants... Hey, tell me something. How come you never talked more about when you were in the war 'n all?"

James rubbed Luke's shoulder. "I think when you come back you won't want to talk about it either. Maybe when you need to, I'll be one you can talk to about it. I'm not trying to scare you, but war is a horrible thing. It's not like in sports when you lose and you just take a shower and go home. In the war, when you lose...well, you know what I'm trying to say."

Sarah cut in. "Do we have to talk about this now? I really want to enjoy the moment. I haven't seen my son in a very long time and I don't want to talk about war during the small amount of time I have with him. Okay?"

Luke and James exchanged glances that said, *we'd best obey Mama.*

They zigzagged through the white limestone parking lot to the entrance of the restaurant, which was a long wooden porch. Neon lights in the window advertised RC Cola and 7-Up next to a wooden sign that read, "No Negroes and No Checks." Sarah and James paid no attention to the sign, but Luke felt a twinge of guilt when he saw it. He flipped Emily over backward and plopped her feet on the porch as they stepped inside.

"Luke, please be careful," said Sara. "She's not a toy, you know."

Emily just giggled.

Just as the packed parking lot had indicated, Swamp Mama's was extremely crowded inside.

"I'm going to use the restroom while ya'll get a table," Luke announced and walked off.

Impatient for someone to seat them, instead of staying in the roped-off waiting area, James spotted a waitress in the far back who was in the process of cleaning a table. Defying Sara's plea for him to stay put, he jumped the rope, walked over to her and asked if they could sit there.

"Sure," said the waitress with a warm smile. "It'll just take me a second, but you can go ahead and sit down if like."

James motioned for Sara and Emily to come on back. The family squeezed in and waited for the waitress to finish wiping down the table. With her final swipe of the rag, she spoke. "My name is Kate," she said, "I'll be serving you this afternoon. May I go ahead and get you something to drink before you order?"

Kate turned toward each of them and wrote down their requests, Sarah first, James, then Emily.

"And," said Sarah, "bring one more iced tea for my son."

"Yes, ma'am," she said as she turned to head back to the kitchen.

Luke came back from the restroom at precisely the same time Kate was returning with the drinks. When Luke saw her, he was taken aback. Her beauty was breathtaking—shining brunette hair, warm and perfect lips, soft fair skin, and sharp green eyes. And she moved so gracefully that to Luke it seemed as if she were gliding. Wearing a white blouse and black skirt, with a small apron around her waist, she was perhaps the loveliest young woman he'd ever seen.

"Excuse me," said Luke, lightly brushing her arm as he sat down. Her scent was intoxicating as he past.

"No, excuse *me*," Kate said, aware that Luke was noticing her.

For a brief moment their eyes met and then Kate's broke away to begin serving the drinks.

"Are you ready to order now, or do you need more time?" she said with a smile as she pulled out her pen and order pad. She tried not to look at Luke directly, all though she seemed to want to. After Sara, James, and Emily finished ordering, Kate turned to Luke. "And what may I get for you?" she asked softly.

"I guess I'll just have what he's having," said Luke, pointing to his father.

Kate nodded and walked away. Luke found it difficult to keep his eyes from following her.

Luke was puzzled by his attraction. When she brought the food, and each time she returned to the table, the two would make eye contact and then Luke would quickly look away. The last thing he wanted was to get involved with anyone. He wouldn't. He had loved Haley and still did. But the way this Kate had looked at him made his throat tighten. The waitresses at the *Frosty Top Café* had been cute, but Luke never thought twice about them. Nor did he think about the girls back at the motel, although they were attractive, too. When the guys back at base had tried to drag Luke out with them to go pick up babes, he would have none of it. These emotions were crazy, he knew. He didn't even know this Kate girl. For all he knew, she could be engaged or something. It was probably purely a physical thing.

Yet, Luke felt there was something pleasantly different about her apart from her striking beauty. She seemed familiar and compelling. Maybe she reminded him of his mother. After all she did have similar dark hair and green eyes. But that didn't quite explain it. Suddenly, it hit him like an iron skillet. Despite the different hair color and skin tone, this Kate reminded him of Haley. Yes, that was it! Haley. For some odd reason, she gave off the same impressions as Haley. It was uncanny.

Battling with these fresh emotions and the guilt of even thinking of experiencing happiness with someone other than Haley caused Luke to lose his appetite. He barely touched his food. Sarah figured out what was going on with her motherly intuition. She had noticed the two eying one another and now her son seemed to be struggling within himself.

"Luke, dear," she said, touching his arm. "You're going to have to let Haley go eventually. It's okay to be attracted to someone else. She seems to be a very lovely young lady. You don't plan on staying single all your life do you?"

"But you don't understand, Mom. I could never love anyone like I loved Haley."

"You're right, Honey, I don't fully understand, but I do know that at some point, you will have to move on. Haley would have wanted you to. If she really cared for you, and she did, she would not want you to suffer so."

This was not the conversation Luke wanted to have. "Look, I don't want to bum ya'll out anymore than I already have," he said. "I'm going to go outside and wait until ya'll are finished."

"That's fine," said James, "We're all about done anyway."

"Can I go with Luke, Daddy?"

"You have to ask him."

Emily looked up at Luke with her gigantic chocolate puppy dog eyes and he was smitten.

"Come on, squirt," he said, taking her hand. As they walked out of the restaurant, Luke turned hoping for a final glance at Kate. To his delight, Kate was walking toward the kitchen and was peering at him through the corner of her eyes. Their eyes met and she smiled softly before disappearing through two double doors.

Walking back to the motel, Luke quietly continued the mental punishment of himself. *You low-life scum. How could you dare think about someone else? You don't deserve to love anyone and you certainly don't deserve for anyone else to love you.... Why should you ever be happy? Haley is dead! Did you forget? You should have known better. You should have known better. You'll never love anyone like you loved Haley.* He shoved the feelings and thoughts he was having about this Kate out of his mind, and pushed onward.

The plan was to spend Friday night thru Sunday morning together, just bumming around town and visiting. Sarah wanted to check out downtown and do some window-shopping. Emily just had to swim in the pool, and James thought a cookout somewhere was in order. Luke suggested a drive over to the beach. They liked that idea, so the family decided that the next morning they would head over to the Gulf for some fun in the sun.

➤➤ ◄◄

Fourteen weeks in the military had turned Luke into a human alarm clock and at 4:30 Saturday morning, he was wide-awake, counting ceiling tiles. Not wanting to wake the others but needing to get up and do something, Luke quietly slid out of the bed and dressed himself. On the bedside table he left a note saying he had borrowed the Chrysler and would be back around seven or so.

It was the first time he had been away from base completely alone. Driving around town, he enjoyed the early morning quiet. Nearly everything was closed except for a couple of coffee houses and the Krispy Kreme donut shop. He stopped and ate a half dozen hot-glazed donuts and two big glasses of milk, then drove down Main Street, around the Square, by the city park, through some of the neighborhoods that sort of reminded him of home, and then to the Victoria State University campus. Luke hadn't been on a college campus since his visit to LSU, and he was curious.

The sun was just beginning to rise. The grounds were warm and inviting, and the antique lightposts that lined the streets were still glowing from the night. Stately buildings were set beneath century-old moss-covered oak trees. The campus reminded him a lot of LSU. In the distance, Luke could make out the football stadium peeking up over the trees. He turned the car and drove toward it. It was a nice, old stadium, concrete, though not nearly as big as LSU's. This one probably seated around twenty thousand, Luke guessed—LSU's could seat sixty thousand. Victoria State was considered a small university. Still, twenty thousand was pretty big for a stadium.

Luke thought about Jake and the other guys who had accosted him and Sammy in the *Frosty Top Café*. He thought about how they had degraded Sammy. It amazed him how intelligent people could justify those kind of actions. In a few hours, the stadium would be filled with people who would come to watch them play, cheering, and making heroes of them. Luke knew the feeling it brought on. He knew it well. At another time, under different circumstances, he would have fit in with Jake and his buddies. Luke shuddered at the thought. However, knowing Sammy and hearing his story had opened his eyes.

Across the street, Luke noticed the baseball stadium. It, too, was very nice, although much newer, giving the appearance that the university was proud of its baseball program. It was much smaller that the football stadium, it seated maybe two or three thousand and that was stretching it. But it was still nice. Several blue and yellow pennants flew over it. *Gulf Coast Conference Runner-Up–1957. Gulf Coast Conference Champions–1961. Gulf Coast Conference Champions–1962. Gulf Coast Conference Champions–1965.*

On an impulse, Luke parked the car, got out, and walked to the baseball stadium. It just so happened that the gates were open. He hesitated for a moment and almost headed back to the car, but he decided to continue exploring instead. Once inside, he turned to face the seats. He took in the breadth of the stadium. He made his way up the steps to the very top and looked out over the campus and back to the playing field. A cool, morning breeze blew steadily, and again he had a fleeting recollection of the fire tower back home, but he didn't ponder on it. Everything was all so beautiful. He had never seen such a well-tended field.

Walking back down the steps, Luke found himself wandering out onto the field toward the pitcher's mound. He stepped up on the dirt, now imagining the stadium filled with cheering fans. The score 1 to 1, top of the ninth. He'd already struck out two batters. The batter up had two strikes against him. Luke did a wind-up and threw an imaginary pitch and the imaginary batter swung. Yes! Luke jumped up and raised his hands to thank the crowd. He then jogged to home plate, his turn to bat. If he could hit a home run, they would win the game and the championship.

Luke gripped the imaginary bat, focusing on the imaginary pitcher, but again, exactly as they had done back at the base, his hands began to shake and his palms started sweating. The scene from Galilee Baptist started playing. Then came the nausea. Luke stumbled back away from the plate and started to bolt from the stadium, but instead this time he stood his ground. "No!" he shouted, loud and firm. The sound echoed off of the stadium seats. "Not this time!" Luke shook his head, clenched his jaw, and forced himself back up to the plate. He squeezed the imaginary bat and swung.

The pretend ball sailed out of the park. Luke Hatcher had done it again. He jogged around the bases waving to the crowd, lost in his created moment. By the time he had reached third base, however, the voices in his head were back—those ever-faithful, nagging, torturous, judgments. *You know Haley can see you. Don't you? Where do you get off, Luke Hatcher? You should have known better. You know you'll never play again. So, stop even thinking about it!* In a full sprint, Luke rounded third, up the ramp leading outside the park, and never stopped running until he was back at the car. "Leave me alone!" he screamed, pounding the steering wheel. "Leave me alone!"

CHAPTER 28

"YOU'RE AWFUL QUIET this morning, Honey. You okay?" Sarah said to Luke, while cutting Emily's pancake into a dozen little pieces. "And you've been picking at your food all morning. That's not like you. Do you need to talk about something?"

"Its okay, Mom," Luke replied. "I'm just not hungry. I stuffed myself on Krispy Kremes this morning is all."

"Mom, I want some blueberry syrup," Emily requested.

"What do you say?" Sarah asked.

"Oh, I forgot...please, may I have some blueberry syrup."

"Yes, you may, as soon as I ask the waitress."

"What'd you do this morning?" James asked Luke.

"Nothing really. Just bummed around. Went up to the college. They have some real nice facilities over there. That was the first time I'd been by myself away from base since...well, you know." Luke crunched down on a sausage link. They were at Swamp Mama's again, this time for breakfast. He had secretly hoped Kate would be there, but was actually relieved when she wasn't; he had resolved to put her out of his mind for good.

"Yeah," James said. "From what I hear, they have a pretty good program. Nothing like LSU though."

"Of course not...Hey, what time we heading to the beach? It's about an hour's drive. I figure if we leave around eleven we could get there by noon. I want to hit those waves with Emily."

Emily giggled. "Can we get a blow-up raft, Mama?"

"We'll see," Sarah said then shifted her focus to James. "They're only about a dollar at Woolworth's."

"Fine with me," said James, then turning to Luke, "Can you get us there?"

"Yes sir. It's pretty easy and I know this great spot, too. Me and the guys went a couple times already."

"The guys and I," Sarah corrected.

"Yes, Ma'am. The guys and I went a couple times already."

It was only 9:00 A.M. so the rest of the morning the family of four just meandered around. Luke took them for a short tour of the town. He drove them by *The Frosty Top Café* and shared about his experience with Sammy. Both Sarah and James shook their heads in disbelief, but Luke couldn't tell whether it was because they were outraged at the injustice or were simply shocked that their son had been kicked out with a colored person. Whichever one, Luke didn't pursue the matter any further.

He took them to the university where they parked and walked around some. The campus was getting fairly crowded because of the football game that afternoon. James was set on getting Emily her raft and having that afternoon cookout, so after leaving Victoria State, they stopped at Woolworth's and picked up the raft, a beach ball, one of those new fangled Styrofoam ice chests, and other supplies before heading out to the Gulf of Mexico.

The weather was absolutely perfect—sun shining with the temperature in the mid-eighties, a much-needed break from the usual mid-to-upper nineties. James drove and Luke sat upfront with him, while Sarah and Emily stretched out in the backseat. Upon arrival, they were met with pristine, snow-white beaches and warm, indigo water. Because of the strong breeze, white caps tipped the four to five foot waves that were crashing against the shore. All afternoon they thundered in a rhythmic pattern that blended hypnotically with the squawking of seagulls circling above. The Hatchers were able to pull the car right up to the beach and a picnic table. Sarah still wore her favorite white cotton sundress with a headscarf and big round sunglasses. She was glad the car was close to the table because she was afraid the wind would blow away all the plates and things. Now, she could just serve out of the car's open trunk. In his faithful khaki pants and a loose-fitting Hawaiian shirt, James began cooking hamburgers on his portable charcoal grill, brought from home. He would never consider going on a road trip without it. Luke wore a pair of cut-off jeans and no shirt, while Emily had on a solid blue, one-piece bathing suit with her hair pulled back in a ponytail. Sarah had made sure that everyone had on plenty of Coppertone.

The afternoon was almost perfect. The breeze kept the bugs away and the burgers were juicy. Luke inflated the little raft. Together he and Emily waded into the Gulf and rode wave after wave back to shore. Hand in hand, big brother and little sister walked down the beach as far as they could in search of seashells. Yes, the day was almost perfect...almost.

"I've been thinking this thing over, Luke," James said, sipping on a bottle of Coke after Luke had ambled back to the picnic table. Emily was content digging in the sand for awhile and Sarah was sitting on a blanket reading her novel. "You know," James continued, then, hesitating a bit, "it's still possible for you to play pro ball or college ball." At that, he reached down in the trunk and pulled out a brand new bat, a couple of gloves, and a new baseball that had been covered up with a tarp. "I've heard of several players that played after they finished their military obligations. What's important is that you don't let your skills get rusty. I'm sure, if we stay in touch with the coaches and the pro scouts, they'll give you another shot. I've even talked with Billy Clark and he said he'd give you another look."

In the background, Sarah had put her book down and stood up. With her hands on her waist, shaking her head, she was shocked at what her husband was doing. "Not now, James!"

James crossed his arms and frowned back at her. "I'm just trying to help him out."

"Well, if you really wanted to help him, you'd just love and support him."

"Sometimes, love must be tough, Sarah. You know that."

"And sometimes it must be unconditional! You know that!"

Emily looked up for a moment, but couldn't hear because of the crashing waves, so she resumed constructing her masterpiece.

Luke hated to see the tension between his parents. Without saying a word, he jerked the bat out of his father's hands and marched to the water's edge. With all the strength he could muster, threw the bat as far into the Gulf as he could. Then he walked calmly back to James and confronted him. "You don't get it, do you? Haley is dead. She's not coming back and I killed her. So, understand this, I am never playing baseball again. End of story."

James stood speechless before his son. He was shocked. It was the first time Luke had ever really stood up to him. Pouting, James stormed off down the beach. Luke stormed off down the beach in the opposite direction. Sara was in the middle, torn. She dropped down beside Emily and started digging in the sand with her.

Down by the water, Luke turned and looked over his shoulder for his dad. James turned too and faced his son, and they walked toward one another, both unsure of what kind of clash would occur. The two of them met, and turned to face the waves. James put his arm around his son and Luke didn't object. Neither of them said a word for a long time. At last, Luke turned to his father and spoke. "I realize what you're trying to do and I'm really sorry. The last thing I ever wanted to do was to let you down."

"All I'm asking is that you simply give yourself some time, Son. One day you may change your mind," James insisted. "That's all I'm asking."

"Well, I think the army will give me plenty of time to think."

"I know it will. There's no doubt about that."

Walking back to the picnic area James looked up at Sarah who was nodding her head. "What?" he snapped.

"You never give up, do you?" Sarah said, wiping her hands on a paper towel.

"He's my boy, Sarah, my boy. Don't you get it? He still has a chance. It's not too late."

"But it's not your decision, James. How many times have we been through this? There's more to life than baseball. Besides, you heard the boy. And frankly, I'm sick and tired of baseball."

James leaned against the picnic table and crossed his arms. He stared out at the Gulf and then to Luke, where he was now burying his sister up to her neck in sand. Emily was one gigantic smile. "I just hate to see all that talent go to waste," he sighed. "We've worked too hard."

Sarah put her hand on James' shoulder, gently massaging it. "Are you thinking of Luke, or yourself?"

He cleared his throat before answering. "I guess a little bit of both. Mainly, I hate to see him struggling so much. It's like I'm expecting him to snap out of it at any moment."

Sarah studied James carefully. "Honey, I hate to see him struggling too, but you know as well as I do, that Luke has to find his own way. We can't do it for him. We have to trust that God is watching over Luke and He is working in Luke's life."

He shrugged and his voice softened, "Perhaps you're right."

➤➤ ◄◄

The sky turned three shades of pink before fading into a deep purple. All four sat on the beach watching the orange ball of fire drop behind the horizon. By the time they got back to the motel, they were exhausted, so it was showers and then to bed without even one bit of protest from Emily.

That night, in the motel room, another nightmare pounced on Luke, the first one in a long time. Somehow, his parents coming, this Kate girl, the baseball stadium, and his Dad at the beach, all together, had caused a fresh wave of sentiment to surge through him. In the dream, he and Haley were standing at the wedding altar. Haley was dressed in a stunning white gown and began to recite her vows, but when she came to the words, "I do" a baseball came flying out of nowhere, striking her on the head. Luke was jolted from his sleep in a cold sweat, screaming, "Noooooo!"

Everyone was instantly awake. Sarah was the first to Luke's side. She didn't say anything, just cuddled him in her arms and rocked. James didn't know what to do. The pain he felt for his son was deep. He wanted to fix the situation like he did when the roof leaked or the car needed a tune-up. That's what he did. He fixed things. But this, this was too big for him, and he felt completely ignorant as how to respond. He slipped on his pants and shirt then stepped out onto the breezeway and leaned over the railing clinching his fists. "God," he cried silently in pain. *"Please, help my son."*

CHAPTER 29

THE LAST TWO weeks of AIT flew by. Luke forced himself to put one foot in front of the other and trudge ahead. On the final Friday, military orders were handed down and true to his promise, Uncle Sam kept Luke and Sammy together. The bad news was, the war was heating up and the United States had had its worse week, losing 12,000 men. Because of that, the AIT graduates were only given one week of leave before they had to report back for the flight out to Vietnam.

Sammy took a bus back home to Kentwood to spend a few days with his family. Luke, however still could not scrape up the courage to go back to Magnolia Springs and face his demons. His parents weren't too happy about it, but tried to understand. So Luke remained at Fort Clements, not leaving the base except one time to take a trip with some of the guys over to the Gulf. He spent most of that day alone wandering the beach and riding some waves. There seemed to be a surplus of girls in bikinis lounging on beach blankets. Their heads turned when Luke walked by, but he never really noticed them. Once he thought he saw Kate, but it wasn't.

James, Sarah, and Emily, did drive to Florida one more time for the few days before Luke was due to fly to Vietnam. On this visit, baseball took a backseat. The seriousness of Luke going to war was really hitting the Hatchers. For three days, they did a lot of the same things they did before. Swamp Mama's had become their favorite restaurant, but Luke never saw Kate again. It was as if she had disappeared off of the face of the earth. Luke was fine with that; now she could be simply a flicker in his memory.

No one was prepared for the scene at the airport, as the soldiers, dressed in their camouflaged fatigues, shiny black ankle boots, and green fedora caps, waited to board the plane. Of the friends and family gathered, not one person had dry eyes.

"Well, I guess this is it," Luke said, trying to hold himself together.

Sarah moved closer, straightening Luke's hat with her fingers and then arranging his bangs. "You be careful, you hear?" A trickle of tears ran softly down her cheeks.

Emily clutched his leg. "Please don't go, Luke! Don't go!"

Luke squatted down, gently taking her face in his hands, brushing the wetness from under her eyes. "Now, listen to me. You have to be a big girl and help Mama and Daddy, okay? And don't you worry. I'll be home before you can say Rumplestiltskin three times."

Emily collapsed into his arms and Luke held her tight, taking in as much of her sweetness as he could. When he rose, James firmly held out his hand. He gripped Luke's and pulled him to himself and the two embraced. James moved back and held his son proudly at arm's length. "You're a man now, Luke" he said.

"Yes, Dad, I am," Luke replied. "And don't worry. Everything's going to work out fine."

Because Sammy's family couldn't come, he hung out with the Hatchers at the airport. "It was real nice getting to know you, Mr. and Mrs. Hatcher," he said, standing up, dwarfing James and Sarah. "Luke's blessed to have you."

James held out his hand and grasped Sammy's tightly. "You two watch each other's back, you hear?"

"Yes, sir. I hear what you saying."

"Oh, come here," said Sarah, reaching out her arms. "Give me a hug." She squeezed Sammy tight and was surprised to find herself thinking, *I've never hugged a colored man before.* "Thanks for being Luke's friend. You're an answer to prayer."

"Yes, Ma'am."

"We will begin boarding flight 119 now," the announcement came.

Sammy stepped aside and the three Hatchers pulled together for one last group hug. Luke pried his family's fingers off of him and picked up his bag. "Well, I guess this is it," he trembled. "I love you guys."

Heading through the outside gate, a gust of wind whipped Luke's hat off. He picked it up, continued across the runway and up the stairs of the plane. Reaching the entrance, he turned around and waved back to them standing at the waiting area that overlooked the runway. Then he ducked inside and grabbed his seat next to Sammy. Pressing his forehead against the plane's window, Luke observed his family. He could see all three of them watching. A knot formed in his stomach.

Though they had not agreed with what he had done, the two visits by his parents—the way they had dropped everything, doing whatever it took to make those trips to see their son, had reinforced his certainty of their unconditional love and commitment to him. It was like when he was growing up and they never missed a single game he ever played in. Whether football, baseball, or basketball, at least one of his parents had always been present. Luke had come to depend on them being present. On many occasions, James, Sarah, and Emily would drive halfway across the state just to watch him play. Once, they drove all the way to Shreveport, some five hours, for a State Baseball playoff game. When warming up before a game, Luke would be anxious and tense until he'd spot his parents in the stands. As soon as he would see them, calmness would wash over him and he was ready to play. James and Sarah had made the sacrifices to support their son, and it didn't stop with sports. In fact, looking back, Luke now realized, it wasn't just about sports. It was about him. It was about them supporting him. Sammy was right; he was very "blessed" indeed.

As the plane taxied toward the runway, he wondered if he would ever see them again. Too soon the plane lifted into the air and they were out of sight. A very scared eighteen-year-old was flying to some distant place where soldiers were dying every day. Would he be one of them? If so, would that be so bad?

CHAPTER 30

BY THE TIME they had reached the fourth leg of their trip, Luke and Sammy had made stops in San Francisco and Guam, and had switched to a military helicopter in Saigon. Along the way they picked up and dropped off other soldiers, most of whom were carbon copies of the ones they'd boarded with back in Victoria—barely eighteen or nineteen, young, and scared.

They were now "in country" the term used for Vietnam. Every horror story Sergeant Millhouse had told them about the place had been vastly understated. It was as close to hell on Earth as they ever wanted to see. For starters, when the GIs were rushed out of their helicopters onto the Cu Tieng base camp, about 45 kilos northwest of Saigon, the 110-degree heat and 98 percent humidity slapped them in the face like steamy, wet towels. Wind whipping up from the choppers magnified the stench of burning human dung. The smell was so strong that

Luke gagged. What do you do when there are thousands of American soldiers and absolutely no plumbing? The military's solution was to gather the human waste in big barrels, saturate it with fuel oil, and set it on fire.

A massive bulldozed clearing, Cu Tieng had about the same number of square miles as Manhattan. Surrounded by perpetual rice fields and luscious jungle terrain, a virtual military city had been erected with wood, tin, canvas, and sandbags. It was big enough for a small airstrip, artillery units, a PX, division headquarters, a mess hall, and medical facilities. Orange dust kicked up from military vehicles that rumbled through the dirt streets was plastered like stucco on the green buildings and tents. Wrapped around the camp's border was concertina wire, similar to barbed wire, but with razor-like blades every few inches. Each of the sandbag bunkers was equipped with grenade launchers and .50-caliber machine guns. Along with the bunkers, soldiers manned the thirty-three watchtowers round the clock. Cu Tieng was the most secure permanent base camp in Vietnam, but for Luke and Sammy it was just a stepping-stone. Normally, the new arrivals were run through a five-day "in country" training course at the base, but because of the urgent need for replacements, this training had been scrubbed. The only additional training these troops would get would come from their unit leader before they hit the field.

An officer yelled through a bullhorn to be heard over the chopper noise. "Move out to the processing building for your orders!"

Luke clutched his gear with one arm and covered his nose with the other as he and the rest of the GIs sprinted to the processing area a few hundred yards away. In the distance, booms of artillery rounds could be heard blasting enemy positions. By the time he made it to processing, Luke was already sopping wet with sweat. In what seemed like record speed he was given his orders and marched to a large dusty tent that was encircled by a six-foot hedge of sandbags. Outside the tent, GIs waited in line while a sunbaked lieutenant barked out names. Hearing his name, Luke stepped into the tent, where he was issued an M16 rife and a .45 pistol, ten magazines, two bandoliers of shells, four grenades, and a flak jacket. Thirty minutes later, he and nineteen others were herded onto two olive-green transport trucks with canvas coverings and a fence like railing around the beds. There was chicken wire over the windows and all other openings. These trucks were being used to relocate the replacement troops, as they were called, somewhere deeper into enemy territory. Luke's vehicle bumped and jerked along a dirt road. Each time the truck hit a pothole the soldiers aboard were tossed around mercilessly.

They had been told that they were on their way to join the Alpha Company, one of the several companies making up the 2nd Battalion of the 21st Infantry. Along the way, Luke wondered if grenades and mortars had caused the potholes, or if they would run into any landmines or booby traps. His biggest fear, however, was of the ambushes that were usually sprung where the dirt roads intersected. These were sudden attacks launched from the flanks. No one ever knew when one would be coming, so each crossroad was approached as if it might be a potential ambush. Luke kept a keen eye out for the enemy, but all he saw were old, wrinkled, Vietnamese farmers shaded by their huge round hats, squatting in the fields.

"What's chicken wire covering the windows for?" one of the GIs asked over the truck's rumble.

"Gooks, man," someone shouted back. "They throw grenades through the windows."

One of the things that was making the Vietnam War so complicated was the difficulty of discerning who the enemy really was. An innocent-looking old farmer just might pull out a grenade or pistol and blow you away. A friendly dog, desperate for affection, could have a bomb sewn onto its belly. Children, while appearing harmless, could either be thieves or the enemy. In Vietnam, hidden dangers could kill.

Luke glanced over at his buddy, Sammy, who had now become more like the brother he never had. His eyes were closed and his helmet tilted to one side. It occurred to Luke how strange it was that he and Sammy had become so close, especially since he had resisted him so much at first.

After a long, sweaty hour, the trucks finally ground their gears to a stop at the Red Eagle Firecamp, a much smaller temporary base camp for infantry ground patrols. If Cu Tieng was considered a small military city, then Red Eagle would be a military village. It housed about a hundred troops and was surrounded by thick, jungle vegetation on two sides and rice fields on the other two. Several slim lines of purple smoke rose up from a couple dozen "hootches," cabin-sized canvas tents and sandbag huts. Bunkers were dug into the ground along the perimeter with sandbags stacked around them, along with more concertina wire. A clearing of about a hundred yards from the fence to the trees had been bulldozed around the camp. Soldiers carrying M16 rifles kept guard on four watchtowers that looked strangely similar to oversized deer stands. This would be home for awhile, until new orders came in.

Walking briskly up to meet the trucks came a short, scruffy-looking soldier who was champing down on a half wasted, unlit, cigar. As the GIs hustled off the truck, he started speaking.

"Okay, men. Gather around," he said, pausing to give everybody a moment to get huddled in a circle. "I'm First Commanding Sergeant O'Brian. You can call me Sergeant O'Brian, or just O'Brian, or Tinkerbell. I really don't give a flip what you call me as long as you follow orders. It's show time, men. All your training has come down to this. But I guess I don't have to remind you of that. Now, my advice to you is that you stay in touch with your family back home, watch your buddy's back, and above all, pray. Those three things will get you through. And one other thing; we're sure glad to see you boys. We need the relief." He pointed to another man standing under a nearby tree. "Staff Sergeant Baker here will show you boys where to go."

The Alpha Red Company was responsible for holding down an assigned area of territory. By day and by night, rotating teams were sent out from base camp on patrols, sweeping villages and certain land borders, attempting to keep the area clean of communist Vietcong guerrillas (VCs). In the thickness of the jungle vegetation, enemy attacks were more frequent and could come from any direction. VCs could be only a few feet away from you, waiting behind trees or hidden in the razor-sharp elephant grass. They could strike before you could even blink.

In this country, anthills were sometimes six feet tall. The snakes were twice that. And at night, it was dark, black, deep pit black. Sometimes, you couldn't see your partner only a few feet from you. Occasionally, although the moonlight did offer a reprieve from the darkness, it only cast eerie shadows along the ground. VCs were adept at living in and moving through this type of terrain like ghosts in the night, often dressed in what looked like black pajamas. They usually struck in the darkness, because in the light of day, they were not a match for the United States' superior firepower.

Luke, Sammy, and six others bunked in a sandbag hootch with a canvas top. It had tables, chairs, mosquito nets, lockers, and dimly shining light bulbs strung like Christmas decorations around the ceiling. Each man's bunk and locker became his own individual shrine.

Sammy hung up a small wooden cross and a family portrait of him, his mother, three sisters, and little brother. Next to them was a yellowing, black-and-white photograph of his father in his prime. Luke taped a couple Polaroid photos of him and his family on his locker. Other than that, his space was pretty plain. Some of the others however, got more creative, with girly pictures, mirrors, and all sorts of paraphernalia. One guy, Gino, had a statue of Buddha wearing a cross and a rabbit's foot.

"You a Christian?" Sammy had asked him.

"I don't know what I am, man," he said, "but I believe."

His response was typical of how many of them felt. They were all terrified that they might be the next one going home in a body bag. As the men continued to settle in, Staff Sergeant Baker stepped into the hootch and made them stop whatever they were doing and listen up. He sat down backward on a folding chair. He had his helmet on and, like O'Brian, he hadn't shaved for days.

"Sergeant O'Brian asked me to come and brief you on a few important details. Again, let me reiterate how glad we are to have you here. We really need the manpower, but you won't do us any good dead. So, if you are going to stay alive there are some facts you need to know about. First, whatever you do, don't get yourself all frantic and frenzied because it will only get you killed. You have to be calm and decisive. Look, you're here now. You can't change that. So, the best way to make your little vacation successful is to face your fears head-on. You do too much flinching and second-guessing and you'll end up with a bullet in your head. The good news is, if you stay alive for the first couple of weeks your odds of survival go up considerably. Now, I want you to take your dog tags from around your neck and string them in your bootlaces. When they're around your neck, they make noise and it will get you killed. In the boots they won't make any noise. Also, I want you to color them with your shoe polish so they won't be reflecting in the sun or moonlight. If you have anything you want to keep dry, wrap it in plastic and put it in the lining of your helmet."

As he continued he stood up and walked over and picked up a soldier's hand grenade. "Bend the pins on all your grenades right now, because when you're out in the jungle, limbs from bushes and trees get caught in the rings and yank out the pins and you get blown away. Remember, it only takes one time and you're history. You may get lucky for ninety-nine times, but it's the one-hundredth time that gets you. So pay attention to the details."

He handed the grenade back to the soldier. "I want you always sleeping with your boots on and don't forget to put your Halazone tablets in each and every canteen of water or you'll get dysentery. Take your malaria pills every day or you'll get malaria and take your salt tabs, too. If you don't remember your salt, I'm telling you, you'll black out from heat exhaustion. And take your helmet off as much as you can. I knew one ol' boy that got his brain fried because he left that metal bowl on all day when it was about 110 degrees. And if you gotta smoke, do it during the day. If you light up at night, you can kiss yourself goodbye. Another big problem when you're out in the field is the leaches. I know you've heard about them. I hate to tell you, but it's true. When they bite you and you pull them off, the heads break off and stay in your skin. You can't let them stay in there or they'll get infected and that can lead to serious medical problems. Usually, a lighted match head will force it to come out, but you can't light matches at night. So look in your C-Rations for your salt. Rub some of it on the head and that'll work too. All right guys, that's about it. Get some rest and good luck. I'll see you in the morning."

CHAPTER 31

AS THE SOLDIERS began settling in for their first night, Luke's attention was drawn to the faded picture of Sammy's father hanging on his locker. He walked over for a closer look and was amazed at the resemblance to Sammy.

"Hey Sammy," Luke asked. "Why haven't I seen that picture before and how come you didn't hang it up during Basic and AIT?

"Kept it in my wallet," Sammy said, lying back in his bunk, his hands behind his head. He didn't offer Luke any more information.

"Ya'll sure did look alike."

"Yeah, we did. He was good-looking, wasn't he?" Sammy chuckled.

"What was his name?"

"Cleo A. Williams. People called him Cleo. The A stood for Alfred."

"How come you never talk about him, man? What's his story?"

"What's with all the questions, Bro? And why you so interested all of a sudden?"

"I don't know, I guess seeing his picture made me curious."

"Like I told you back in Victoria. I'll tell you when the time is right. His story is too powerful to be wasted." He rolled his back to Luke. "Now go to sleep, man."

They tried to sleep, but sometime in the early-morning hours, rain began pounding against the canvas top so hard that it sounded as if the whole thing was going to collapse. Lightening flashes lit up the hootch like strobe lights, creating eerie shadows.

"Gook in the corner, man!" one of the GIs shouted into the darkness. Terrified, he rolled out of bed and grabbed his rifle. A wave of paranoia spread across the room. Lighting flashed again, momentarily lighting up the area. Several more picked up their weapons. Sammy however, very calmly crouched his way over to a light cord that was hanging down and pulled it. When the dim bulbs shed light on the situation, there was no enemy in the corner, only a chair with a helmet and jacket hanging on it. Relieved, the men tried to settle back down for sleep in spite of the spine-chilling atmosphere.

Luke was now suffering from the most serious case of homesickness he had ever experienced. Curled in the fetal position, he longed for the warmth and security of home—to take a hot shower, to sleep in his soft bed, to stuff himself with his mother's baked bread...

Everyone slept on edge for the rest of the night, Sammy being the only exception. At the crack of dawn, Sergeant O'Brian charged inside the hootch wearing a forest-green, hooded rain poncho. He was carrying a wooden crate and an M-16 rifle. His square jaw bore five days of stubble and he still chewed on what appeared to be the same unlit cigar.

"Rise and shine, ladies! It's time for C-rations and assignments." He dropped a crate on the floor. Then took his M-16's three-pronged flash suppressor and cut the wires on the case. Packets of meals fell out into a pile.

"Choose your breakfast and meals for two days. We're going on patrol."

Moans and groans ricocheted through the cots.

"But we just got here," a muffled voice came from under a blanket.

Sergeant O'Brian walked over to the cot and shoved the guy on the floor with his foot.

"Get up you lazy scumbag! You think this is a game? If I was the enemy, you'd be dead already." Again, the Sergeant addressed the group. "All right, after you've got your rations get your gear together and meet the rest of the team outside. We're moving out in fifteen."

Within seconds the unit was gathered around picking out their rations for the next two days. When Luke read the labels on each packet, his homesickness intensified—Ham Patties

& Lima Beans, Beef Patties & Potato Slices, Hotdogs & Beans, Pork Chunks & Beans, Ham Pieces & Scrambled Eggs.

The evening meals at base camp had always been cooked and hot, with coffee and iced tea, but field meals were light-weight and dehydrated. They fit into the soldiers' backpacks to be mixed with water and eaten in their pouches. Each meal also came with various desserts and all contained cigarettes, gum, candy, waterproof matches, instant coffee mix, salt, pepper, and a small roll of toilet paper.

With the rain still drizzling steadily, the men grabbed their gear and headed out to meet Sergeant O'Brian and the rest of the team.

"Reconnaissance," O'Brian said. "For the next three days, we'll be on a reconnaissance observation mission." He squatted down and pulled out a map of the terrain. The rest of the team participating, fifteen in all, huddled in a half circle around him. "We're covering this area over here. It's about a thirty mile radius," he said, drawing a circle on the map. "And it goes all the way down to here, the Mil Lo River. We'll move along a well developed trail that moves down this way." He drew a line on the map. "Then, we'll hit route 9 at the village of Ca Lu which will bring us back." He exhaled and clutched his hands into a fist. "Okay, here's the deal. Intelligence sources believe there's new VC movement going on somewhere in that area—new camps and village manipulation. Because this is a scouting and not an ambush mission, our job is simply to locate the enemy and chart it. Cappelli here will radio in their position for the flyboys to drop the napalm." The sergeant pointed to another soldier standing next to him. "This is Gino Clark, our medic. He'll keep you patched up when you need it. You already know Staff Sergeant Baker here. The only weapons you'll need to carry is your M16 and pistol, plus grenades—anything else will slow us down. Our goal is to keep a distance of 100 to 200 meters from the enemy, *but*—and it's an important but—if we walk up on any, we'll have to take them out ourselves. If you want to live, then you do exactly as Sergeant Baker and I say. You take all those mushy feelings in your mind and you stuff them. This ain't no training exercise, it's the real thing. Out here, if one of you screws up, somebody dies.

"Where have I heard that before?" thought Luke. For a moment he just stood there. Just three and a half months before he had been a naïve mama's boy, nervous about asking Haley out for a date....

➤ ◄

For the first two days the team trudged along the dense jungle trail and waded through rice fields. Four experienced point men led the way with mine-sweeping equipment. As fate would have it, the rainy season had begun and the soldier's feet stayed wet and muddy, making walking uncomfortable and blisters inevitable. If that wasn't enough, it appeared that if the enemy didn't get them, the leaches would—just as Sergeant Baker had said. By the second evening, the black, slimy creatures were everywhere, crawling up the soldier's pant legs and in their boots and between their shirts, latching onto stomachs and backs. The good news was they could anticipate a quiet night made even better by the fact that the rain had stopped for a while. The team hunkered down alongside a river ravine for the night. They tried their best to wring out their clothing and get rid of the leaches. That night, Luke pulled the 0200 to 0400 watch on the rear post, but it didn't really matter to him, because between being wet, the leaches, and now the shivers, it was difficult to get much sleep anyway.

When on night watch during a patrol run, one of the great challenges for the soldiers was keeping their minds occupied as the hours slowly crept by. They had to lie motionless, anticipating imminent enemy contact at any moment. In the towers back at camp, one could at least walk his post. In the bunkers, they could move around, talk to the guy in the next hole, take five-minutes to relieve themselves or even have some coffee. But none of that is possible on patrol.

Luke was on his belly along a furrow, his finger on the trigger, watching and waiting for anything that moved. Grass shoots protruded from his helmet. He had smeared green and black camouflage stick all over his face. The only sounds he could hear were tree frogs croaking alongside crickets chirping. They harmonized together while the steady droplets of water trickling from the leaves kept time. The moon peeked from behind the clouds, illuminating the sky. Streaks of moonlight filtered down through the trees casting those eerie shadows. If Luke didn't know better, he would swear that he was back in Florida or Louisiana.

Movement in the grass-field caused him to refocus on the task at hand. Then it sounded as if someone coughed. He froze in position, his heartbeat racing, as his finger twitched against the trigger. He couldn't make out if it was animal or human. It seemed to move swiftly like a deer, but deer didn't cough. He feared it was the enemy marching down the footpath, most likely a point man. Whatever it was, it was heading for the camp at a leisurely but steady pace.

Now it was closer—forty, maybe fifty yards away, yet Luke still couldn't see anything. He ran in a crouched position a distance of about a hundred feet and woke Sergeant Baker who alerted the rest of the team. By the time Sergeant O'Brian made it to Luke the movement had stopped. Sergeant O'Brian gestured for the rest of the team to take their positions. Everyone lay deathly still and quiet. Feelings of anticipation pulsed through them as they listened intently for the slightest movement.

Swaying of the bush again and what sounded like someone stepping lightly through the woods convinced them of the likelihood that VCs were advancing on their position. Whoever or whatever it was, it didn't seem to know they were there and it was going to walk right up on them. It was at that moment they all heard it—a loud squeal. It wasn't a VC point man. It was a small herd of wild hogs! When the biggest boar, the one with tusks, dangerous and vicious, noticed them, it began to rush toward them.

"I can nail 'em Sarg," said Luke. "Just like I did that eight-pointer back home. We could have us some barbequed pig."

"You shoot that pig and we give away our position," O'Brian said. "Gooks'll be swarming around here like yellow-jackets. Grab some sticks or rocks to throw at him and hopefully all of them will go away."

The soldiers all grabbed whatever was near them, branches, rocks, sticks, and began throwing them. That did the trick. The big boar turned and the whole herd wandered off with him.

"Congratulations Hatcher," said Sergeant O'Brian, slapping Luke on the back. "You woke up the whole team for a bunch of pigs."

Luke responded with one of those, "I feel like such an idiot" grins.

"Don't worry, private. You did the right thing," said O'Brian. "It's always better to err on the side of caution and live than on the side of negligence and die. Know what I mean?"

"I know exactly what you mean," said Luke.

CHAPTER 32

"BET YOU NEVER thought you'd end up here in the jungle like this, coming face to face with a big ol' boar hog?" Sammy asked Luke as the soldiers walked in pairs down a mucky trail the next morning. "That was something else. Wasn't it? All that training so we could find us a bunch of pigs. I wish we had shot one. Man, I can almost taste that barbeque right now. Cain't you?"

Luke didn't respond, only grunted and adjusted his backpack to ease the rubbing under his arms. The early morning's sun was turning the moisture from the recent rain into steam. Even though the rain had stopped, everyone was soaked and the wet gear had become much heavier. Luke's pant legs were pasted to his skin and the heat was baking the back of his shirt. His feet seemed to have shriveled and were slipping from side to side in his boots, creating big blisters.

There was silence for a long while as the trail began to take on a steady incline and the marching became more of a climb. Luke slapped a mosquito that had lit on his neck and refocused on the trail ahead.

Shifting his gear on his back, Sammy began to sing and hum a stanza from his favorite hymn. *"It is well with my soul,"* he sang. *"It is well...umm, umm, It is well, oh yes it is, umm, umm, ...with my soul. When peace like a river attends my way, When sorrows like sea-billows roll, Whatever my lot, Thou has taught me to say: It is well. It is well with my soul."* He sang and hummed the verses over and over.

"That doesn't sound like something you'd sing," said Luke at last. "That's a white folk song."

"It may be a white folk song the way ya'll sing it, but we put jive into it," Sammy said, snapping his fingers and doing a little dance move.

Luke tilted his helmet back and scratched his head. "It really is well with your soul, isn't it, Sam?"

"I believe it is. Yes, sir, Luke, I believe it is."

"Tell me something then. Are you scared of dying out here?"

"You know it, but you can be scared and still have peace." Sammy shifted his stance, working out the stiffness in his legs. "I'm scared *and* I have peace. I guess that's the best way to describe it."

"I'm scared, too, Sam, man, but I don't have peace."

"Look at me, man," Sammy said. He stopped walking and pulled Luke's head in his direction. "But you can, Luke. You can have peace."

"I'm not like you, Sam. You have faith 'n all and I respect that, but it comes natural for you, because you're so..." Luke caught himself in mid-sentence and changed his words. "I just have questions, that's all... Like why are we here in this godforsaken mosquito factory guarding our lives, probably going to have to kill someone if we're going to get out of here alive? And don't forget, those VCs have families, too. We may have to kill someone's son or father or husband. I've already killed someone's daughter. There's too much pain and suffering and injustice in the world. Something's gone wrong. And you above all people ought to know about that. Where's the justice in life, Sam, the justice?"

"You think faith comes easy for me?" Sammy answered with sharpness in his voice. "I know what you were about to say about me. You think I'm simple-minded, that I'm just a good ol' black boy, that I just have faith because I'm naïve and don't know no better."

Luke kept silent, looking out into the jungle.

"That's it, isn't it Luke?"

Luke sighed. "After all we've been through, Sam, you of all people ought to know I'm not like that. I treat you just like I do anybody else."

"Let me tell you something, Luke. The God of the universe gave me a brain and I have faith because of common sense and because He's been faithful to me again and again. Like

289

I told you before, God met me in that prison and he took care of me there."

"I'm not questioning your intelligence. I just don't see things like you do. Life's more complicated for me."

"Shhh," Sammy whispered placing his index finger over his lips. "You hear that?" Machine gun fire could be heard faintly in the distance.

"Sounds like they're moving this way," said Luke.

For several minutes, the team marched in silence, keenly listening, until the sounds became further and further away. Then it was quiet again.

"He was killed," Sammy said, still looking forward up the trail.

"Who was killed?" asked Luke.

"Papa."

Luke rested his rifle on his shoulder and turned. "I'm sorry, man."

"I was seventeen years old when he died. Papa was pastor of Mount Zion Missionary Church, and he didn't just preach it, he lived it."

Luke nodded his head indicating to Sammy that he was listening.

"I'm a preacher's kid and Papa taught me the Word of the Lord from the time I was knee high to a rooster. He gave me many reasons to believe... I remember one day when we were walking out in this field and he said, 'Son, whenever you need to find God, you don't need to go far, just look around and He'll be right in front of you.' He picked up an acorn off the ground and held it in his open palm. Then, he looked up at one of those big oak trees and said, 'You see, Son, inside this tiny acorn is everything it needs to know in order to become a big strong oak tree like this one right here.' He pointed out the sturdy trunk and sprawling limbs that stretched out over us. 'It do amaze me,' he said, 'how man, with all his fancy learning and sophisticated inventions can't seem to make one single tree. What causes the acorn to grow into an oak, or an apple seed to grow into an apple tree, or a pumpkin seed to grow into a pumpkin plant?' Then, he got all excited, took off his ol' brown hat, and started waiving it around, shouting, 'Praise God! Thank you Jesus!' Then he calmed down, took hold of my shoulders and said, 'Samuel.' That's what he called me. 'Jus' like God put the know-how into a tiny spider in order for it to build its web, he put that know-how in each seed. It's a miracle.' Then he told me, 'Samuel, now you is a seed and God created you for a divine purpose. Don't go trying to be no oak tree if God made you to be a pine.' I never forgot that day."

Luke was transfixed by his friend's words, but Sammy wasn't finished. He had much more he wanted to say—much more that needed to be said.

"You know, Luke, the Scriptures say, 'Without faith it is impossible to please God, that we must first believe that He is, and then that He is a rewarder of those that diligently seek Him.' The very first thing to faith is seeing God's existence. Another thing Papa used to do was to hold out his hand and make a fist. Then he'd slowly open and close it again and again, saying, 'Samuel, we be creatures of great design. There is so much design just in this hand right here. First, there is my fingers. Now, you'd think we'd get along just fine without no fingers.' I'd just shake my head and shrug my shoulders. 'Each one of these fingers bends at just the right place, so we can grab things. And there's the skeleton with all the joints. On top of that are the muscles that keep tension on the skeleton to help it move. Then there are these little electric wires that connect our hand to our brain and the brain sends out electricity when it tells the hand to move. Our body is one fine machine. Not even them new space rockets that orbit the earth are as fine.' Papa, he'd take off his hat again, and start dancing and shouting, kicking up dust from the ground. Papa read a lot of books and made sure all of us kids learned to read. He'd always end by saying, 'Samuel, where there is a design, there is a designer and where there is a designer, there is a purpose.' He got that out of a book. 'Find your purpose Son, it'll keep you from floundering,' he said. I've pondered those words for all my years."

"That's interesting," said Luke, "and I'm not trying to put you down or anything, but it doesn't really help answer my questions about pain and injustice in the world..." Luke hesitated, pondering whether or not to ask his next question, then went ahead. "So, how'd he get killed anyway?" he said softly.

"Shot."

"By whites?"

"Nope," Sammy said with a slight tremble. "He was shot by some brothers—killed by his own people."

"Hey, man, we don't have to talk about it if you don't want."

"It's OK, Luke. I brought it up first. It's the right time because you're ready to hear now. Before, I wasn't so sure." Sammy wiped the sweat from his face. "He was shot during a robbery at the Crossroads Corner Store. Jo Jo, my little sister, was sick with the flu and was running a high fever and Papa ran out to get some medicine for her. Mama wanted me to go, but I sassed back at her that I was too tired. Papa told her, 'let the boy rest,' and went out to get it himself... If I'd just obeyed my Mama, Papa would be here today—kind of like with you and Haley."

"Why didn't you say something before?" Luke pressed. "You could have told me this weeks ago."

"Just being patient. Like I said, I was waiting for the right time. That's something else Papa taught me—always be wise with your words. Don't be throwing pearls among the swine. I always knew I'd tell you, like I did about my prison. I was just waiting for God's timing is all. You see, there's much more about God that you need to know, Luke—that you must know. I think His story will change your life. I know it did mine."

"I'm listening," said Luke, but just as Sammy started back with his story, Staff Sergeant Baker motioned for everyone to stop for a much-needed lunch break.

→ ←

Herman Riley looked down from his can of cold spaghetti as the gaunt gray dog, matted and mud-caked, with saliva dripping from its mouth licked his boots. It had ambled up on the squad while they were taking their break on the dirt trail, regrouping from the heat.

"Get now! Go on you old mutt," Riley muttered, shoving the dog away with his foot. "You're drooling all over my boots, man." He stood and shook his leg, but the dog only took a step backward and growled.

"Give the thing a break," one of the other soldiers said, "Your boots are already covered with muck anyway."

"I don't give a flip. I don't want that mangy thing's spit on me. Probably got rabies or something."

Luke, stretched out with his head propped up against his backpack, flipped the dog a spoon full of beans, but it just sniffed and scratched at it with its paws, then looked back up at them with a "come on boys, that's not good enough" expression on its face.

Luke slapped his thigh laughing. "Look at that, would you? A starving dog won't even eat this mess!"

"Ain't it the truth," said Sammy, "ain't it the truth."

After a while, the dog wised up and figured out it wasn't going to do any better so it lapped up the beans. When finished, it tilted its head and gave Luke another beggarly look. Luke set his can of beans on the ground with a cracker and let the creature finish them off.

Riley stood and stretched. He tossed his empty can of spaghetti down for the dog to lick and then walked off the trail into the bush. To the west a ditch separated the trail from what appeared to be miles of rice paddies with a few Vietnamese farmers working in knee-deep water. To the east, there was a large undeveloped field of tall elephant grass with a small trail meandering through it and several clusters of trees dotted along the way, one of which Riley stepped into. A couple of miles in the distance, the field backed up to some steep, thickly vegetated foothills that had large gray boulders jutting out from them.

"Riley! Where you think you're goin'?" Sergeant O'Brian yelled out.

"When you gotta go, Sarge, you gotta go," Riley shouted back with a goofy-looking grin on his face.

"Get back over here, now! Follow the procedure. That area ain't been cleared!"

Riley turned and began lanking back to the rest of the team, but he never saw the Bouncing Betty land mine hidden underneath the patch of grass. The blast sprayed burning shrapnel up through his thighs and into his stomach, ripping his arms and legs away from the rest of his body. Pieces of his skull and torso flew off like a shredding rag doll.

Sergeant O'Brian mumbled some expletives under his breath while staring up at the sky with clenched fists. Then, almost as if possessed by some outside force, he seemed to have been overcome by a violent hatred that surged unbidden, causing his ruddy complexion to turn bloody. "Idiot," he muttered. "Cappelli! Call in an extraction chopper at once to get us out of here. But we're going to have to retreat on foot for a good two or three miles, then meet up with the chopper there. If we meet here, they'll shoot us down. They know we're here now. That mine was set up as a warning to let them know we're in the area. They're probably watching us right now."

Standing over by what was left of Riley's torso; Sergeant Baker dropped his head and slowly exhaled. "Men, you know what we have to do before we take off."

"Don't have a body bag," Clark, the medic, said. "All I have is an extra poncho."

"That'll have to do," said Baker. "Let's get it done."

About thirty yards in the opposite direction from where Baker was, the old gray dog was licking one of Riley's blown off legs. Sergeant O'Brian slowly brought his M16 to his shoulder. Squinting through his scope, he squeezed the trigger. The gun let out a single pop and recoiled slightly. A few yards away, the bullet found its target. The old gray dog lie spread out on the ground, its limbs twitching, and then they became still. "Get away from my soldier, you mangy mutt," the Sergeant said, as he lowered the rifle down from his chest. Luke fell to his knees and started to vomit. This was no training exercise. It was the real thing. It was war.

CHAPTER 33

NOT MUCH WAS spoken on the two-mile trudge to meet the chopper. All the while they were being airlifted back to Red Eagle, the GIs stared vacantly at each other, at the floor, at the walls, and out of the open side doors of the chopper. The reverberating sounds of the whirling propellers had a hypnotic effect, even as the shock and utter terror of Riley's death weighed down on them. When back at camp, Sergeant O' Riley wasted little time addressing the new replacements.

"What you saw out there, men, was repulsive. It was a meaningless tragedy. Yet the whole incident could have been easily prevented! Do you hear me? It could have been prevented! Riley's death was stupid! When an order is given, no matter how absurd it may seem; it is for a good reason. Never, and I mean never, when on patrol, do you leave the group unless it's been cleared! I don't care if you have to relieve yourself in your pants. You understand? And another thing, don't feed the dogs!"

Most of the men simply stared back blankly at their leader trying to make some sense of what had happened. A couple of them mumbled the words, "Yes, sir."

"Good. Now get some rest. Tomorrow is another day."

→→ ←←

Luke soon found out one thing about this war: it consisted mostly of long periods of tedious routine and boredom, living like an animal under appalling conditions, interrupted by sharp moments of sheer terror. Unless you were on a patrol run in the field or on a night watch, you slept in your hooch, got up each morning at daylight, followed a set routine of chores around the camp, and then sat around in the evenings shooting the bull and drinking beer or soda, sometimes playing games like checkers, chess, or cards, maybe writing letters. At any rate, you marked the days off the calendar until your orders changed and you were off to another assignment. There was a lot of time to think about the disturbing images you had seen, like your buddy's corpse being picked up in bits and pieces and rolled up in a poncho.

There was also a lot of time to talk. Sammy had piqued Luke's curiosity about his father. He wanted to hear more, especially now.

The next afternoon after Luke had finished cleaning and inspecting his rifle, he found Sammy sitting on a pile of unused sandbags alone reading his Bible. Shirtless, with his M16 leaning against him, he looked worn. Less than four days in country and the physical and emotional strain was already unbearable.

"Hey, man," said Luke softly. "Am I interrupting?" The sun was beaming down.

Sammy closed the Bible and looked up, squinting. "Doing some reading is all. Whatcha got?"

"You got a minute to talk?"

"I always got a minute for you, Luke."

Luke scooted up an empty wooden ammunition box and sat down on it facing Sammy. "Tell me more about your dad. You got my curiosity up. And the way things are going, you better tell me now, 'cause I may not be here tomorrow."

Sammy scratched his head and thought for a moment, sort of teasing Luke. "All right," he said, opening his Bible back up and flipping through the pages. When he found a certain spot, he stopped and handed the book to Luke. "Read verse eight."

I wasn't expecting a Bible lesson, thought Luke, but he searched for verse eight like he was told and began reading aloud. "We are confident, I say, and willing rather to be absent from the body, and to be present with the Lord." He handed the book back to Sammy. "Yeah? And what does that have to do with your father?"

"Absent from the body, Luke, means we are present with the Lord. When we leave this body, we go right into His

299

presence. And at this very moment, my papa really is in Heaven. He's not dead…and neither is Haley. It's real, Luke. Heaven is real."

Luke looked a bit surprised. "Is that all you wanted to tell me about your dad, that he's in Heaven? I kind of figured that you thought that."

"Well if it is true and you already knew it, then why do you live like it's not? And answer me honestly."

Luke thought for a moment. "I guess because I don't know if I really believe it or not. Like I said back in Basic, it all seems like a fairy tale to me, now, since Haley and all." Luke held his hand over his eyes to shield the sun. "Really, Sam, is that all you wanted to tell me about your dad?"

"Well, not really. I just wanted you to see it in Scripture before I told you his story. You see Papa saw Heaven."

"If that is what you believe," said Luke a little disappointed. "I mean I respect your viewpoint and all."

"No, Luke. I don't think you understand what I'm saying. My papa died and saw Heaven then he came back to life and told us about it."

Even though you're a great guy, now I know you are batty. "Okay…" said Luke slowly. "If you say so, man… Look Sam, I really didn't mean to disturb you. I need to go help J.C. and Edwards dig that foxhole."

"No you don't," Sammy said forcefully. "You're on your R&R time. Now just hold on. I'm not finished yet."

"All right, all right. I'm all ears."

"You see, Papa didn't die right away when he got shot. They carried him to the hospital over in McComb, Mississippi. While he was in the emergency room, he died. His heart actually stopped—flat-lined and everything. They covered his body up with a sheet and wheeled him into another room to wait for the morgue to come get him. The nurse had come out in the waiting room and was telling us that Papa had passed away. Mama was going into convulsions and stuff, when another nurse came running up to her and said, 'we don't understand it, but his heart is beating again!' They rushed him up to surgery and operated. After the surgery, and the anesthesia wore off, he was in recovery and regained his consciousness. Mama, Jo Jo, and me was gathered around him."

Whether he believed it or not, Luke was now enthralled by the story, leaning forward, with his elbows on his knees and his chin in his hands.

"When Papa finally did speak his words were slow and a bit slurred, but his eyes were sparkling like a little baby. He said, 'I've been with one of the Lord's angels, and he told me to come back and tell you what I saw.' Papa struggled to get the words out, but we could understand him fine. 'First, I was floating up above my body. I could see everything that was going on. I saw two nurses and one doctor working on me. The doctor was tall with snow-white hair. One of the nurses was black and the other was white and real little, like a little girl almost. I saw them put the sheet over my body and then push my bed into another room. One of the nurses, the little white one, went out to the waiting room to talk to you. Mama had her hand on her forehead and was jerking all around. I got real sad when I saw her.' He looked over at Mama, just sitting there with this look of anguish across her face. 'I tried calling out to you, not to cry that I was fine, but you couldn't hear me. After that, the most beautiful, brightest light surrounded me. It was warm and I was filled with a peace like I've never felt before. Samuel, it wasn't a dream. You have to believe me. It was more real than anything I've ever seen. I thought the light should be destroying my eyes then I realized I had a new body—a glorified one. The light was flowing in and through me. I was filled completely with love.' Then Papa looked up at all three of us. 'I never felt so alive. And then an angel came to me in this light. It had the most beautiful eyes and golden, flowing hair. I fell on my face but it lifted me up and said, 'Do not worship me, for I am but a creation like you.' I reached out and took the angel's hand. We traveled fast—like the speed of one of them rockets. 'Where am I?' I asked. But before the angel could speak, the answer was right there in my mind. *Absent from the body, present with the Lord.*'"

"'Suddenly, we was standing in the most lovely valley filled with flowers, plants, and trees. Everything was perfect. There was not a dead branch or leaf or flower anywhere and there were no bugs.'"

"'There is no death here,' the angel said to me."

"'And the colors, Samuel. They were unlike anything I ever seen before—brand-new colors that don't exist on Earth. There was no Sun like there is on Earth either. Everything seemed to produce its own light. Me and the angel were inside the light, a part of it, living and moving and being. In the distance, a golden color somehow radiated within the light. Then I could hear the most glorious music, again unlike anything I'd had ever heard.'"

"'That's the Heavenly City,' the angel said to me. 'Many are waiting for you there. But before you enter, you must go back and tell your family what you have seen.'"

"'When the angel said that, I was back in my body again. So, I guess I'm telling you what I seen. I don't think I'm going to be here much longer.' And Papa was right. We all hugged him gently. Mama sat by his bed and the next day he died. Now, I know what you may be thinking, Luke. You are probably thinking my papa was just hallucinating, but he wasn't. You see, Dr. Kennedy said there was no way my papa could have described what went on in the emergency room and in the waiting room because he was unconscious the whole time, with his eyes closed. But Papa described everything to a 'T'. And you gotta know; my papa wasn't one to lie or exaggerate. In fact, he hated exaggerations. No, Luke, my papa was really present with the Lord just like the Bible says, and that gives me a lot of hope."

Luke nodded his head, his expression one of deep thought.

"Heck, Luke, I don't know anymore than you do, why all the bad stuff happens, but I know my papa wasn't lying and I know that somehow God is working in all of this... You know, Haley is with God right now. She really is."

"I don't know, Sam. I have to think about all this. It's kind of heavy."

"But it's true."

CHAPTER 34

SARAH LOVED EVERYTHING about
Christmas. She loved the weather, the bright lights, the front-
yard manger scenes. She loved the carols, and waiting for Santa
Clause to come, drinking hot chocolate with buttered toast, and
stringing popcorn with the kids. She loved sitting together, wide-
eyed, looking at how beautiful their Christmas tree was, all lit up.
Each year, James and Luke would go tromping through the
woods in search of the perfect tree. When they finally carried it
in the house, it was usually so tall that it had to be cut off to
make it fit into the living room. It was never really perfect, but it
was always big. For James and Luke, bigger was better.

Anticipation would fill Sarah's and Emily's hearts as the
two men worked to make sure the tree was standing up straight
and turned just right so the bare spots were not facing the front.
Then, there were always those couple of branches sticking out

awkwardly like wild hairs that needed to be trimmed. In the end, the tree was a reflection of their home, not flawless, but simple, warm, loving, and inviting.

This year, however, with Luke's absence, the season hadn't held its usual luster. Of course, there was Emily, and this Christmas would be mostly for her. But even she didn't seem to have the same enthusiasm as in times past.

On this particular day, Emily was visiting at a friend's house, James was working at the mill as usual, and Sarah found herself home alone. She stood back, observing the tree. It was Okay, she thought, though it wasn't quite as big as usual and didn't appear to be shining nearly as brightly. She adjusted the colorfully wrapped presents stacked underneath that were from an array of friends and relatives. Over half of them were for Luke. From her apron pocket, she pulled out his most recent letter and read it for about the tenth time since receiving it.

December 9, 1966

Dear Mom, Dad & Emily,

I hope you had a wonderful Thanksgiving. Uncle Sam sent us special turkey and dressing dinners. It was nice, but not as good as yours Mom. We are getting ready to be airlifted by chopper out of Red Eagle. We're going out about seventy-five miles north to set up a new base camp and then search and clear a mountain. Believe it or not, they have mountains here. But they're still covered with jungle. This mountain is supposed to be a hiding place for the Vietcong. So maybe we'll see some action. I'll be there for at least three months. So far, since I got here, we've lost seventeen of the eighty or so men in this platoon. One guy stepped on a land mine. I've been in the field for about two months now so I'm getting pretty filthy. The flies and insects here are terrible. They are constantly swarming around and landing on us. Most of us have sores and cuts and a thing called jungle rot all over our bodies. The flies love it. Ha. We spend more time swatting the insects than we do the enemy.

Thanks for sending me the pictures. Keep them coming. They really help me fight off the homesickness. Emily, you are getting so big and pretty. I know you have two or three boyfriends at least. I was proud of your pictures and showed them off to all the guys. Your cookies are a big hit Mom! Send them more often and in bigger batches. The guys say they're the best. I haven't been inside a PX since I got over here so I'm running out of a lot of things. One thing I desperately need is socks. My last pair rotted off, so my feet are in pretty bad condition right now. I could also use some towels—not white. Green would be best. It seems there are never enough. We use them for everything, from wiping away sweat, to pads for our machine guns. Please send some M&M's. They don't melt and are easy to keep. And if you can I would like a Frisbee. It would give us something else to do when not on patrol. I just ran out of ink in my pen, so I could use some pens also.

Tell everyone that I'd appreciate them writing me. I'd be glad to write back when I find the time. You wouldn't believe how much good those letters do. About the only thing a soldier has to look forward to is mail call. Take some pictures on Christmas morning and send them with my package. I want to see what all Santa brought. I hope I didn't ask for too much. If I did, that's Okay. Just *send whatever you can. Have a Merry Christmas. Sorry I won't be*

there in person, but I'll be there in my heart.

> *Love,*
> *Luke*

Sarah folded the letter, placed it back in her pocket, and checked her mental list. Luke had sent the letter on December 9th, but it had just arrived two days ago on the 20th. She had started filling his request that very day and had put in Luke's package everything he requested except the pictures yet to be taken.

Come Christmas morning, Emily was pulling Sarah and James out of bed at 6:00 A.M. Sarah put the coffeepot on, and they all shuffled to the living room in their pajamas. Emily was ecstatic and she jumped all around when she saw her brand new Schwinn banana-seat bike under the tree. After she gave her bike a thorough examination and seemed satisfied, the three of them sat in a semi-circle to open the rest of their presents, leaving a space where Luke usually was. Emily was designated as the official gift passer-outer. When there was one for Luke, it was stacked in his spot. In the end, Emily had gotten the most gifts. James and Sarah contended that the kids get too much stuff each year, yet they were the very ones always insisting on buying those few extras as security to make sure Christmas was indeed special. Next, they each took a couple of Luke's gifts and opened them for him. Sarah would take pictures of the gift and write a note on the back telling whom it was from. When they had finally finished with all the gifts, James spoke up.

"Before we finish, we need to pray," he said, holding his hands out for Sarah and Emily to take. The three grasped each other's hands. James was never one for long drawn-out prayers. "Lord Jesus, we come before you and thank you for the greatest gift of all—the gift of yourself. Because you died on the Cross for our sins, we are forgiven and have eternal life. And that is what Christmas is all about."

Sarah nodded her head in agreement. "Yes, Lord," she whispered, while Emily wiggled and squirmed a bit.

"And Lord, we lift up our son, Luke to You. Please watch over him in Vietnam. Protect him from the enemy and let him know how much we love him and You love him. Bring him home safely, Lord. In Jesus name, Amen."

The moment James said "Amen," Sarah released her hand, jumped up from the sofa and literally ran down the hall to their bedroom. She slammed the door and flung herself across the bed, sobbing loudly. James slowly began picking up the wrapping paper that was strewn all over the living room, unsure about what to do, but Emily made her way to the bedroom door and started knocking.

"Mama, it's gonna be okay," she said through the door. "Please don't cry, Mama. Luke is coming home soon. I just know he is. I love you."

James walked up and put his hand on Emily's shoulder. "Your mother will be okay, Honey. We just need to leave her alone for awhile. Come help me pick up the wrapping paper in the living room, and then you can go outside and ride that bike. Okay?"

"I don't feel like riding right now, Daddy," she said. "I miss Luke."

James knelt down so he could be on his daughter's eye level. "I miss him too, Honey," he said with a gentle hug.

➤➤ ◄◄

Christmas had come and gone and after five months in country Luke was still with the Alpha Company even though they had moved to set up the new firebase camp called Red Fox. They worked for two weeks nonstop, constructing the camp, building bunkers, foxholes, watchtowers, and hooches. Materials were hauled in via helicopters and trucks. When finished, Luke felt more like a construction worker than a soldier. Soon, however, he was jerked back to reality.

By March, he had been on over fifty patrol runs and involved in half as many ambushes. He was constantly hungry and fatigued and had witnessed enough death to last him ten lifetimes. Bouts of anger, combined with growing fears—both fear of death and fears of living—were dragging him into a downward spiral of depression.

While he was forever burdened by the fact that he had been the cause of Haley's death, the things he was seeing in this war were challenging him on a whole different level. Now, he was coming face-to-face with half mutilated corpses and seeing people shot or blown up on a daily basis. As a result, he was becoming more cynical and callous with each passing day, losing faith and questioning not only God but humanity as well. Here was evil, up close and personal.

And all too often the killing was senseless. Like one evening at dusk when they were in the field walking through a village, Luke had the feeling that somebody was following them. He turned around to say something to someone and he saw two Vietnamese about fifty yards back running toward them, following them. The road curved, so Luke and a couple of others got off the road and hid behind some trees while the rest of the company kept walking. When the two Vietnamese made it to the curve, Dale Maxwell, one of the guys with Luke, jumped out and confronted what turned out to be two kids. Both were girls, and they couldn't have been more than thirteen years old. One of them had a grenade in her hand and was waving it around as if she were going to throw it, yelling something in Vietnamese. Nobody could understand her. Not knowing if she was going to throw the grenade or what, Maxwell just shot both of them in the head. As it turned out, they were friendly. The pin was still in the grenade. One of the GIs had dropped it and they were bringing it back, doing them an act of kindness. But nobody could risk checking to see what they were up to. The two girls could have just as easily been the enemy.

Luke had stood in horror as the mother of one of the girls ran up to her dead daughter screaming and shouting and crying, making fists at them, cradling her in her arms, rocking back and forth.

Later that night in his sleeping bag, Luke held a grenade to his chest contemplating whether or not to pull the pin and just end it all. At that moment, the only thing that kept him from actually going through with it was thinking about the agony his dying would put his family through. Also that Scripture that Sammy had told him—"Absent from the body, present with the Lord." For some odd reason, Luke could just not get that out of his mind.

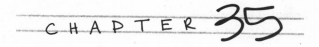

CHAPTER 35

ON MAY 29, 1967, Alpha Company was carrying out its mountain-clearing operation. The terrain included a mixture of thick jungle vegetation and high rocky ridges, and it offered excellent concealment to the enemy. The foliage was so thick that it was not uncommon for the VCs to spring an ambush when an American unit was only five to fifteen meters away.

On this day, the ridge they had been walking on dropped off into a marsh. The unit trudged through knee-deep water filled with decaying underbrush. Whenever they patrolled in the thickets, the soldiers walked in single file, ten or so yards apart so they could make sure the person in front and behind was still there. After a couple of hours, the underbrush thinned and the troops found themselves climbing a steep incline. Mixed in with the heavy vegetation were huge gray boulders. Hills jutted up all around them.

At the top, the incline flatted out and the vegetation became much thicker. Luke and Sammy, along with ten or so other GIs, were the first ones to make it up. A good thirty men were still climbing up behind them. The ones that made it up walked to a clearing about fifty yards away and sat on the ground taking the weight of their 60-pound packs off their shoulders and catching their breath. No sooner had they gotten their packs off but one of the point men motioned toward them to take cover.

"Hey, I'm positive I saw the trees moving back over there where we came up," he half-whispered and half-called out.

Command Sergeant O'Brian crawled over to check it out.

"See that," the point man said pointing to a cluster of elephant leaves back at the incline where more soldiers were coming up. "Over there, see, it moved again."

O'Brian had a sickening feeling in the pit of his stomach. He knew that often the VCs wore freshly cut foliage on their helmets and all over their bodies. He figured they were all just watching them and waiting. He had a gut feeling that they had walked into a trap. They were sitting ducks. He used hand signals and motioned for Sergeant Baker and the men to take cover. It was a tense moment. Everybody quietly hit their bellies and snaked into the brush, careful not to make a sound. The problem was, the troops still climbing up the incline had no idea what they were heading into. A messenger was sent to warn them, but before he made it to the edge, machine guns began ripping through the area at the incline. Out of the bushes came VCs swarming everywhere like angry bees. Then, the explosions began. Grenade launchers that were hidden in the vegetation barraged those on the incline. The guys who had barely made it to the top got hit and began convulsing and shrieking in agony. Luke crawled behind a nearby boulder, clutching his rifle with sweaty palms. Back where the soldiers were still coming up, he could see machine-gun fire through the dense vegetation.

"Back to the edge!" Sergeant O'Brian barked. "Get them boys some help!"

With adrenaline pushing through his veins, Luke and the others crept back toward the gunfire, shooting everything that moved along the way. Luke heard a crunch behind him and jolted around. It was Sammy. Sammy nodded and the two began to creep forward toward the ridge, their heads on a swivel.

Nearing the battle's hub, the two hunkered down behind another group of waist-high boulders with patchy green slime on them. Bullets were cutting through elephant leaves, popping the barks from trees, and ricocheting off the rocks. Grenades and mortars went off every ten or fifteen seconds. Fear gripped Luke as he unloaded a round of bullets and slid down, slamming his back against the rocks to reload.

Running up beside Luke, blasting the enemy, was Sammy. "*Yea, though I walk through the valley of the shadow of death,*" he quoted, as he let his machine gun rip. "*I will fear no evil.*" He let it rip again. "*For Thou art with me.*" He, too, slid down behind the rock to reload. "*The Lord is my refuge and my fortress. In Him I will trust.*" Sammy's bloodshot eyes stood out against his black skin. Sweat poured from his face. He glanced at Luke. No words were necessary; his terror was clear. "*God is my refuge and my strength, a very present help in trouble.*" He shifted back into position and fired another round.

A runner from Sergeant O'Brian crouched down besides them. Huffing for air, he relayed a message for them to hold the line a little longer, that the Air Force was on the way.

Luke pulled the pin on a hand grenade and lobbed it in the direction of the gunfire. When it exploded, two Vietcong came running out of the jungle, flailing around, their bodies bloodied and disfigured.

"*Lord, forgive me,*" Sammy yelled out, as he opened up with his machine gun, chopping them down.

"I can't hold on for much longer," Luke shouted.

From his right flank, three VCs rushed out of the brush to attack him.

Sammy was shooting forward, but happened to glance over in Luke's direction. "Look out!" he screamed, empting a round into the enemy before Luke even realized they were there.

Seconds later, the beautiful sound of U.S. fighter jets were heard overhead and the enemy began retreating. Five dead VCs lay at Luke's feet. Sammy had saved his life. It was when Luke turned to thank his best friend for what he had done that he saw what had happened.

➤➤ ◄◄

"Oh, Sam. Oh, God, Jesus!" Luke cried out. "Medic! Get a medic over here! Medic! Can somebody get me a medic?"

Several bullets had punctured Sammy's chest and the wounds were bleeding profusely, his breaths short.

Luke ripped off his shirt and started applying pressure to the red splotches across Sammy's body. "Where's the medic? Medic! Man down! Medic!" He pressed on the wounds and looked down into his eyes. "You're going to make it, Sam. You just hold on. You hear me? Don't you go and die on me!"

Sammy lifted his eyes toward Luke, love piercing through his pain. He panted for more air. "Don't you...worry about...me...Luke," said Sammy, his words sluggish and slow. Shivering, he raised his head to look down at himself, but he was too weak and his head fell back down into Luke's arms. In a whisper, he continued. "Get...out...of this...jungle." He gasped for more breath. "And get...back...home...You hear?........ God has...a...great...purpose for...........you."

"What about your purpose?" Luke cried, tears flowing abundant. "God didn't create you to die out here like this! What about your purpose, Sam? What about you? Don't you give up on me! *Don't* you!"

"This...is...my...........purpose," Sammy panted. "Right here...with you...to...let...Christ...live...through... me...God...loves...you...Luke...let...Him...give...you........... peace."

"God could never love me. I could never make up for all I've done...You be quiet and rest." Luke held Sammy's head up to his chest and caressed it.

"Luke...my...............friend...it's not...about...what you...did...but what...He...did." Sammy's eyes closed and his breathing slowed.

"Sam? Sam? Wake up! You hold on." Luke gently shook Sammy's head. "Medic!"

Sammy's eyes barely opened back up. "Don't...cry... for...me...You...know...that...peace...I...was...telling...you... about?"

Luke just held his friend and rocked.

"It's here...Luke...just...like...............He............ ....promised...I.................feel...............it...Luke ...It's....wonderful....Don't...you...........................see?...It's ...about...eternity....Life's about..........................eternity... You...can't...live............................until...you're...ready... to.........................die...I'm...ready...Luke,...and Haley.................she..." Flinching from the pain, Sammy closed his eyes again. "It...hurts,...Luke. It...hurts...real ....bad. But...soon...the...hurt...............be...... ......gone."

"Stop it, Sam. Stop it, right now." Luke wiped his face.

With another surge of strength, Sammy pulled Luke closer. "All we.................got......is...the............time... God...gives.........us...............You......be.........true...with... what...God's.........given.........you.........You...may...be...bre athing,......Luke,...but...you're...not.................really......... ......living."

Luke gazed down through his tears. "But..."

Shivering because his body was going into shock, Sammy lifted his own blood-drenched hand to Luke's face. "God.........loved...you...this.........much," he said, then, slowly and purposely smeared his own blood across Luke's cheek. Sammy grasped Luke's chin in his hand, squeezing. Their eyes locked. Calm filled Sammy's face, but terror filled Luke's.

"Hey...............Luke," said Sammy, "I see an............angel...just.........like.........Papa.........did....... I'm...not...lying,...Luke. It's...right...............here............tell my...Mama...about...the............angel." Sammy's hand dropped, and he fell limp.

"You're my best friend, Sam, my very best friend," Luke cried. On his knees, with his best friend's blood across his face, Luke lifted his arms toward the sky. "Nooooooo!!!" he screamed, his voice echoing through the jungle. Seconds later there was a loud blast and Luke felt intense burning on his skin and pieces of shrapnel entering his body, then everything went black.

CHAPTER 36

A SINGLE RAY of sunlight beamed through a crack in the Venetian blinds directly into Luke's face. He blinked and squinted. Images were blurred and he couldn't make out the figure leaning over him. As he lifted his hands to rub his eyes, he discovered that an IV tube was connected to his wrist. Then he felt the pain—throbbing, aching, burning, searing pain all over his body.

"Wh...where am I?" he asked faintly, his eyes coming into focus now.

"There, there, now," a sympathetic nurse who was attempting to take his vital signs said. She was dressed in a green army jumpsuit, with a Red Cross patch on her shoulder. "I see you decided to join us?" She reached for a cool, damp, cloth, and began dabbing his face. The smell of fever reeked, while the sounds of moaning could be heard from the other beds in Luke's area as well as up and down the hallway. "You've been out of it for about two days. Of course, we helped a little bit by giving you all these medications to fight the pain."

"What happened?" asked Luke.

"You were almost killed. That's what happened. Yes sir, from what I hear, you're one lucky soldier."

"Cu Chang base hospital?"

"Oh, no. Quang Tri...the 18th Surgical." She leaned over and fluffed Luke's pillow. Placing her hands on her hips, she looked down on him with empathy. "This hospital is better equipped for your type of wounds."

"I can't hardly remember anything," Luke strained. "We were in a fire fight and I was holding Sa..." His face turned ashen with recollection. It was coming back to him and he simply turned his head toward the wall, eyes fixed in a blank stare. "Sam," Luke mouthed in a whisper. "I'm going to miss you, man."

The nurse patted him again with the cool cloth. "Okay," she said. "That oughta do it. The doctor will be here in a bit. He wants to talk to you. Now you get better. That's an order." At that, she scribbled something down on her clipboard and then turned to tend one of the other soldiers.

Luke wanted to weep, but couldn't. He had seen so many tears in the last eleven months of his life—more than he thought any person should ever have to see. Today he was empty and tired—poured-out, drained, exhausted not only physically but weary of the inner struggle. Barely nineteen years old, and all he wanted was to go to sleep and not wake up again. What a difference a year can make.

The wounded soldier in the bed next to him mumbled something incoherently. Luke tried to speak to him, but the fellow was too far gone to carry on any type of conversation. Luke found himself lying in silence, like he had so many times during the past year, enduring his own pain while taking in the sounds and smells of the suffering surrounding him. His eyes wandered around the room first to the soldiers in their beds. One had had his legs blown off. Another's head was wrapped in gauze with blood soaked splotches all over it. Luke's eyes continued past the five or six occupied beds, to the large window, where giant green elephant leaves blocked the view. After attempting to gaze out the window for a minute his eyes moved back inside the room, scanning the whitewashed stucco walls. They were practically bare, except for the round white-faced clock with black numerals that made a click each time the hands moved, a couple of medical charts, a full color poster of the beach in Honolulu, Hawaii, and a single Catholic-type crucifix, toward which Luke's eyes seemed to be pulled.

Not small, its wooden cross was about two feet long and a foot or so wide. Hanging upon it was a meticulously detailed bronze sculpture of Jesus. Apparently, it had been placed there by a priest or missionary or perhaps was donated from someone back home. Luke studied the figure hanging. How many times had he seen it before? Hundreds, maybe thousands of times, he guessed, in picture books at Sunday school, in the church sanctuary, in a portrait at home that Sarah had hung in the hallway. His mother's had a little light that shone upon Jesus hanging between two thieves and it served as a nightlight in the hall. Through many a dark night, as far back as he could remember, the light shining on Jesus had guided him to the bathroom and kitchen in the night. Yet, he had never given much thought to what it actually meant. This time however, he paid careful attention to the nails that pierced Jesus' hands and feet, the crown of thorns pressed down on his head, and the rip in his side. Yet, it was the anguish in Jesus' eyes that seemed to speak the most, as if they were looking right through Luke, reaching down into the depths of his soul. It was the same anguish that Luke felt.

At that precise moment, gazing at the crucifix and thinking of Sammy, something happened that Luke could only describe as a miracle. In an instant, Luke's mind was filled with clarity and understanding. It was as if someone had lifted a veil off of his eyes. An epiphany, some would call it. *Injustice; Jesus knew more about the injustice of life than anyone. They killed him in such a terrible way. Jesus was no stranger to pain. Jesus knew pain. He knew suffering and He endured all of it for me?*

Luke had heard the stories. Every Christmas it was the virgin birth and on Easter it was the crucifixion and the resurrection. Heck, he had played Jesus in the Sunday school Easter play one year. Yes, Luke had grown up in church, made a verbal commitment, and had even been baptized in the sixth grade. Yet, it was all just something to please his parents—something that good kids did. But Jesus had no real relevance to him back then. How could a man who died so long ago help him with his pitching and batting? That was how Luke thought about it, and what little faith he did possess had died along with Haley and all of the horrors he'd experienced in Vietnam.

An angel did not appear, nor did Luke have a miraculous vision. Yet right there in that hospital room, something happened. Maybe Sammy's words were hitting home. Whatever the reason, Luke began to understand the magnitude of what Jesus did. And right there in that hospital room, Luke Hatcher became ruefully aware of his own personal bankruptcy, that there was nothing he could ever do to make things right. He could never be good enough—never do enough good deeds— never do anything to wipe away the stain of his failures. Luke touched his own face, recalling how Sammy had smeared his blood on him. *That's why Jesus had to die. There was no other way.* Luke had heard it before, but now he got it.

Out of his brokenness, Luke fumbled for words. *Dear Lord Jesus, there's so much I don't understand. I've made a total wreck of my life and I'm responsible for the death of two good people and all those VCs. Jesus, if you are really alive and love me, like Sammy said, then please come into me and change me. Take my sins and give me that same peace that Sammy had. I'm desperate for you, God.*

Luke felt a weight lift from his soul. He couldn't explain it, but as surely as he was in that hospital bed, he knew he had been washed clean and God's spirit was soothing him. God was embracing him and breathing His life into him. Luke wanted to laugh. He was filled with joy. Where was all this unexpected joyfulness coming from? With each breath came illumination of what Sammy had told him. God's Spirit was bringing his words back to life. *"I lived most of my life in anger and hate, until God took it out of me. He just reached down into me and pulled it right out. Now, I don't live all torn up inside... It ain't about Sunday school Luke. Goes way deeper than that, Bro."* Luke yet again wiped the tears from his eyes as Sammy's words ran lucid through his mind. *"Right there in that prison, God showed himself to me... You really can't live, until you know you're ready to die."*

A resurrection of the heart took place. The peace that Sammy had talked about enveloped Luke. He remembered Sammy's last words, something about seeing an angel. Luke knew that Sammy would not lie or make things up, so he reasoned it was true. An angel had come to get him. *Surely, one came for Haley as well? It's really real. Heaven is really real.* As impossible as it may seem, Luke was a new person and understood clearly what he had to do. He had to live the rest of his life for God, do what God wanted him to do, not because he was forced to, not out of guilt from his past, but out of gratitude, fulfilling the purpose for which he was created. He couldn't let Haley and Sammy die in vain.

"Excuse me?" the doctor asked, breaking Luke's meditation. "Am I interrupting something?"

"No, it's okay," said Luke. "I was just praying."

"Well, Private Hatcher," he said, "flipping through his charts. "I have some bad news and I have some good news."

"Give me the bad news first, Doc."

"All right, it seems that you have several shattered bones and shrapnel embedded in numerous places. We can't take much of the shrapnel out, because we would have to dig it out and that would be like wounding you all over again. You have 2nd-degree burns over a good portion of your body. Plus, your left leg was badly mangled. The shrapnel ripped through muscle and bone. It will take several reconstructive surgeries and months of therapy to get you walking again. That's the bad news." The doctor sat down on the edge of Luke's bed. "The good news is you're alive and somehow, the burns didn't touch your face and they will eventually heal, leaving only minor scarring. Your broken bones will heal and your leg will eventually heal also. However, like I said, it's going to take at least eight to ten months of rehab and then you probably won't have full use of it."

Luke's face contorted. "Will I be crippled?"

"Depends on how you define cripple. You'll probably walk with a limp. How bad will depend on how hard you work at rehab and how your leg responds."

"Will I be able to run?" he asked, suddenly thinking about baseball.

"Don't push your luck. If I were you, I'd be happy I was alive and didn't have to spend my life in a wheelchair like that guy's going to have to do." He shot a glance over at the soldier who had lost both of his legs.

"Yes sir, I understand what you mean," Luke said. He was truly grateful, yet at the same time, his heart sank. Unexpectedly and miraculously he was thinking about playing baseball again and now the doctor was telling him this. "What if I work extra hard at rehab?"

"With hard work and perhaps a miracle, you might be able to regain eighty to ninety percent usage."

"So, I could run, just not as fast?"

"I figure it's possible, but like I said, it depends on how hard you work and how the leg responds."

"Thanks, Doc."

"We're going to monitor you for awhile and then try to move you outta here. We need the space."

"To Cu Tieng?" Luke asked.

"No, son. You're going home. You can't do rehab here. We don't have the facilities and it doesn't make sense for you to stay in Vietnam for a year just to rehab. By the time you finish your rehab, you'll have served your time." He patted Luke and started walking to the door.

Again joy rushed through Luke's soul. He was going home. Images of his family flooded his mind. For a moment, he was caught up in a cloud of cheerfulness, but then his mood abruptly switched back to somberness as thoughts of Sammy came back to his mind. He raised his head. "Hey, Doc?"

"Yeah?" the doctor answered, standing by another bed, looking back.

"Never mind, it couldn't," Luke reasoned, dropping his head back on his pillow.

"I'll be checking up on you tomorrow. Hopefully, we can get you out of here soon." He started walking away.

"No, wait!"

The doctor turned around. "Yes, Private? Spit it out, son. I've got a ton of wounded soldiers to see."

"Did you by any chance treat a Private Samuel Williams? A huge black man."

"No. Not that I recall. There's no Private Williams on my list. I'm sorry."

Luke laid his head back down in deep sorrow at the loss of his best friend, all the while enveloped in this new and strange peace.

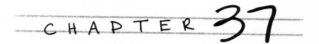

CHAPTER 37

IT WAS WINDY and drizzling rain when the Hercules C130 touched down. A specially manned hospital in the air, it was well equipped for the task of transporting wounded military personnel. Along the way, they had dropped off soldiers in Seattle, San Francisco, San Antonio, and Shreveport before landing back in Victoria where Luke and three others would be admitted to the McGinnis Army/Community Hospital at Fort Clements. As Luke was being moved from the plane to the hospital vehicle, he sucked in a long, deep, breath of refreshing air. It was good to be back on American soil.

James, Sarah, and Emily were already waiting at the hospital when Luke was wheeled in. His body was well-bundled, and his left leg stuck out straight with all sorts of wires and pins attached to it. The three engulfed him, but tried not to hurt him by hugging him. There were more tears. This time, they were tears of joy.

Sarah bent down and gently placed her palms on each side of Luke's face. She looked intently into his bloodshot eyes while James and Emily looked on. "My precious, precious boy," she said. "God has brought you home alive. You will never know how worried I was about you, but now you are here."

"I'm sorry I caused you to worry and I'm sorry I've caused so much trouble for everybody."

"Shhhh," Sarah said. "All of that is in the past now. All you need to know is that you are loved." She kissed his forehead and stood back up.

Luke's expression changed, his eyes narrowed, taking on a more determined look. "Something happened to me over there. I'm not the same Luke that left here a year ago."

James and Sarah exchanged glances, both wondering what their son could mean.

Studying the three people standing in front of him, Luke's lips broke into a grin. "It's really great to see you guys, you know that?"

"All right everyone," one of the attending nurses said. "I need to get soldier boy here to his room. Ya'll are more than welcomed to come up with us."

For the next two days, James, Sarah, and Emily stayed at the motel and spent their days with Luke in the hospital. Then they went home to Magnolia Springs, with the intention of coming back as often as they could.

➤➤ ◄◄

It took over eight weeks as an inpatient for Luke's burns and broken bones to heal to the point where rehab could be started. His hamstring and thigh required three different reconstructive surgeries. The only time that he got out of his hospital room during those eight weeks was when an aide pushed him around the halls in a wheelchair, or when James or Sarah pushed him around while they were visiting. The days were long and boring. However, the enforced solitude gave Luke ample opportunity to read the Bible and think, which he did all day long, absorbing Scripture like a sponge and soaking up its truth.

For one three-week period, Sarah came to help out. During that time, the two often read the Bible together and discussed it. Luke had a plethora of questions and still frequently battled with guilt and nagging doubts that from time to time jumped on him like demons. Yet despite the battles, Sarah could see her son transforming before her very eyes, and Luke was pleasantly surprised at the depth of understanding that his mother possessed. Their relationship reached a depth that neither had experienced before.

"I know that what happened to me in that hospital bed back in Vietnam was real, Mom," said Luke, sitting up in his bed. Sarah was seated in the visitor's chair with an open Bible across her lap. "The peace that came over me that day, it wasn't from me. There's no way I could have created that. It was the peace that Sammy was always talking about."

"That's the Holy Spirit," Sarah said, flipping to a particular passage. "Here, listen to this; 'And the peace of God, which passeth all understanding, shall keep your hearts and minds through Christ Jesus.' That's Philippians 4:7, one of my favorite verses. When we turn ourselves over to God, he sends us his supernatural peace. And it is supernatural."

"Let me ask you this, Mom; do you believe in angels?"

"Of course I do, silly."

"So, you actually believe they're here right now, and we just can't see them?"

"I don't know if they're here right now, but I believe God sends them at certain times."

"I haven't told anybody this, except Sammy's Mama in a letter. When Sam got shot, right before, you know, he died, he told me that he saw an angel. Made me promise I'd tell his Mama. Part of me really wants to believe it was true. And in the hospital that day I did, but now, a part of me thinks he might have been hallucinating."

"Why would you think that?"

"I don't know, maybe the loss of blood or something caused his mind to see things. Once, he told me this wild story about his Dad. Said he died and came back to life, that his spirit floated up out of his body and he saw an angel and a bright light and then parts of Heaven. It's kind of hard to believe."

"Well, what does the Bible say about it?" Again, Sarah started flipping the pages. "Here listen to this one: 'For when they shall rise from the dead, they neither marry, nor are given in marriage; but are as the angels which are in Heaven.' Jesus said that. He said there are angels and that there is a Heaven." She scooted her chair over to be a little closer to Luke. "You know your Grandmother's sister, my Aunt Queenie?"

"Now Mom, you know I know Aunt Queenie."

"Well, she swears she saw an angel. And I'm inclined to believe her."

Luke perked up. "She did?"

"Sure did...and there was no finer lady than my Aunt Queenie. She was a schoolteacher and I don't think she was the type to be making up stories like that. In fact, she was rather shy."

"Why didn't she talk about it more?"

"It's not one of those things you just go around spouting off or people will think you're a bit out there. But she told enough people at the appropriate times."

"What happened?"

"Well, your Grandmother's Grandmother Sarah, who I'm named after, had been fighting pneumonia for a long time. She was 87, at the time and she was running a high fever. This particular day, my Mama and Aunt Queenie, both in their teens, were over visiting, helping out and whatnot. Queenie was instructed to run out and draw a bucket of water from the well. They didn't have running water at the time. So, she hurried out to get the water. Mama was taking care of some other chore. On the way back from the well, Queenie looked up at the house and right above the tin roof, just a pretty as you please, was an angel.

When she saw it, Queenie said she thought to herself, 'I guess it's coming for Grandma Sarah.' She dropped the bucket and came running in the house crying, saying that she had just seen an angel. And sure enough, when she got back in the house, Grandma Sarah had passed away."

"What'd it look like? Did she say?"

"She said it had golden hair and the most beautiful feet. She went on and on about its beautiful feet. Like I said, Aunt Queenie was one of the sanest people I know and she held to that story her whole life."

"But if all that is true and God is real, and I believe that He is, then why does all this bad stuff happen? It just doesn't make sense to me."

"You know Luke, the Bible is a very honest book and when you read it you'll see that bad things happened to people all the time. God never told us that during our time on this Earth things would always be easy or that we would understand everything. But He did promise to help us through it, if we let him."

Sarah turned the pages to find yet another passage of Scripture. "Listen to this one; '...the God of all comfort; Who comforteth us in all our tribulation, that we may be able to comfort them which are in any trouble, by the comfort wherewith we ourselves are comforted of God.' Common sense tells you that if bad things are never going to happen, then that Scripture should not even be in the Bible. And if we never had any trouble, we could never know God's comfort. Notice God didn't say we wouldn't have hard times, but that He would help us through them."

"You really know the Bible."

"Been reading it all my life, since I was seven or eight. Mama used to make us read a whole chapter every night before bed. I guess it paid off."

"But Mom, the night that Haley died, I read a Scripture that said if I called out to God that he would help. I've even got it memorized. Can't forget it. It said, 'In my distress I called upon the Lord and he heard me.' I called out to God." Luke's voice began to tremble and crack. "I asked him again and again to make Haley better, but she died. Why? Why did she have to die? Why did all those things happen to Sammy? And why did Sammy die? And why does war have to happen?"

Suddenly, something broke inside Luke, as it had done in the past, He began to weep uncontrollably. "You can't imagine what I saw over there!" he yelled out. "You'll never know!" Sarah took his hand and squeezed it tight. "It was horrible, Mom, really horrible. I'll never forget their faces—the fear on their faces and the mangled bodies—all the mangled bodies." Luke dropped his head back on his pillow and closed his eyes.

Sarah stood up and gently kissed her son on the forehead.

⇥ ⇤

When Luke's bones and burns were almost healed, and the 759 stitches were removed from his leg, he began the long, arduous task of rehabilitation. Not only had the explosion ripped through his thigh and hamstring muscles, but atrophy had set in. His left leg looked like a skeleton's leg, as opposed to his right, which was normal and athletic-looking.

At nine weeks, he began a vigorous regimen of therapeutic exercises and treatments. The long process was tedious, and painful, but by the end of the twelfth week, he could stand on his own and walk at a snail's pace with the aid of a cane. After that, Luke was officially declared to be an outpatient and moved back on base into a special barrack with several other unique cases. He was assigned a four-hour-a-day desk job on base, allowing him to complete his three hours of physical therapy each day and to get adequate rest. Compliance to military rules and regulations was still enforced. However, his life now was much more flexible and free. It was shortly thereafter, some fifteen months from when Luke had joined up in Houston that Sarah and James left Emily with Aunt Lydia and again drove over to see him, this time, with a little surprise. They knew when Luke would be in rehab so they purposely met him at the hospital.

"I told you guys, the wheelchair is not necessary. I can walk," said Luke.

"Yeah, but we want to get you there as quickly as possible," said James.

"Get where? What are you talking about?" Luke laughed.

"You'll see," said Sarah, pushing the button for the elevator. "Just be patient." When the doors opened they rolled him in.

"What are you guys up to? I know ya'll are up to something," Luke said, the elevator creaking downward. They were on the second floor, so the ride to the lobby was short. The elevator dinged and the doors reopened.

"Now close your eyes and don't open them. You hear me?" Sarah joked playfully.

James zigzagged the wheelchair through several rows of parked cars.

"Aw, come on. When can I open them?"

"Obey your mother and keep them shut," said James, coming to a sudden stop.

"Now can I open them?"

"No. Not yet," said James, "Hold out your hands."

Luke held out his palms and a big smile broke across his lips as James placed a set of car keys in them. "Now you can open them."

Luke could not believe his eyes. Parked before him was the candy-apple-red 1953 Chevy coupe convertible he and James had started working on two years prior, except now it was completely restored. It was like brand new. James had finished the project for his son while he was in Vietnam.

"So, what do you think? She's a beaut, isn't she?"

"She looks incredible Dad." Luke ran his hand across the smooth paint job. "You must have spent hours on it."

"Let's just say it helped keep my mind occupied," said James. "You know, I had to stay busy doing something."

"Thanks so much you guys. I don't know what to say."

"You don't have to say anything. Just enjoy it," said James, rubbing Luke's shoulder.

"Well," said Sarah, "I think I'd like to take a little spin around town."

"Sounds good to me," said Luke. "By the way, how are you guys getting home?"

"Our plane leaves Sunday at 4:00 P.M."

"Ya'll are the best parents a guy could ever have," trembled Luke as a wave of realization surged over him—realization again of just how much his family loved him and how truly blessed he was to have them.

They got into the car and Luke took the wheel. This car was such a welcome surprise; however, another surprise lay just ahead.

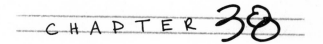

C H A P T E R 38

"SEVENTEEN! EIGHTEEN," LUKE groaned, as he strained to lift his leg straight out on the leg extension machine.

"Come on, now, just two more reps," Charles, the physical therapist, encouraged.

"Nineteen...aaahhh...twenty!" Luke's leg dropped, clanging the weights against each other.

"Good work, Luke. I think we can add a little more weight next time. You're making great progress."

"Thanks, Charles," Luke said, grabbing his leg with his hands and dragging it off the machine. After pulling himself up, he leaned against the padded vinyl seat until he could adjust his leg underneath himself to where he could stand. Then, he shifted his weight to his cane.

"Look, starting tomorrow," the therapist said, "instead of me, an intern from Victoria State is going to be assisting you."

Luke rolled his eyes back and sighed.

"Don't worry, it'll be fine. I've done some rotations with her and she knows her stuff. Plus, I'll still be available if you need me."

"Whatever you say, man. But you're letting me down. You know that?"

"I think you'll make the adjustment just fine," Charles laughed. "Besides, she's a lot easier on the eyes than I am. That's for sure." He patted Luke's back. "Come on; let's get some heat on that leg before you do your walking exercises."

＞＞　＜＜

Luke was not prepared when she walked into the room, nor was she. Neither one of them moved as they stood transfixed, gazing at each other in disbelief.

"It…it's you," she said, adjusting her hair, now suddenly conscious of her appearance.

The same curious fluttering Luke had felt when he'd first met her rushed through his being. "Kate?" he asked apprehensively. "Is that you?"

"You remember my name," she said, their eyes locking once again, just as they had done a year earlier. "How could you possibly remember my name?"

"Wasn't that hard. You were…" Luke couldn't quite get the words out, but somehow, Kate knew what he meant.

"I take it you two already know each other," said Charles, walking up to them.

"Yes," replied Luke, "We've met."

"Good afternoon, Kate," Charles said, shaking her hand. "This is Luke Hatcher. You should be familiar with his charts and since you already know him. I'll just leave you two alone. I've got something pressing I need to work on. If you need me for anything, I'll be in my office."

"Thank you Mr. West," said Kate. She glanced down and observed that her hands were trembling slightly and she laughed to herself. It was odd; she had worked with many wounded soldiers before but normally she wasn't this nervous. No doubt, Luke's injury was serious, but he still maintained his rugged good looks, even when leaning on a cane in his gray, military workout sweats. Though not yet 20 years old, his face displayed a hard-earned, rough maturity.

Looking at her, the same features that struck Luke the first time again called out to him—her shiny brunette hair, her soft, fair skin, her delicately boned face, her intense green eyes. Today, she even appeared softer somehow, her expression warm and familiar.

"Okay, then," Kate said. "Let's get started." She scribbled something in her notebook and assisted Luke as he hobbled to his first exercise.

CHAPTER 39

SEPTEMBER ENDED WITH an unseasonable cold front, something that hadn't happened in northern Florida in quite a while. Jeans were pulled from bottom drawers to replace shorts, and lightweight cotton shirts were swapped out for jackets and sweatshirts.

Wearing a short jacket today, Kate Robinson walked across campus. Each day, she was finding that she was trudging through her classes, glancing at her watch every few minutes, in anticipation of meeting Luke at the hospital rehab center. Their favorite time was after the strength workout and treatments, when Luke had to walk for extended periods. Kate would walk by his side, being there for him to lean on when he needed it, and they would walk and talk. It was a great way to get to know each other. Up to this point, however, Luke had remained quiet and mysterious, conversing about only surface things. He had mentioned nothing of Haley, not too much of the war, and had only briefly touched on Sammy. Kate, on the other hand, had exposed deep things about herself. She felt safe with Luke.

Her home was Tallahassee, less than two hours away. She was attending Victoria State on an academic scholarship, majoring in physical therapy. She began in the School of Nursing, but had transferred to physical therapy because the field was new and wide open and she like helping people overcome their physical and emotional barriers. Her father, believe it or not, was a Methodist minister, so she was glad to hear that Luke had come from a Christian background and that he seemed to love God. Kate was a pure, young woman who had grown up in a loving family with rock-solid values.

It was obvious to both of them that they had feelings for each other, although their dating relationship was somewhat unconventional. Everything had to revolve around Luke's therapy. When walking around the hospital grounds became monotonous, they would embark in the Chevy in search of more interesting places to walk and talk. More and more, they found themselves at the Victoria State football stadium. They would walk around the track and onto the field. Kate would almost always challenge Luke to walk up the stadium steps as well. He would struggle, his leg shaking, but Kate would push him until he made his goal. Each day they would try for a couple more steps. When he reached the limit of his strength, they would just sit and enjoy the breeze and the view of the campus. Because the stadium was usually vacant when they were there, it had a surreal and romantic feel, especially at night.

After a while, however, Kate noticed a recurrent glitch in the progression of their relationship. She wanted to move forward. Luke however, often sent her mixed signals that would leave her unsure about how he truly felt. It was as if he wanted to jump into the deep water, but for some reason always opted to wade around in the shallow where it was safe. Why was he walled up? Kate wondered. Why wouldn't he let her in?

→ ←

One November afternoon, the sun was starting to dip below the edge of the stadium, and was casting a deep pink across the sky. Luke and Kate strolled casually around the track. Because of the high characteristic Florida humidity, the 49-degree temperature felt much colder. Kate wore jeans and a hooded navy and gold Victoria State sweatshirt. The chill in the air made her rosy cheeks and lips stand out against her light skin and dark hair that ruffled at her shoulders. Her eyes, glowing as usual like priceless green gems, added the completing touch. Luke, on the other hand, wore his faithful army sweats, his army jacket, and, of course, his shiny black army boots.

That evening, a blustery wind blew, and while they walked, they remained close to each other to stay warm. Kate looped her arm through Luke's and they walked slowly, even more slowly than usual. Luke's muscles were stiffening up. Maybe it wasn't the best idea to go out in the cold....

Both of them were abnormally quiet as they walked. For the very first time since their meeting, an awkwardness was caging them in. Kate's senses were telling her that yet again, something was troubling Luke—something deeper than his injuries, and she was determined to find out what it was. However, she also knew she did not want to push him further away.

"Luke," Kate asked tenderly. "I wish I knew what was going on in your mind. Lately when we've been together, it's like your body is here, but your mind is elsewhere. Why are you so distant?"

She held his hand in hers, interlacing their fingers together. "What's going on with you, Luke? Do you ever think about where we're going with all this?"

Luke listened, but didn't respond, his face turned forward avoiding eye contact.

Kate continued, "I've been thinking that we've been seeing each other for a couple months now. I know you enjoy being with me or you wouldn't keep spending time with me. You could easily do all your walking without me now. You give me signals that you have deep feelings for me, and that makes me happy—happier than I've ever been in my life. Each day, I can't wait to be with you. But after all this time, I have no clue where you stand and in the last week or so… I don't know… It feels like you're backing away from me…and you haven't even tried to kiss me, Luke. Not once. What am I doing wrong? Do you want to just end it now and get it over with?"

Kate felt tenseness in Luke's body. "I do care about you, Kate, if that's what you want to know."

She blinked, then, closed her eyes for a second before answering, as if reaching for some inner courage.

"No, Luke, that's not it... I want to know if you're serious about us or are you playing some kind of game. I don't know if you've noticed, but I... I've fallen in love with you Luke Hatcher!"

He stopped walking and drew her to closer to himself, gently caressing her hair.

"You know I'm serious about you, Kate. But..." Luke paused for a moment and an uncomfortable silence hung in the air. Kate could feel Luke's chest rising and falling with each breath.

"But what, Luke? But what?"

"You don't know me. There are things about me I haven't told you."

"Like what, Luke? What could be that bad?"

"Kate, I don't deserve to be happy and I don't deserve someone a wonderful as you. It's that simple."

"Luuuuke! You're scaring me."

Luke's leg was improving by leaps and bounds. He was actually, now considering throwing the baseball around some and starting some light batting practice. It had been well over a year and a half since the accident with Haley. It had also been that long since he'd been home and now that he was mobile, the pressure was on for him to return for a visit. The truth was; although Luke had made his peace with God, he still carried the emotional scars of Haley and Sammy in his heart, not to mention the horrible things he'd done and seen in Vietnam. The nightmares had returned with a vengeance and he had realized that they might never go away. Things he thought he could shake off after his spiritual rebirth still tormented him from time to time, sometimes even worse than before. And Haley's death, as horrible as it was, was now just one of several traumatic experiences that he could not forget.

As a result of the inner struggle he was experiencing, whenever Kate tried to move the relationship to a deeper level, Luke would invariably pull away, almost as if he were trying to sabotage it. One of the doctors had diagnosed Luke with Post Traumatic Stress Disorder, a new term attached to many of the returning vets. The doctor recommended psychotherapy and so Luke went to counseling on base. His official diagnosis was PTSD, yet Luke knew something more was going on inside of him. A life-threatening spiritual battle seemed to be raging.

"Look, Kate," Luke said abruptly, "I don't know any other way to put it, but maybe we just need a break from each other."

Kate stopped dead in her tracks. She couldn't believe her ears. "Please don't say that, Luke," tears now welling up, "Please..."

"Let's go," Luke said, matter-of-fact. "I'll drop you off at your dorm."

"Why are you doing this?"

"It's for the best, Kate. It really is. You can do so much better than me."

Luke said nothing as he drove Kate back to the dorm while she silently cried in the passenger seat. When the car stopped, he got out and opened her door. "Good bye, Kate," he said, cold as a stone, then climbed back in and drove off. Kate ran to her room in tears.

This was Friday afternoon. Throughout the whole weekend, Luke felt absolutely miserable. The one thing he wasn't experiencing was peace. That was for sure. There was no phone in the barracks so Kate could not call him or come on base without a pass. Luke never went to the pay phone or attempted to call her. He knew that he had hurt her and that hurt him, but he reasoned that a clean break was for the best—she would get over it.

However, something was happening that Luke had not counted on. Every time he closed his eyes, he could see Kate's beautiful smile and warm eyes. When he opened his eyes he thought about her. Regardless of how hard he tried, he couldn't get her out of his mind. It was clear that he too was falling in love with her. There was such a comfort level when they were together, just as it had been when he was with Haley. Each time he tried to let go and abandon himself to love, however, feelings of disloyalty and guilt about Haley would rise up. He loved Haley too. He would always love Haley. This wasn't fair to either one of them.

It was about ten on Sunday evening and sleep was out of the question. He couldn't take it any longer. Luke got up and made his way to a pay phone at the PX and dialed the numbers. After four rings someone picked up.

"Hello," The voice was soft and soothing.

"Hey, Mom, this is Luke. How you doing?"

"I'm fine, Honey. Why are you calling so late? Is everything okay? Are you all right?"

"Mom, I really need some help. I think I've messed up, but this time I think I need to talk to Dad."

"Sure Honey, he's right here. You don't want to tell me first? I might be able to help."

"I know you can, but I need to talk to Dad on this one."

"Here's your father." Sarah handed the phone to James while whispering, "He needs some help."

"Luke, Son, what can I do? You need some money or something?"

"No Dad, I have plenty of money, but I think I did something really stupid."

"I'm listening," he said. Sarah had moved her ear up to James, trying to listen too.

"I broke up with Kate and I don't know what to do. I think I hurt her pretty bad."

"I'm sorry, Son. I had a good feeling about her. Did you two get into a fight?"

"No. I just broke it off."

"What did you go and do a dumb think like that for? You're not going to find another one like her, you know. That I can tell you for sure."

"Thanks Dad. That's what I really needed to hear," said Luke sarcastically.

"Do you love her, Son?"

"I think I do, Dad, but it's Haley. Every time I try to let go, I feel guilty and stuff. I still love Haley and can't let her go."

"Son, I'm going to tell it to you straight. You may not like what I'm going to say, but you need to hear me—you've really got to hear what I'm saying. Haley is gone. She was a great person, a wonderful person. There was a tragic accident and she was killed. It was horrible. I'm not making light of it and no one is telling you to forget her. You can never do that, but now it is time to move on with your life. You have grieved enough, and I think if you let Kate get away, you will be even sorrier. She's a fine one, Luke, inside and out. And let me ask you this; do you seriously think Haley would want you to be miserable all your life because of her? Of course she wouldn't. She wasn't that kind of a person. Think, Luke, think. If you don't move on, you might as well dig a hole six feet deep, crawl in, and cover yourself up. This is one time you need to have courage. Time is ticking, Son, and a girl like Kate isn't going to be available for long. I can assure you of that, too." This was a long speech for James to make, and he spoke every word with passion.

"You sure?"

"Of course I'm sure. Hey, I know what I'm talking about. I almost lost your mother once. We broke up and I can't imagine what would've happened if we hadn't gotten back together. She's the best thing that ever happened to me." Sarah leaned into James, placed her arms around his waist, and started nibbling on his neck. "In fact, she's got her hands all over me right now. I can't keep the woman away," James said, with a snicker.

"This is serious, Dad."

"I know, Son. I know it's serious. Have you told Kate about Haley?"

"No."

"Don't you think it's time? Listen to your heart.

"Bye, Dad. Tell Mom and Emily that I love them."

"Will do, Son. Bye now."

As Luke hung up the phone he realized that his father had never been more on target. He would never meet anyone like Kate again. This was his chance. He realized what a fool he'd been and all the unnecessary pain he had put Kate through. He desperately missed her now, feeling like a part of him had been ripped away.

Still in a reflective mood, he decided to go for a ride in the Chevy. As Luke crawled in, he remembered something that he had put in the trunk. Something within his spirit nudged him to open it up and look at it. Luke got back out of the car and walked around to the trunk, inserted the key and popped it open. Tucked away neatly in the very back was a brown cardboard box. He reached for the box and pulled it forward, then opened the folded ends. Inside, on top of some other stuff, was Sammy's old Bible. It was the one thing that he had of Sammy's, other than the photos he'd taken. His anguish about losing Sammy had kept him from touching it. When he wanted to read the Bible, he opted for a new Bible his mom had bought him.

Because of his fresh injuries, Luke had been unable to attend Sammy's funeral, but after Mrs. Williams had read Luke's seven-page letter, including Sammy's angel experience, she had mailed the Bible to him, insisting that he have it.

"Sammy would want you to have it," she had said in the letter. "He talked so much about you, Luke. You were a good friend—a good friend indeed." Luke had just put the Bible in the box with some other things, out of sight.

Now with Sammy's Bible in his hands, Luke drove to a spot under a street lamp and parked so he could see. He began flipping through it. He couldn't help but see how certain passages were underlined and circled and notes were written in the margins. Notes had been jotted down everywhere. Even the blank pages in the back, where the maps were, had all been filled up with notes. He'd noticed them before, but he had never really read them, preferring to keep the volume more as a shrine to his friend.

On this night, in desperation, something clicked in Luke's mind and he began consuming Sammy's notes. Tears streamed down his face as he read. It was as if his friend had come to life again and was sitting in the passenger seat talking to him. God's Spirit was there, too—thick and compassionate, just like He was in the hospital room back in Vietnam.

As Luke made his way through the worn pages, stopping at underlined passages, one particular page kept bidding for his attention. Sammy had scribbled what appeared to be a rough outline for living through tough times on one of the note pages of his Bible.

What hard times do for us:

1. Removes all crutches

2. Makes us stronger

3. Teaches us to desperately depend on God

God wants us to be a giver of life to the hurting.

Allow God to send his comfort

Allow God to show you the needs of other folk around you

Allow God to use you in the healing of other folks

Luke let Sammy's words fill him and also his parents' words as well. He became acutely aware of his own selfishness. By focusing completely on himself and his own pain, he was preventing God from working through him and was also blocking his own healing. The only way for him to deal with all the pain would be to reach out to those around him. Like Sammy did. That's what he meant when he had said, *"I'm fulfilling my purpose, Luke, right here with you. My purpose is to glorify God wherever I am, to let Christ shine through me."*

Luke was seeing that God's purpose for his life had little to do with baseball and things of that nature. It had much more to do with blooming where he was planted, letting God use him to be a conduit of His love to serve others wherever he may find himself. *That's what life is really about. If God allows me to play baseball again, that'll be great, but if not, it really doesn't matter.* Luke knew he must allow God to filter and remove his pain. He had to become a giver of life to others instead of a taker. That's what Sammy and Haley would want. That's what Sammy and Haley had done.

He thought of Kate, of how she had given so much of herself and he simply took and took and took, soaking up her affection like a sponge, but giving nothing in return. *How in the world could she forgive me and love me?*

Luke knew his soul was at peace with God again. But this time, he wanted it to be different. Sitting in the car under the streetlight, he prayed for God to take his self-centeredness and to change his heart and make him the man He wanted him to be.

He checked his watch: 12:31 A.M. As late as it was, however, this couldn't wait until morning. He couldn't bear Kate being in pain one more second. He had to talk to her—now. He started the car and drove up and down streets until he tracked down another pay phone. With anxious fingers, he dialed the number to Kate's room.

Kate fumbled around for the phone. "Hello," she said, sleepily.

"Kate, it's me."

"Luke," she responded tenderly. "I knew you'd call."

"Can we talk?"

"Sure, I'm listening."

"Not over the phone, in person, tonight?"

"Is everything all right, Luke?" She said.

"Things are better than they've been in a long time, but I have to talk to you… Its really important or I'd wait till tomorrow afternoon."

"I have an eight-o-clock in the morning, but I guess I could skip it if I'm too sleepy. And I think there's no front desk person on duty, so I don't have to worry about our dorm curfew."

"Are you sure?"

"Yeah, Luke. I'm sure."

"Great. I'll pick you up in ten minutes."

"You can't see me like this. I need to get ready."

"Kate, you're always beautiful."

CHAPTER 40

THE CHEVY WAS good and warm when Kate crawled in. "This better be good," she said, giving Luke a cute little wink.

"Do you have all night? Because it's a long story."

"Anything for the man I love."

"Before I start, there's something I have to do." He leaned over closer to her and paused a moment, then smiled and brought his hand to her face, caressing her cheek softly with his fingers. He then pressed his lips up to hers, and kissed her slowly and tenderly. "I love you, too, Kate Robinson."

She pushed him away, looking intently at his features. He pulled her back and kissed her again, this time stronger, more passionately. Kate kissed him back, just as passionately. When Luke pulled away, he had a serious look about him.

"Now that there's no question how I feel about you," Luke said, "We need to talk."

"Are you up to walking?"

"I am, if you aren't too cold."

"Ah, it's not that cold. You'll help keep me warm. Besides, we're in Florida, remember?"

They drifted along the cracked cement sidewalks of Victoria State and somehow made their way to their favorite spot—the football stadium. Kate put her arm around his waist and pulled closer. "All right Soldier Boy, spill the beans," she joked, then turned serious, "Really Luke. You can tell me anything."

"I don't quite know where to begin," Luke said.

"How about the beginning? I'm in the listening mood," Kate replied.

"Okay," Luke inhaled and exhaled deeply. "Here goes... All my life, I have been a baseball player. Growing up, I ate, drank, and breathed baseball. It's like that's what I was created to do. My dad worked with me and it paid off. My senior year at Magnolia Springs I was All State, All American, and had signed a scholarship to Louisiana State University."

Kate's expression lit up with pleasant surprise. "Oh really? I'm impressed."

"After I signed with LSU, a scout from the Atlanta Braves called me and told me they wanted me. I was going to the Braves camp. I was so excited."

Luke took a deep breath and continued his account. "Before you, there was someone else, someone that I loved dearly. In a many ways, Haley was a lot like you. We grew up together, and yes, Kate, she was wonderful. She was beautiful. Haley was funny, smart, and I loved her. She was really the only girl I loved...until I met you. I still love Haley. But not like you may think. You see..." He paused searching for the right words. "Haley is... She's dead, and I killed her."

Kate was stunned. The twinge of jealousy she had started to feel disappeared into the night air. This was bigger than anything she'd expected. "Go ahead," she encouraged, ready to hear more.

"Like me, Haley was also quite a ballplayer. Softball, one of the best Magnolia Springs had ever seen. On one Sunday, over a year ago, June 16th to be specific, some jerk in Sunday school said real loud so everyone could hear, that Haley could strike me out. Well, that stirred the pot and soon Haley was on the mound pitching to me with half the church youth group looking on.... The first two pitches were strikes, but to be honest, I wasn't really trying. But on that last pitch, I was thinking I'm going to show everyone how great the mighty Luke Hatcher is by knocking the stupid ball out of the park...."

Luke stopped walking. "Kate, it hurts so much. I wish I could do that whole day over again. I wish I could have a second chance."

"It's okay, Luke. It's okay," Kate said, clutching him tighter.

"That's what everybody says, but I knew better, Kate, I knew better. If I wasn't so proud, none of this would have happened...so stupid... Anyway, as you may have figured out, I hit the ball. It was a line drive and it struck Haley in the head. The next day she died. And Kate, her mother said to me, 'Luke you should have known better.' I'll never forget the pain in that woman's face. I took her baby. I killed Haley. And I loved her. I don't know if I would have married her or anything like that, but I sure did love her....

"I swore baseball off for good. I mean, why should God let me play when I killed Haley? Why should I have a life, when I deprived Haley of hers? Do you know, the day of her funeral, I almost killed myself. It's true—put a shotgun barrel in my mouth and came within a breath of pulling the trigger. Instead, I ran away to the army. And now, whenever I feel myself beginning to enjoy life, like I do with you, I am overcome with these feelings of guilt."

Kate stopped walking and looked him in his eyes. "I'm so sorry, Luke. I don't know what to say."

"While I was in the army, I met Sammy. Or rather God sent Sammy to me. I've told you about him."

"I remember. He's the black man who died."

"Yes. He was a great big guy, and he was my best friend. We spent Basic together and stayed together all the way to 'Nam. He taught me many things and showed me the way to God. But..."

Kate clutched Luke's arm.

"As you know, Sammy died, too. But Kate, he died in my arms, after saving my life." By this time, Luke was weeping, and so was Kate.

"Oh, Luke, I had no idea."

"Now God has shown me how selfish I've been and He's shown me the answer for my life. It's to let God use me to help others. It's all written down in Sammy's Bible... I'll show you later."

"Luke, I believe in miracles," Kate said. "And there are certain things in life, that when they happen, we feel God's peace... You know what I think? I think God put us together for a purpose. And I want you to know, that I love you no matter what."

Luke pulled her into his arms. "You never cease to amaze me, Kate Robinson," then tenderly he kissed her.

They didn't speak for a long while. Eventually, they strolled back toward the car. On the way, they sat down on a wooden bench underneath a cluster of oaks, beside a flickering antique sidewalk lamp. Kate sat on one end and Luke laid his head in her lap.

When Luke started to speak, Kate placed her finger over his lips tenderly.

"Shhhh," she whispered, "Not yet." Then she began to sing, softly, with the most angelic voice:

> *When peace like a river attendeth my way,*
>
> *When sorrows like sea-bellows roll,*
>
> *Whatever my lot, Thou hast taught me to say:*
>
> *It is well, it is well with my soul.*
>
> *It is well... It is well... It is well with my soul.*

Then, Kate began to hum the tune ever so gently, until a peace enveloped both of them.

"Wha...how...You know that song? This is incredible, Kate! You have no idea what that song means to me. Sammy always sang that very song. I think its God's way of letting me know He's here, that everything's going to be all right."

Running her fingers through Luke's hair, she said, "My daddy used to sing me that song when I was growing up. Whenever something bad would happen and I thought my world was falling apart, like the time Josh Kennedy asked another girl to the homecoming dance, I would sit in his lap and he would sing that song. One day, he told me the story behind it. There was this man in the 1800's who lost all four of his daughters in a shipwreck. He took a ship to the very spot where they died. As he looked out over the ocean, God filled him with an incredible peace and he wrote that song."

"Sounds like you have a pretty special dad," Luke whispered, gazing into Kate's eyes.

"He is special," she said, standing up, holding out her hand. The gesture was more than "Hold my hand," it was "I want to share a lifetime with you."

Luke stood slowly and took Kate's hand, and they began walking on their new journey, together.

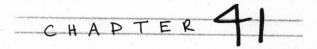

CHAPTER 41

"I'M SO GLAD that you're going with me, Kate," Luke said as he threw her suitcase in the trunk of his car. "Mom and Dad are going to be glad to see you, not to mention Emily."

"I'm glad, too. I've missed them so much." Kate looked up at him, her dark hair blowing in the breeze, "and I want to help you through this." She gave Luke a peck on the cheek and hopped in.

The weather had turned unusually warm, so they were able to ride with the top down for part of the way. They drove straight through to Magnolia Springs, only stopping for gas and food.

The sun was just beginning to set when Luke and Kate turned onto White Street. They were completely unprepared for what awaited them. The whole neighborhood lined the sides of the street, cheering and clapping as they drove by. Several boys on bicycles rode alongside them. Pulling into the driveway a mob of neighbors rushed around the car. It was a glorious homecoming. Everybody was hugging and kissing both of them. Even his high school buddy, Jimmy Pikes, was there.

Noticing Luke's limp, someone helped him up the steps to the front porch. Sarah and her neighbors had prepared a potluck dinner for everyone.

There was a ton of home-cooked food, and an equal amount of wonderful conversation. Most folks wanted to know about Vietnam and how Luke got wounded. He told them all about Sammy. Kate filled the folks in on how they had met. As the night wore down, eventually everyone except family had gone home. Not once had Haley's name been mentioned. Sarah and Kate went to clean up the kitchen, and James and Luke sat in the living room to talk.

"So," Luke said with a sigh. "How are the Sparks doing? I didn't think they would be here tonight anyway. I imagine they hate me."

"They moved, Luke. I didn't tell you that?"

"No, sir."

"I'm sorry. It must have slipped my mind." James rattled the ice around in his tea. "Moved to Tulsa, Oklahoma, of all places...to start over."

"Oh..." Luke replied.

"Well, son, I'm glad you're finally back home. Even if it is for a short time...How's the leg coming?"

"Slow, but it's coming… I can jog very, very, slowly. My therapy tech says progress will go much faster now, though."

"You think you'll be ready for baseball season next year?"

"Dad, I'm hoping so. But I'm trying to make some major decisions. I'm thinking about going to college and get my education. The GI Bill will cover it and I'll try to play baseball as a walk-on…. When Kate graduates, she can get on just about anywhere there's a good hospital. We're going to shop around some schools to see the best place for me to have a shot on a team. I really don't think it's realistic for me to try out for the pros, yet. If my leg heals up and I do well in college, then maybe, but all that's in God's hands."

"Sounds great, Luke." James stood up. "I'm real proud of you. Yes I am, real proud. And that Kate, she's something isn't she?"

"Yes she is, Dad."

"Well, I don't know about you, but its way past my bedtime." James stood and walked toward the hallway. "Good night, Son."

"Good night." Luke looked up from the reclining chair he was sitting in. "Hey, Dad?"

James turned around in the doorway, eyes heavy, "Yes."

"I love you."

"I love you, too, Luke."

Sarah had prepared the guest room for Kate and she had readied Luke's old bedroom for him. He walked in hesitantly. It was the first time he'd been in his room since the day of Haley's funeral. When he walked in, sure enough, he was hit with a surge of tormenting images and feelings. He remembered waking up in the darkness that morning of the funeral, finding the shotgun, putting the barrel to his mouth—coming so close to pulling the trigger.

He opened one of his dresser drawers. There was his senior yearbook lying on top of the clothes. He picked it up and scrutinized the cover before opening to look for Haley's picture. There she was. It was the first time he'd seen her face since the funeral. He couldn't breathe. His mind was flooded with memories. He took the yearbook over to the edge of his bed, and began to weep.

His door was still open. Kate heard him and rushed to his side. Sarah also heard him and started toward his room, but when she saw Kate go in, she stopped. Luke needed Kate now, more than he needed his mother.

"I don't know if I can do this," Luke said. "On this very bed, I almost blew my brains out."

"You were grieving, Luke." Kate reasoned, compassionately. "And it's all right to have the feelings you're having now. You have to work through them."

"Look at her picture." He handed the book to Kate. "She was so beautiful—so full of life."

"You're right, Luke. She was beautiful." She took Luke's hand. "But I think we need to pray."

Father, Luke and I need you to give us strength right now... She prayed, then paused, reached over, and pulled Sammy's old

Bible—the one that Luke now read from daily—out of the open suitcase on the floor. Kate turned some pages and stopped at a particular verse. "Here. This is it. 'For God hath not given us a spirit of fear, but of power and love and a sound mind.'" She looked up at Luke. "Luke, we have the Holy Spirit in us. That means God has given us what we need to beat this thing. We can do all things through Christ who strengthens us. You don't have to let this destroy you." She paused, thinking intently. "And do you know what we are going to do tomorrow?"

"What?"

"We're going out to the cemetary...we are going to settle things about...Haley... And then we're moving on."

Luke stared at Kate, a mixture of fear and irritation written across his face.

"Luke, don't be upset with me. You know it's time to let go."

"Fine, I'll do it," he said walking out of the room.

The next morning, Luke was extra-quiet at the breakfast table. Sarah had prepared a feast of homemade biscuits and gravy, with cheese grits, eggs, and bacon, Luke's favorite. But instead of devouring it as he had always done in the past, today he only picked at it. Again, Sarah knew something was up.

"So, what do you kids have planned for today?" she asked.

Luke shrugged his shoulders. "Stuff."

"Luke and I are going to practice pitching and hitting later today while you girls go gallivanting or something," said James.

"Ah, that's great Mr. Hatcher," Kate said. "But Luke and I have something very important to do this morning. Right, Luke?"

"Whatever you say, Kate."

"Don't worry, Mr. and Mrs. Hatcher... It shouldn't take that long."

Luke breathed deeply, letting the air out with a sigh.

➤➤ ◄◄

Gravel crunched under the tires of the Chevy as it inched its way along the cemetery road. Luke slowed the car to a stop and killed the ignition.

"Well," he said, "I guess this is it."

Kate took hold of his hand. "You can do this, Luke. I'll come with you."

"No, you stay in the car. This is something I have to do on my own." He slipped his hand out of Kate's, kissed her softly, and opened the door.

Lush, green, grass cushioned his steps as he meandered through the numerous gravestones, searching for that special one. The smell of flowers was heavy in the air. As with the rest of Magnolia Springs, oak and magnolia trees created parasols of soothing shade. Luke didn't notice anything except for the way he felt; this walk through the cemetery was painfully similar to his walk down the church aisle to Haley's casket. His heart raced and palms became sweaty. Then, on the very back row of gravestones, underneath one of the biggest magnolia trees, Luke saw it. Several fresh flower arrangements had been placed around the headstone. On top of the headstone there was a white granite cross about three feet high. At the very center of the cross was a laminated color picture of Haley.

Luke ran his fingers over her picture, not knowing what to say or do. Instead of feeling anxiety anymore, though, Luke was surprised at the calmness that had come over him—a calmness he knew must have come from outside himself. He remembered that song, *It Is Well With My Soul*, and he thought of the man on the ship who had lost his four daughters. Luke sensed God's presence all around him. Tears welled up in his eyes, but this was different from before, almost welcome. He was profoundly sad, but he also had a certain peace and knowing that Haley was in a much better place.

His mind flashed back to the funeral and the words of Pastor Taylor: "We can truly rejoice because Haley is with God in Paradise.... 'To be absent from the body is to be present with the Lord.'..."

Luke pondered the changes that had taken place in his heart when he finally turned his life over to God. And the peace he was experiencing almost overwhelmed him, right there, at Haley's grave...it was nothing less than supernatural.

Gazing at Haley's photograph, Luke began to talk.

"Haley, I know you're not really here. But I've come to settle the score with my guilty conscience. I'm so sorry for what happened that day. I know it was an accident, but I also know I could have prevented it. Haley, I would give my own life, if I knew it would bring you back, but I can't do that. The best I can do now is to live the rest of my life for God and to honor your memory. My friend Sammy told me, 'All we have is the time God gives us. Be true with that time.' If you can, you should look him up. He's up there in Heaven, too. You will really like him. Haley, you lived your life to the fullest, not for yourself, but for others and God. I learned so much from you."

Luke knelt down on one knee, resting his arm on his leg. *"Lord, I want to be a Godly man. I want to live my life to make a difference just like Haley did, and be true to what You created me for."*

He lifted his head and saw Kate standing a few feet away.

Looking back at Haley's picture, he quietly said "I have someone new in my life, I think you would have really liked her." Luke stood and held out his hand toward Kate. Kate reached out and took his hand.

"Kate," Luke said, as he plucked a long blade of grass and placed it in his mouth, "there is someone I would like you to meet."

READING GROUP
DISCUSSION QUESTIONS

1. What *was* "*Luke's Passage*"? From what place to what other place did Luke's "passage" take him? (See chapter 14 for some ideas.) Could the word "passage" be a play on words? (Look up the word in the dictionary to get ideas about alternate meanings.) What part did baseball play in *Luke's Passage?*

2. Luke's life was radically affected by Haley's death. In your own life, trace a chain of events that stemmed from a difficult incident. Consider the following aspects of your own experience: (a) What might have happened in your life if the difficult incident had not occurred? (b) Do you feel that you missed a golden opportunity because of what happened? (c) Do you feel that the resulting series of events made it possible for something good to take place? (d) In retrospect, can you see God's hand of protection, guidance, and control in the events?

3. As a high school student, Luke was a responsible young man with high moral principles. He took advice from his parents, his coaches, and his teachers. He considered himself a Christian. What kind of faith did he have? What needed to happen to it, and why? Trace Luke's spiritual growth from his experience in the hospital chapel until he read Sammy's Bible notes.

4. When he becomes a husband and father, do you think Luke will turn out to be like his own father, James? Why or why not? Do you think he will find it difficult to show emotion or to communicate, as his father did?

Will he be likely to follow in his father's footsteps in terms of living out a dream vicariously through one of his children? What are some of the admirable qualities shown by James?

5. Put yourself in the shoes of Haley's parents, Harvey and Virginia Sparks. How do you think you would have reacted to having your only daughter killed in a freak accident? Would you have moved to a different town to "start over"? What part would your faith in God play in your grieving and decision-making?

6. What role does *hate* play in this book? Who and what did Luke hate? Who and what did other people hate? Talk about racism, as portrayed in this book. Consider how hate seems to be selective. Compare and contrast Sammy and Luke. Re-read their conversation in chapter 17 and review the incident in the café in chapter 24. What might you have done if you had been in the café that day?

7. Contrast Sergeant Millhouse and Sammy Williams with regard to how they handled their respective tragedies. (See chapters 21 and 24 for profiles of each man.) Why did they react so differently to their traumatic circumstances?

8. There are many kinds of grief, not only grief because of death. What other kinds of losses and grieving did you see in this book? What losses did James and Sarah Hatcher grieve about? Sammy Williams? Other people? What else did Luke and his fellow soldiers lose besides some of their buddies? How did Luke handle his grief? Can you think of any positive value in grief? How have you responded to losses in your own life?

9. The book repeatedly mentions Luke's obsessive competitiveness, his pride, and his out-of-control anger. Were these sinful characteristics, as he often thought they were? Did any of Luke's traits prove to be helpful sometimes? Did they mellow over time? If so, how?

10. Shame, guilt, and remorse—Luke felt profound shame at his role in Haley's death, and he castigated himself: "Stupid idiot..." Whenever something reminded him of the reason he had run away from home, and his first reaction was always burning shame. Sometimes he was completely overwhelmed by his guilt (for example, at the baseball game in chapter 20). Were his feelings justified? How did Luke's shame relate to his *pride*, on which he blamed his actions? Was his shame in any way redemptive of his situation?

11. Throughout the story, trace the role played by the words of the Bible. Which passages were particularly important? How did they help, or seem to hinder, Luke's eventual acceptance of his difficult circumstances?

12. Sammy told Luke that God works all things out for the good. He learned this from the Bible, specifically Romans 8:28, which reads: "We know that in all things God works for the good of those who love him, who have been called according to his purpose" (NIV). Discuss this concept in the light of what happened in the story. Is "good" the same as "comfortable"? What can be meant by "good"? Did *all* things work out for the good—for everyone? How did they work out for the good for those who were "called" by God?

AN INTERVIEW WITH AUTHOR MAX DAVIS

1) When did you first realize that you wanted to be a writer? Was there anything in your childhood that influenced you to become a writer?

In my junior year of high school I had a radical conversion experience with Christ. Shortly afterward God placed in my heart a burning desire to write. I had never experienced this desire prior to coming to Christ. When I was seventeen years old, I recall sitting at my desk at Central High School in Baton Rouge, Louisiana writing a book and even designing the cover, completely convinced that God had called me to be an author. Not knowing a thing about writing or how one makes a career of it, I began writing out of sheer obedience to God ...unaware that it would take years and bring me through many deep trials in order to develop my gift. It was only by His staying power that I stuck with it. God allowed me to keep those original high school writings so that after all these years I could look back and know it was Him calling me. I often encourage aspiring authors to not let go of their dreams, if it is God, He will open the doors in His perfect timing. One of my mistakes has been trying to kick down doors that only God could open. I'm learning, project by project, to trust Him more and more, because only He could have released all the doors that have opened for me.

2) Although you have written a several books, *Luke's Passage* is your first novel. Why did you decide to venture into fiction?

For years I began to see the tremendous power and influence that "story" has in our world. Someone once said, "I can't hear what you are saying because your life is speaking so loud." So often we want to preach our message and no one is really listening because they want to *see* the message lived out in our lives first. Yes, there is a time to preach truth straight out, but people are not going to listen if our lives aren't lining up. The same is true in books. Many people will not read non-fiction, but they will engage in a story where the character's lives are speaking through the situations they are put in. My nephew is a case in point. He would not touch my non-fiction books, but he glanced at *Luke's Passage* one day when it was up on my computer screen. About an hour later I had to pull him away. The characters were speaking to him. With story, you can let the characters work out their own doubts, trials, triumphs, and faith in a way the reader can relate. The challenge for me is to abide in Christ and then allow His spirit to flow out of me into what I write.

3) Which writers have influenced your writing and in what ways?

Though I've read hundreds of books more nonfiction than fiction, there are seven that stand out from the others as having a profound influence on me. In the nonfiction genre, *Mere Christianity* by C.S. Lewis, *Celebration of Discipline* by Richard Foster, *The Ragamuffin Gospel* by Brennan Manning, and *Living in Harmony*, formerly *The Rhythm of Life* by Richard Exley. In fiction it is John Grisham's, *The Testament*, John Irving's, *A Prayer for Owen Meany* and Barbara Kingsolver's, *The Bean Trees*. As far as learning different writing styles, I read a variety of books, from William Faulkner to Frank Peretti, gleaning something from all of them.

4) **Why did you write *Luke's Passage* rather than some other story?**

Stories come to me in different ways. Usually they begin as a seed and then begin to grow inside of me eventually causing me to birth it. And believe me giving birth to a book takes much labor and travail. *Luke's Passage* is inspired by a true story. When my daughter was in high school, one of her best friends was hit in the head with a baseball and died a few days later. The young girl's boyfriend hit the ball that struck her. Our family along with the whole community was in shock and asking the question 'why?' It was then I knew I had to write the story. The seed was planted and begin to grow inside me and take root. Upon hearing that the girl's boyfriend had been suicidal and had given up baseball, I decided to write from his perspective. How would it feel to be him? How would I react?

5) **Your characters are compelling and tangible. When reading you become attached to them, just as you would family members. What inspired the development of these characters in your story? Are they based upon people you already know?**

I come from a very large, colorful, loyal, and spiritual family that has deep history and character. Much of my inspiration comes from their stories either directly or indirectly. I keep a running file of stories that people relay to me. The setting of Magnolia Springs came from my memories of the city of Hammond, Louisiana where my Mother grew up and my Grandparents lived. We used to ride our bikes all over Hammond and I can remember vividly the old stores and people sitting on their porches, etc. One of my distant relatives, a man I knew as Uncle Harry, owned an old grocery store with wooden floors and glass casings. I can still remember the smell and feel of that old store. Uncle Harry always wore a white apron and was ready to give us kid's candy. Also, I gather a plethora of information from studying old family photos, newspapers, and magazines.

6) **You managed to capture both a tragic and nostalgic period of American culture and history, which encompasses the Vietnam War and growing up during the 50's and 60's. What kind of research did you do to make this era so real?**

As a kid growing up in the sixties and early seventies, it was a magical time for me and I can remember it all well. But to capture both the tragic and nostalgic feelings and be true to the time period, I have to depend on more than memories. To be as accurate as possible I combine interviewing people who lived in that time period with additional historical research. Research gives you facts, but in an interview you capture the emotion along with other little tidbits of information that helps put you in that setting. Obviously, you can only do that with fairly recent history. That's why I tend to be drawn more toward generational history. To try and capture the feel of pro baseball in the sixties, I interviewed a man who was actually drafted straight from high school to the pros in 1966. Additionally, I interviewed a couple former LSU baseball players who played during that time. The same was true with the Vietnam War.

7) **How do you develop your plot and your characters?**

I like to compare my writing to painting. First, I get an idea then I do a rough sketch—very rough. I throw a lot of ideas against the wall, most ideas don't stick but some do. I keep what sticks and repeat the process over and over, reading and rereading the rough draft, each time correcting and adding.

Over time a pattern begins to develop and then something miraculous occurs, the story takes on a life of its own. At that point, I go with the flow and let the characters write the story. Writing fiction is about problem solving. With each new development, there is a problem that needs to be overcome.

8) **How would you describe your writing style—not your literary style—but the actual writing itself? What kind of techniques do you use.**

I've developed a system that works for me. Writer's block almost always occurs at a transition point in the story. When that happens it does absolutely no good to sit and stare at the computer screen. At this point, I take my notebook and pencil and go for a walk or do something where I am in motion. I have certain places I go to walk. I live on seventy acres and will walk around the property or go up to the school and walk around the track, or I'll walk the river walk downtown. There's something about being in motion that causes creative juices to flow. I can't tell you how many times thoughts have come to me while working on the tractor or working out. Some of my most effective writing times have been when I'm driving cross country. Sometimes, I will literally walk for hours and when the thoughts come, I jot them down. I've walked for hours to get one little paragraph, but it was a transitional paragraph that set the next phase of the book in motion. Once I'm through the difficult transition, then I can get back on the computer and the writing flows. It's a good habit to carry a pen and notebook with you at all times to catch those golden thoughts that come during the day. Many times a thought will come to me in the middle of the night and I have to get up and write it down or it will be lost forever.

9) **There's obviously more to a novel than just an entertaining read. What do you want the reader to take away from *Luke's Passage?***

I want readers to have the realization that they are not alone in their pain. Even though life sometimes doesn't make sense, God is there and that true faith makes a difference in how we respond to pain. Sammy experienced similar difficulties as Luke yet because of his faith, he responded differently. Also, God was working in Luke in the midst of his anger, questions, and pain using them to bring him to a deeper understanding of Himself. Another thing I want the reader to take away from the book is an appreciation and deeper love for the people who are in their lives. Life is fragile and we need to soak in every second we have with our loved ones.

10) **We've talked about the authors who have most influenced your writing. Now on a more personal level, as an adult, what one person has been most influential in your life?**

It's hard to narrow down to one person because down through the years God has always had someone influential in my life for that moment to keep me encouraged in my faith and calling. Upon entering college, I told my parents that God called me to be a writer. Though they surely thought it was a passing phase, they never discouraged me or broke my spirit. Not once did they ridicule my sometimes seemingly unrealistic dreams. One time in seminary a professor wrote on the back of one of my papers, "Your writing is crisp and alive. You use good imagery. Never neglect your gift." This was like pouring gasoline on a fire. I still have that paper today because those few words kept me going. At one point in my life when I was discouraged, I became part of a writer's group headed up by best-selling author, Gilbert Morris. Like my professor in seminary, Gilbert's words of encouragement and constructive criticism encouraged me to keep going. There is no way you would be holding this book in your hands today if not for the constant support and teamwork of my wife, Alanna. There have been times I've wanted to toss in the towel and she wouldn't let me. My father and mother-in law believed in my vision and have supported me. God seems to always place the right people in my path at the right time, friends and fellow writers like Richard Exley and Larry Koenig. .

11) **In conclusion, tell us something personal about Max Davis that most people may not know?**

I've battled with ADD all my life. For years I didn't understand what was going on. And yet, now I see it as a gift rather than a frustration. I believe having ADD has actually contributed to my writing and creativity. God has turned my weakness into a strength.

ACKNOWLEDGEMENTS

As with all my books there are always many people to thank. Well, it's especially true with this one—my first novel. It didn't take me long to discover that writing fiction takes quite a bit more skill than writing nonfiction and I had much to learn. *Luke's Passage* is a reality because of the help of several key people.

Jeff Dunn—a superb fiction editor, thanks for coaching me through the roughest of drafts, for listening and encouraging me so many times when I was about to pull my hair out. I understand it now, "show me don't tell me."

Richard Exley—author, minister, and friend. Thanks for being my pastor of writing and for the many hours reading over my work, giving me honest feedback, and helping me keep my priorities straight.

Mark Gilroy—agent and publishing guru, thanks for continuing to believe in me and for keeping the vision alive.

Debbie Justus—Vice President of Whitestone Books. All I can say is WOW! I can't think of a better person or publisher to launch a first novel. Your work on the cover was unbelievable, a true gift. The way you have championed and marketed the book has made me feel like a John Grisham. Let's sell a million!

Larry & Nidia Koenig, Sharon Phares, Jonathan & Desiree' Chamberlain, Nell Davis, Frank Schroeder, Karen Harden, and Mary McNeill. Thank you all for reading my work at short notice and giving me your feedback.

Alanna, Alanna, Alanna—my wife. I know people are getting tired of hearing me go on and on about you, but I just can't stop. You have been a warrior and champion through this whole process. Of all my editors and readers, you are the rock. I dare not submit a chapter to anyone until you have read it first and have added your insight and balance. Really, the name on the cover of all my books should read Max & Alanna Davis.

MAX DAVIS BIO

 **MAX DAVIS** is a full-time author and speaker. He holds a bachelor's degree in Journalism from the University of Mississippi and a master's degree in Biblical Studies from American Christian College and Seminary.

He has authored several books both fiction and nonfiction, travels speaking to audiences across the nation, and is often featured on numerous radio and television shows including *The 700 Club.*

In addition to writing and speaking, Max has been a collegiate football player, coach, as well as a pastor.

He and his wife, Alanna, live in Greenwell Springs, Louisiana on seventy beautiful acres. They have three children, Kristen, James, and Treva along with a wonderfully spoiled poodle named Trinity.

Max loves the simple life—spending time with his wife on their picturesque property, occasionally wandering into town for a romantic dinner with her, being plugged in to his children's lives, spending time with good friends and family, sharing his faith, reading good books, working out, and of course, writing. Max is also an avid Ole Miss, LSU, and New Orleans Saints football fan.

For additional information on seminars, scheduling speaking engagements, or to write the author, please address your correspondence to:

mdbook@aol.com

OTHER GREAT READS FROM EMERALD POINTE BOOKS

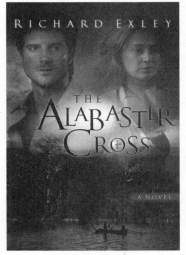

0-9785-370-3

Trapped in a world of anger, 29-year-old Bryan Whittaker cannot move on with his life until he takes a journey into his past...a dangerous journey that will lead him into the heart of the Amazon Rain Forest. Instead of the revenge he seeks, Bryan finds redemption and in the process makes peace with his past.

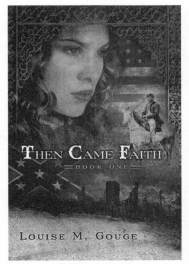

0-97851-372-X

Following the Civil War, Juliana, a beautiful, young abolitionist seeks to help the South heal and repent of its past, when she meets a former Confederate naval officer, Andre, who swears never to forgive the North for the devastation to his family. The question is whether these two strong -willed individuals will be able to swallow their pride and discover a common path to rebuilding the city—and their own lives.

Additional copies of this book and other titles by
Emerald Pointe Books are available from your local bookstore.

If you have enjoyed this book, or if it has impacted your life,
we would like to hear from you:

Please contact us at:

Emerald Pointe Books
Attention: Editorial Department
P.O. Bo 35327
Tulsa, OK 74153-0327

Emerald Pointe Books